MW01599646

Touch And Go

Vanguard Towers: Book 1

Aiden Bates

© 2020

Disclaimer

This is a work of fiction. Names, places, characters, and events are all fictitious for the reader's pleasure. Any similarities to real people, places, events, living or dead are all coincidental.

This book contains sexually explicit content that is intended for ADULTS ONLY (+18).

Contents

Chapter 1 - Derek

"Blood pressure?" I pressed hard on a bleeding wound and glanced up at the nurses rushing to get two large-bore IVs and additional monitors fitted to the patient.

"Eighty over forty, Dr. Carlisle."

"Shit. Touch and go. Get that infusion in *now*. Saline, point nine percent."

"Yes, doctor." A nurse handed me a fresh wad of gauze. I ditched the bloody wad I'd been using to compress the stab wound, and the patient rolled his head and let out a pained groan before slumping back into unconsciousness. He'd stumbled into the ER with an abdominal wound bleeding through his shirt, collapsed in front of the intake desk, and was now on the verge of going into hypotensive shock if I couldn't get him stabilized.

It wasn't the first trauma case of my twelve-hour shift, but I prayed it would be the last. Judging by the violent injuries I'd seen, it had been a nasty night in Washington, DC, and while I thrived working on the frontlines in the ER at Georgetown University Hospital, there was only so much blood I could see in one shift without exhaustion setting in.

"IVs are in, administering crystalloid infusion."

"Thank you, Nurse Harris. Mask fitted?"

"Yes, doctor. Oxygen running."

I lifted the gauze and found the entry wound still spurting deep red, way too much for me to even begin to think about stitching up. "I'm worried about this hemorrhage, Shae."

My favorite nurse clicked her tongue and quickly rushed to get the antifibrinolytic drug ready for injection. "Yes, doctor!"

Two hours later, the patient was stabilized and transferred to surgery, I'd washed the last of the blood off my arms, and my shift was almost over. Heavy with fatigue, I stopped short in the break room and held my breath as a nurse fed dollar bills into the haunted candy machine. "It's not going to work, Shae. I'm telling you, you're wasting your hard-earned cash."

Her braids swayed as she shook her head and punched the number pad with a short, manicured fingernail. "Uh-uh, Dr. Carlisle. I'm telling you, tonight's the night. That candy bar is *mine*. I'm feelin' lucky."

"You're dreaming if you think it's going to fall clean—"

"Ha!"

Astonishingly, the confectionary in row D-4 dropped into the tray without getting snagged on its way down, and Shae shot me a smirk as she peeled back the wrapper with a flourish.

"Damn. I stand corrected, Nurse Harris. Doesn't hospital lore say that you get a wish for that little miracle?"

"Mm-hmm. You want it?"

"The candy bar? More than life itself."

She snatched it out of my reach as we walked to the triage desk. "Dream on. You want the wish, though?"

"Nah, I'm good. You have to make your own luck."

"Oh, c'mon." She slapped my shoulder as we came around the corner to the triage station. "You're what, thirty? Too young to be so damn cynical."

"Thirty-three. And if you *insist*, then I wish for a bite of that candy bar."

She flicked crumbs from the corners of her mouth. "Uh-uh. There are rules to wishing! You can't wish for more wishes, and you sure as hell can't wish for *my* hard-earned chocolate."

"This is getting more and more complicated, Shae." I was about to waste the wish on something like true love when my phone dinged with a text from one of my brothers. Eli worked search and rescue with the National Parks Service in Maryland and Virginia, and he was gone as much as he was home, but he was currently at the Tower and cooking breakfast, if the photo he sent through was anything to go by. An overflowing plate of Eli's special chicken waffles were apparently waiting for me once I got home…if the horde of brothers didn't get to them first.

There were seven brothers, my foster family, and all of them were experts at sniffing out Eli's incredible cooking.

I groaned. "How about I wish for no new trauma cases this shift? I'm thirty minutes from clocking off and there's breakfast waiting for me at home."

Shae looked me up and down. "We've got to get you out of emergency, Derek."

"Hey, you're worried about me? Think I'm going to burn out? Or has it already happened?"

"You? Oh, hell no, you're strong as an ox. But you never think about moving up in the world?"

"Up? There's no hierarchy when it comes to saving people's lives. We're a team, aren't we?"

Shae howled like I was telling a joke. "Let's compare your paycheck to the head surgeon's, and then we can talk about Georgetown University Hospital's so-called 'flat hierarchy,' okay?"

Nurse Carter, scowling as always at our banter, handed me a file from the triage desk and motioned to the far bay where my next patient was waiting. Shae chomped up the last of her candy bar and followed me as I flipped through the chart.

"I'm just saying." She paused to chew, then swallowed and went on. "You're one of the best, but you're stuck here, patching up these ER patients and shipping them off to the surgeons who get all the credit. You should be up there with the big guys and their big cash bonuses."

"Hm, sounds like you're trying to get rid of me, Nurse Harris."

She clucked her tongue. "Sensitive."

The truth was I loved being in the ER in one way or another, I'd been training to be on the frontlines since I was a kid, and the ER was a lot easier to navigate than the foster system I'd been through. Surgery was an option but working in emergency kept me on my toes. Sure, every day when I went to work I knew I'd been dealing with drug overdoses, gunshot and stab wounds, and mental health crises, but there were plenty of curve balls, too.

Curve balls like the handsomeness of the young man who sat in bay six, and the shockingly bright green eyes he flashed at me as I pulled the curtain back. His beauty hit me like a slap to the chest and for once, I was lost for words.

"How you doing, Mr. Lane? That pain relief kicking in?" Shae nudged me as she pushed past and broke me out of my trance.

"Yeah, it's feeling okay, I guess." His voice was gravelly but lilting, hoarse in an airy way.

With his gaze on Nurse Harris, I was able to collect myself and take in what was written on his chart. Sebastian

Lane. Twenty-two-year-old male with a suspected broken wrist.

Action time. Stage smile. A happy doctor leads to a chatty patient, and chatty patients reveal more about the causes of their injuries, which leads to better healing. In theory. "Sebastian. What have we got here? Injured wrist, huh?"

"Hey, doc. Call me Seb."

The minute he turned his gaze back to me, my knees attempted to buckle. Sheer will alone kept me standing. *Get it together, Derek.* I was out as gay, but I'd never crossed the line with a patient, and I sure wasn't about to start now. Not for fatigue. Or hunger. Or low blood sugar. Or the fact that he was beautiful.

"How'd this happen?" I pulled up a stool and scooted to take a look at Seb's wrist, resting on a pillow in his lap. I lifted the ice pack he was holding against it. Bruised. Swollen. Tender to touch. My gut said sprained, but it looked nasty, and I wasn't surprised the triage nurses suspected a fracture.

"Ah, it was just a stupid accident. I took a tumble off the curb. Fell right onto my arm. I'm really, *really* clumsy lately."

Nope. This was a well-practiced speech if I'd ever heard one. And I'd heard plenty. I caught a glimpse of older bruises on his other arm as he laughed nervously and ran a hand through his blond hair. Most certainly his story was bullshit.

I sat back and looked him over. I'd seen plenty of similar injuries in my time in foster care, and even now the roar of white noise filled my ears and the first nips of panic bit at me. Even with my brothers all grown, and even after the number of cases I saw as a doctor, signs of abuse still triggered me. I bit down the rising tide of nausea in my gut and returned Sebastian's everything-is-fine smile with an understanding nod.

"Nurse Harris? Could you get us a new ice pack, please?"

She took the hint and skedaddled, the candy bar wrapper poking out of her pocket as she went. I wanted him to look at me again, but his eyes were trained on the floor.

"You're nice to your nurses." His voice was soft, and he dragged his gaze up my body to look at me from under his raised brows. I hoped he liked what he saw, and then admonished myself for the thought.

"*My* nurses?" I pasted on a smile and cocked my head. "Do you know where you are? My name isn't on the door."

"No? You're not Dr. George Town?" He smirked through a pained grimace that twisted his face into an adorable wince and made my heart beat faster.

"You're clumsy *and* bad at telling jokes? They didn't note that on your chart."

He smiled and it was as attractive as the wince. "Hey! I came here for healing, and now you're hurting my ego."

A witty comeback was right on the tip of my tongue, but he met my gaze and the intensity of his eyes struck me mute. A tiny smirk fluttered at the corner of his lips. Adorable.

He broke eye contact when a woman groaned in the next bay, and I was able to get my head back in the game.

"Any tingling?" I lingered over the soft skin of his thin fingers, and hoped he'd chalk it up to me being thorough. "Or any other sensations there?"

He wiggled his fingers. "Nah."

"Is the pain in the wrist sharp or throbbing?" These were the standard questions to determine a break or sprain, while I considered how to best ask about the bruises.

"Uh… both? Worse when I move it like—" He flexed his hand back and a small, almost silent groan filtered between his lips. As a doctor, I didn't react to the sound. As a man, my body tightened.

"Don't—" His face scrunched as I reached to stabilize his arm before he did more damage.

"Ah! Fuck." He winced and held his wrist to his chest. "Guess those pain pills they gave me weren't too hardcore."

I chuckled and made notes on his chart. "No, the nurses can't give out the heavy stuff."

"Damn…" His eyes met mine and my pulse skyrocketed as I took my hands from where I was holding his elbow and braced myself to ask the questions that gutted me every time.

I softened my voice and stayed close to him. "You want to tell me anything about the bruises on your other arm?"

"Huh?" He cocked his head, then glanced at his arm as though seeing the bruises for the first time. "Oh, shit. Yeah, like I said, just really clumsy. It's a character flaw. I don't have many, but being a klutz is a big one."

I gave him plenty of silence for him to fill with the truth and when he didn't take the invitation, I nodded and cleared my throat. "I'm going to order some X-rays, but I'm almost certain this is a sprain."

Sebastian sighed. "That's a relief. I need both hands for the computer."

"Oh, yeah? Gamer?" I put his chart down beside him on the bed and wheeled my stool toward the cabinet to grab dressings.

"Hacker."

I did a double-take. "Oh, yeah?"

"White hat."

I stopped short and raised my eyebrows, suddenly worried he was talking nonsense. Maybe he needed a neuro consult after all. "Did you hit your head when you fell?"

His laugh was so loud I felt it in my belly and couldn't help but smile. "Ha! White-hat *hacking,* doc. It means that I'm one of the good guys."

"Right... You work with the FBI or something?"

I wheeled back with a bandage and a sling and started to wrap his wrist as gently as I could. The radiologist would remove it, but I wanted it stabilized while Seb waited for his X-ray.

"FBI? Nah, but that's the dream, I guess. Just graduated from UDC, so I'm working freelance and slinging drinks at a bar downtown until I get a full-time gig."

I smirked as I fitted a sling around his shoulder. "The only *slinging* you'll be doing from now on—"

"Oh, no! Dr. Funny over here. Where's Patch Adams?" His face lit up brighter than the exam room lighting, his eyes wide as his smile, and I couldn't help but beam back at him.

"Dr. Carlisle trying to be charming again?" Shae stuck her head into the bay and handed me a fresh ice pack.

I gasped in mock offense. "*Trying*?"

"He's doing a pretty good job of it, actually," Seb said quietly.

"It's his specialty. Anything else I can get you, doctor?"

"Could you let radiology know that we'll be sending Seb for an X-ray? And send an orderly?"

"Of course, doctor." Shae gave me a sassy look before she jerked the curtains closed.

"Thank you, nurse."

Sebastian's cheeks were flushed, and I did my best not to look at his face while I finished wrapping his wrist. I adjusted the sling around his shoulders while he pressed the fresh ice pack to the injury. Dressing an injury like this was usually a nurse's duty, but I had a reputation for spending extra time chatting with patients, and this way at least I could be useful while I did it.

"How's that?" I slid back and checked the angle of his arm in the sling.

"Feels okay, I guess." He moved his arm to demonstrate, but his wince said more than his words.

"Too tight?" Maybe I'd been distracted by his eyes—bright, sparkling green—or his smile.

He shook his head. The move small. Tentative. "Nah. Just, you know…sprained"

"It's going to hurt for a while longer, I'm afraid. Keep it still, use ibuprofen, and ice for fifteen minutes every hour. You got an ice pack at home?"

"Yes, as a former and current klutz, I keep a spare bag of frozen peas on standby at all times."

"Ah. The classic medicinal vegetables." Had to love those home remedies. I almost let my mind go there, but instead, I nodded. "They get mushy. Better take that pack with you, switch it out with the peas when they melt."

That grin was back. And a cock of his head let the overhead light catch another sparkle in his eyes as he spoke. "You're too generous."

"I like to think so." My cheeks burned. I hadn't flirted in a while. If that was even what this was.

He wet his lips and the glisten on his bottom lip was as transfixing as the light in his eyes.

My tongue felt heavy and awkward in my mouth, and I was searching for something appropriate to say when the curtain flew open and cranky old Barney, my favorite orderly, shuffled in and motioned to the wheelchair with a nod.

"Barney will take you to radiology."

"Hey, Barney, what's up?" Seb turned back to me when the orderly responded with a deadpan grunt. "Will I see you after the X-ray?"

I shook my head. "My shift ends soon. You're out of my hands now."

"Damn." The disappointment flashed on his face before he grinned sweetly and moved past me to the wheelchair. "Well, thanks for patching me up, doc. Maybe I'll see you again."

I hated how much I hoped that would be true, and I cleared my throat as I pulled the curtain wide for them to navigate out of the bay. "Come in if you need us but try to stay out of trouble."

He lifted his hand in goodbye as Barney wheeled him out and called back to me as he rolled down the corridor. "One can only hope!"

Chapter 2 - Sebastian

Damn, that ER doctor was *hot.* Sore, tired, and feeling sorry for myself, I pictured his handsome face as I made my way home from the hospital on foot. No car for me, and I didn't want to risk getting my sprained wrist smacked on public transport, so I pounded the pavement and kept my eye on the curb…which looked more dangerous since my fall.

What I'd told Dr. Dish was almost one-hundred percent true—I was on a run of bad luck, and I had no idea why life had taken such a recent shitty turn. All since that one life-fucking moment four years ago when my parents died. Car accident. Big Ben and I all alone. Was that not enough bad luck? I had a soft spot for my brother, even though he was a real man's man—translation: homophobic asshole. Lucky me, he was the only family I had left.

And now it seemed I was on a fresh roll of bad juju. The doc clearly hadn't bought my story, but I really *had* tripped on the curb and landed hard on my wrist in the street. After a late shift at the bar, I'd turned up my street and stood at the curb to wait for a gap in the traffic. Right as a truck rumbled past, I was about to make a dash across the two-lane road when I slipped and fell. I swore someone shoved me, but by the time I'd cried out and blinked through the pain, there was no one in sight.

As for the bruises, I'd told a little fib when he questioned me. A few days earlier, a guy mistook me for someone else. He dug his fingers into my arm and shook me like I was a rag doll before he put his cigarette breath in my face, ranting about a debt I needed to pay. I never thought of myself as having one of those faces everyone said looked like someone they knew, but this guy was adamant. I was his man, and I owed him big time. Maybe I had a debt-ridden doppelganger. Just my luck.

But there was always a little bit of good mixed in with the bad. As my apartment building came into view, I tallied my recent wins against the losses.

One: Roughed up by someone trying to get money out of me, *but* I didn't really owe him, I was debt-free…except for student loans, which I refused to acknowledge and prayed every day for a collapse of the banking sector.

Two: Wrist sprained, but not broken. Had to go to the hospital, but I got seen by a hot doctor. And damn, was he ever good-looking. I liked older guys, and he was exactly my type. Mid-thirties with a few of those sexy creases framing his magnetic, deep blue eyes. He was lean, not built, but I had a feeling there were some rock-hard abs hiding under his scrubs. He was a real dish. Dr. Dish. Mm, tasty.

As I walked to the entrance of my apartment building, a shiver ran from the base of my skull to my gut and I was yanked out of my Dr. Dish daydream. I spun around. Someone was watching me. I scanned the street. The usual assortment of business folks in suits talking into their ear pods, homeless guys wheeling carts of trash, cars, trucks…no one paying attention to anyone outside of their own little bubble. No one even glanced my way. Maybe the pain was getting to me.

I fished out my keys and wrangled the door open with just my right hand, then headed up the stairs to my crappy studio apartment.

A waft of damp air hit me when I stepped into my place, and I tried not to think about the mold probably growing in hidden spaces throughout the building. The one-room studio with its worn-out, brown shag carpet that hadn't been replaced since the '70s, a sofa someone had left behind, and years' worth of smoke yellowing the ceiling was what I could afford with my bar job and inconsistent freelance tech gigs. Living there might have been a health hazard, but at least this place was mine. Home sweet musty home.

Straight to the linoleum-tiled kitchen with its half-broken electric stove and window that provided only a view of the stucco wall next door, I waited for the kettle to boil and passed the time by practicing my glass-wrangling skills with a sturdy mug. I tested the weight of it in my left hand. Not bad. I chucked it up in the air and caught it again with no problem. Maybe I'd be able to manage at the bar with just one hand after all. Or maybe not…I put a spin on the next throw, cried out as the motion yanked something in my wrist, and the mug bounced on the linoleum floor with a dull thud. Broken handle. Chipped rim. Great.

I settled onto the threadbare sofa with my cup of tea in my broken mug and a Dr. Dish daydream brewing when a heavy thump rattled my door. Mid-sip, I paused, and my pulse pounded in my ears as loud as the knocking continued.

"Seb! Open the fuck up." Big Ben's voice blasted through the thin hollow-core door like an active volcano. If he kept banging, his big meaty fist might just pound right through the wood.

"Yeah, yeah. Hold on."

"Open up!"

"I said hold *on*, I'm coming!" I was so dozy I didn't bother to set the cup down before trying to stand. With just one hand and legs tired from my long walk, getting up off the deep-set couch was a gymnastic feat, and I sloshed warm tea all over my arm in the process. At least the sofa was brown and wouldn't show the stain. I was still flicking warm tea off my good hand when I opened the door.

"I need you to fix this shit." Ben shoved his laptop at me, and I barely dodged it so it didn't hit my sling.

"Whoa, I'm kind of limited, bro." I held up my injury so he could have a look. Not that I expected more than a grunt in reply.

He sneered. "What's wrong with you? You look all…twitchy."

"I'm fine. Just fell off the curb." I held up my bandaged wrist again, and he pulled his head back and widened his eyes like he'd only just noticed before he reached out a trembling hand, and quickly yanked it away again. Was he actually worried?

I couldn't meet his gaze without blurting out that I thought I was being followed and maybe it was related to my accident. He would laugh it off. He'd make sure I knew he thought I was a sissy. A pansy. A Nancy-boy. Weak. And Big Ben didn't like weak. Not one bit. I wrangled the laptop under my arm and ushered him inside. "Just some bad luck. What's going on with this piece of junk? Didn't I tell you to get the RAM upgrade, like, last month?"

"It's frozen, and I need it thawed, like, yesterday." Of course he did. Big Ben needed everything done yesterday.

"Uh, sure, I'll see if I can *thaw* it." I was exhausted, but we didn't exactly have the type of relationship where I could say no without it becoming a whole *thing*, so I stacked the laptop on top of mine at my desk, and flicked it open.

Ben stood over my shoulder, and his towering frame shaded most of the light from the bare bulb hanging down from the ceiling behind him. He bit his nails loudly near my ear while I tried some key combinations to unfreeze the screen that was stuck on a spreadsheet report in a program I wasn't familiar with. I was happy my wrist didn't hurt too badly while I typed, but none of my usual workarounds were working.

"What were you doing when it froze?" I kept trying key commands, but the screen remained stuck.

"Working," he snapped. "I need to get it back in."

"Calm down, I'm working on it—"

"Fuck, Seb! You don't fucking understand!" His escalation wasn't unexpected. When Ben wanted something, he wanted it now.

His tirade was cut off by his ringtone—a Drake song—and I slumped back into my gamer chair and took a couple of calming breaths, pumped my good hand into a fist while he answered his phone. I hated when Ben raised his voice, because my bouts of nerves made me feel wimpy around him. When he stormed outside to take the call, I was able to concentrate on what I was doing.

I held my breath and forced a manual reset, praying he'd backed up his work because if he hadn't, it would all be lost, and he'd kick my ass. With a bright and happy *ding*, the screen repowered, and the spreadsheet looked exactly the same. I ran my good hand over my face with relief, and I was about to close the laptop when something caught my eye.

There was a spreadsheet tab beside the one that was open, titled *Dummy.* Not very subtle. It looked nearly identical to the one opened when Ben handed me the laptop, records of transactions from different bank accounts, manually created by Ben. He was an accountant and did freelance bookkeeping for a bunch of companies, and I recognized a few names of his clients he'd complained about recently—Galway, Inc., Maurice French PTY, LTD., and Kerning Trade… Big names tied up with serious shit in DC. But the transactions on the spreadsheet seemed off.

All the money seemed to be flowing through to a third spreadsheet that tallied the total. At the top of the third was a single ten-digit number. I was more familiar with 001 combinations, but I recognized this one—the account number on the deposit slips I used to put my paychecks into. Ben's account. Ben was siphoning money from his clients.

My stomach clenched.

No way. He couldn't be that stupid, could he?

I caught a glimpse of his bulky frame through a gap in the door, still on the phone as he paced in the hallway. Good, I had time. My heart was racing, and my leg started bouncing. I had to act fast.

With a deep breath, I bit through the pain in my wrist and keystroked my way into Ben's hard drive with rapid-fire keyboard shortcuts, quickly searching for evidence he wasn't seriously stealing cash from major players in DC. My stomach sank when I got into his bank accounts and found the opposite—the transactions were for real. He was cutting a little off the top of his clients' accounts and accruing a hefty balance for himself.

"You idiot, Ben." I sighed and ran a hand through my hair.

"I wish you hadn't seen that."

I jumped and shouted when his voice hissed from over my shoulder. "What the fuck? You're stealing from your clients. Why would you do something so stupid?" I needed to hear him say it wasn't what I thought it was, what my brain told me it was. I needed my brother not to be a thief on top of every other thing I already knew him to be.

"This is none of your business." His chest puffed up and his hands clenched into fists as he looked me over. A vein pulsed in his neck. I shrank back, even though I hated looking weak, but I was trembling and he'd no doubt notice, so my slight prep to duck and cover didn't matter much. Such were the excuses I made for myself.

He let out a low growl. A threat, but he didn't hit me. He reached to slam the laptop shut before he snatched it off the desk and stalked toward the door.

My relief was quickly followed by genuine concern. Whatever he'd gotten himself into was…bad. Illegal at best. Dangerous at worst. I spun my chair and stood. "Hey! Talk to me. You're asking for trouble, Ben."

He barked with laughter. "You wouldn't know the first thing about it, *Sebastian*."

Of course, I wouldn't know anything about it. I was too dumb. Too naïve. Too young to understand. Same old war cries he'd been throwing at me since he was a teen, and I was still a scrawny runt, trying desperately to be his friend. Maybe back then, he was right—I hadn't known much about sports, girls, or beer, because I was a dorky kid who didn't take his nose out of my computer screen, and he was the big man on campus. But this—numbers and spreadsheets—was in my wheelhouse and I could read. Decipher. Snoop. This was different.

"I'm a fucking hacker, dude. Of course, I know about cybertheft, are you kidding me? My people practically invented it." *My people* being the computer geniuses who bailed out accountants who got locked out of their programs. We were the gurus. The cutting edge Einsteins of today who could go undetected for years because we understood a language no one else did. And anyone who looked at his shit would know he was in over his head.

"You don't know shit about my life."

"Maybe not." I bit my lip and tried not to show how sad that fact made me. "Can I help, though? You need better security around your digital footprint if you're going to be wrangling cash out of accounts like that—" This once, I could do something for him. Something valuable that could keep him out of prison if he listened to me.

"Help? You?" His fresh bark of laughter earned him my glare and he looked me up and down, ending on a scowl. I'd been found lacking.

I clenched my jaw and swallowed thickly. "Yeah, me. Or am I so useless I can only unfreeze your piece-of-shit laptop?"

"Just shut the fuck up, all right?" He sniffed arrogantly and headed toward the door. "About all of it."

The words flew out before I could stop them. "Or what?"

"Or *what*?" He spun, eyebrows raised, fists clenched.

"Yeah, *or what*? Have you thought about what's going to happen if your secret gets out? How bad it'd be on you if someone finds out about this?"

"Don't fucking threaten me, Seb."

His voice was icy, and he stepped toward me. I should have backed down. Every instinct in my body told me to duck and cover. But my anger rose up and out of my mouth, and I snarled. "*Or what?*"

The laptop hit the floor. His boots squeaked against the floorboards as his heavy frame rushed back into the room. Fear weakened me, my knees gave out, and everything went black.

Chapter 3 - Derek

Home sweet-smelling home. I let myself into the Vanguard Tower after my shift and took a deep breath. My brothers and I had used a lot of bare cedarwood beams in the conversion of this old warehouse into a communal apartment building, and the wood made the whole place smell warm and welcoming, exactly what I needed after a long, bloody shift. It had taken a lot of work to build a hollowed-out warehouse into a set of six apartments, and I was grateful every single time I came home.

The old building at the docks of the southwest waterfront had been somewhat of a wreck when I'd inherited it from a grandfather I never knew I had. My mother had died in front of me when I was eight, from a home invasion gone really, really wrong and with no dad or other family, I went into the system and got shuffled between foster homes for the next ten years. Life had been tough back then, but I'd met my brothers—the foster crew who had helped revamp the warehouse we now affectionately called the Vanguard Tower, a nod to the fact that we all worked on the frontlines as first responders.

It was close to midday by the time I slipped the key in the lock of my apartment at the back of the ground floor—hours after I should've already been home. I'd stayed back to see Seb's X-rays … Not that I'd had to, and not that he'd known about it. I was confident in my diagnosis of a sprained wrist, but I couldn't leave before I knew for sure he wasn't suffering from a fracture that needed to be set.

As soon as the results came in clear, my tiredness, crankiness, and hunger really set in, and by the time I got home, I was exhausted.

Inside my unit, I shook off my shoes and started to strip before a stifled cough made me jump. My brother, Braxton, sat on the ottoman with a grin stretched from ear to ear, while Eli was in the kitchen at the far end of the open-plan living area, rooting through my fridge.

"Privacy?" I scowled. I shouldn't have been surprised. We were constantly in each other's spaces. Personal space meant nothing here. I usually loved how close we were, but after twelve especially bloody hours at work and not a single candy bar in my belly, I wasn't in the mood for company. And my head was still stuck on Sebastian. Stuck on his case. Not on him. On. His. Case.

"You're *way* too late for chicken and waffles, Derek." Braxton licked his fingers and moaned like he could still taste the maple syrup.

"Yeah, big shift at the hospital today." I picked up my shirt from where I'd tossed it on the floor and threw it at my youngest brother. My aim was way off, but he caught it before it flew over his shoulder.

He took one sniff of it and gagged then tossed it back at me. "I've got something for you."

"And I've got some food coming up." The kitchen island was covered with ingredients, and Eli was fishing a skillet from the rack above the stove when Uno, his German Shepherd, bounded out from behind the counter and rushed to say hello to me.

I gave her a cuddle then collapsed onto the couch and grunted something I hoped sounded like appreciation, while Braxton fished through his bag, and Uno rested her chin on my knee for more pats. Brax chucked a rolled-up shirt at me, and I let it slap against my chest before I unraveled it and admired the intricate hand-painted design of figures and symbols.

"You like?" His voice quivered. My heart panged whenever my little brothers looked to me for approval, even now when they were all grown.

"Very cool." It was. Braxton was the baby of the brothers at only twenty-four, working as an artist, and the only one of us who wasn't on the frontlines. He'd been designing his own clothing recently and this one looked like a work of art I could hang on the wall.

"Batik technique from Indonesia, but I used some ideas from Japanese and European folklore. Kind of a mishmash. Like me." He was of Caucasian and Asian descent…and that was as specific as his record in the foster system got when it came to background details on his heritage.

"I love it." My enthusiasm hadn't fared well in the last few minutes, and I yawned when I should've smiled.

Brax frowned. "Uh, sure. It sounds like you *hate* it."

Uno nudged my hand for more affection, and I could barely keep my eyes open as I stroked her fur. "Sorry, Brax. I just had a long shift."

"I haven't seen you this drained for years." Eli tied his long dark hair up into his signature bun and threw a handful of garlic into a pan sizzling with oil. "Tough cases? Tougher than usual, I mean…"

"Mm. Lots of trauma… The usual. One was a bit tough on me personally though, I suppose." I pushed Uno's ears back and scratched her chin. Tough because I knew he'd be back with more bruises, more injuries he would explain with falls and accidents. I'd seen worse cases, this shift even, but his stuck with me. "Younger guy came in with a sprained wrist and bruises on his arms. You know…" We all knew. The foster care system was fraught with "accidents."

They each nodded silently. We'd all seen it before. The shit I'd experienced in foster care was part of the reason why I went into medicine, to do my best to intervene in the cycle of abuse.

Not that it was that easy. When I aged out of the foster system at eighteen, I wanted to go into healthcare. As a mid-level basketballer with good grades, I had offers for full scholarships from five top tier colleges. But the offers didn't include housing, and I couldn't afford to make it on my own. I was steeling myself to reject all the offers and take up a job at a coffee shop. And call it a twist of fate or a stroke of dumb luck, but just as I was about to make the calls, a lawyer tracked me down. My mother's father had recently passed away, and he'd left me a building. A warehouse that should've been condemned. But I spent my first semester of classes working on my essays by the light of a kerosene lamp, huddled in a sleeping bag, and inhaling dust in the middle of the worn-out warehouse.

If it hadn't been for my two eldest brothers, Sean and Matthew, it would have stayed that way through my entire college career, but with their help, I worked my butt off to convert the place into a series of apartments, three units on each of the three levels, and maintain a solid 4.0 GPA. Mine was the first to be built—a pod at the back of the ground floor, peaceful and quiet.

It had taken us a hell of a long time, but with the building done and our lives on track, we got it to the point where we could prove that we were capable and stable enough to foster the rest of the younger brothers who now all lived there in one way or another, and we still kept a spare unit on the top floor as a safe space for anyone in need.

"You can't save everyone." Eli whisked eggs, and Uno looked up at the sound.

Braxton scoffed. "Like you can talk, Eli. You're just as addicted to saving people as Derek is."

"Yeah, well, it's a better addiction than most." Eli picked up the pace on the eggs and Uno started panting excitedly.

Brax flicked his hand at Eli. "That's relative. You throw yourself off cliffs to save people, that's dangerous as hell."

Eli pointed at him with the whisk dripping with egg. "Not as dangerous as being bored."

I nodded in agreement, and Braxton did a double-take between us.

"You two are so weird." Brax softened the insult with his trademark crooked grin.

The smell of warm garlic made my stomach growl, and Uno sniffed the air as Eli poured eggs into the pan. He expertly filled and flipped the omelet, and I wondered if there was anything he couldn't do with graceful ease.

When he'd plated the omelet and served it at the dining table, I hauled myself up and pulled him into a hug. He'd been away for months for his work in search and rescue in national parks, and I never appreciated how much I missed him until he was back. "It's good to see you, brother."

He thumped my shoulder. "You too, man. Eat up, let me feed you, it's the only way I can tend to my savior complex while I'm away from work."

He pulled out my chair and shoved me into it with a firm grip on my shoulders, while Braxton skulked around the kitchen and picked at the leftovers of the vegetables on the chopping board.

"You're *still* hungry?" Eli asked him, staring at our little brother with wide eyes and a half-opened mouth. In his defense, Brax was only twenty-four and hadn't quite outgrown his metabolism yet and needed to be fed every few hours to maintain his constant energy.

"Yeah, man. What do you think, I'm going for the starving artist persona? I've got a physique to maintain." Brax flexed, and Eli rolled his eyes.

I chuckled into my mouthful. It wasn't that Braxton wasn't built, he was just the smallest of us at five foot seven and the youngest, and as he rifled through the kitchen, he was dwarfed by Eli's mountain-climber frame of over six feet.

"Go sit down, I'll make you one, too." Eli nudged him away from the counter.

"Nah, I'll find something in the fridge—"

Eli slapped his hip with a rolled-up dish towel. "Get the hell out of the kitchen, little bro. I'll cook, I don't trust you with these pans. Or maybe Derek will share—"

"Mm-mm. No way. This is mine." I wrapped my forearm around the plate and made a production of shoveling in a bite while they watched.

When Brax made a move to come closer, I waved my fork like a Musketeer's sword, and Uno followed it with hungry eyes.

"Yeah, *Derek* has a physique to maintain," Eli said. I wasn't bodybuilder buff, but I could hold my own.

Braxton grumbled and pulled out a chair opposite me, and another beside him. With a snap of his fingers, he had Uno sitting up beside him, panting happily at the table.

"Really?" I raised my eyebrows as the German Shepherd eyed my meal.

"She's a good girl." He gave her a scratch, and she licked his cheek.

"Hey, she's a working dog, don't teach her bad habits." Eli pointed at Braxton with a spatula from behind the stove where he was cooking more eggs for the youngest brother.

"What's bad about sitting at the table like a person? Looks sophisticated to me." Brax gave Uno another stroke behind her ears then shot me a wink.

"I don't want her getting any ideas about being part of high society or some shit. We don't have dining tables where we stay near the woods, and what if she starts refusing to eat out of her dish?" Eli spoke with authority but also joy. He loved his dog, his job and his brothers. Probably in that order.

I focused on my meal and tried to drown out their prattle until Eli slid a plate in front of Brax, and another beside my first.

"More? For me?" He had the best instincts.

"You look like you need it." He sat down beside me and pulled his long brown hair into a bun at the nape of his neck. "What've I missed while I've been gone?"

"This is about it. Work, sleep, and putting up with these idiots."

"Work… Family… What about *love*?" He drew the word out, an exaggerated thought.

I almost choked on the bite I'd just taken, and then raised my eyebrows at him while I took a sip of juice. "Something you want to tell me about?"

"Why are you being evasive?" He cocked his head, and I couldn't tell if he was hinting or prying.

"Why are *you* being evasive?" I went with hinting.

"Is he seeing someone?" Eli asked Braxton.

"Derek? C'mon, man. You haven't been gone that long. He's a player. For as long as we all shall live. Four months won't change that shit."

"Hey, I'm not a *player*." Except, I kind of was. Relationships were time consuming. And exhausting. And I had brother and a job to tick off those particular boxes. So, check and check.

Braxton laughed. "Fact: in *all* the time I've known you, you have never gone on a second date. Fact: that makes you a player."

My ethos in life didn't fit with commitment. Nothing ever managed to last. The only constant in life was change, so why would I try to stick a pin in something that was meant to ebb and flow? As far as I could see, that was a sure-fire path to heartache and disappointment. But I wasn't going to get into the truth of it with them over breakfast at the end of an arduous shift. "Maybe I'd get a second date if I wasn't so busy taking care of you horde, fixing up your boo-boos and healing your broken hearts."

"Hey, don't blame us for your commitment issues!" Braxton slapped the table.

They cracked up while I rolled my eyes and finished the last bite of my meal. I wiped my mouth with a napkin then chucked it at Braxton. Uno edged toward the plate and lapped up the crumbs as I stood and headed toward the bathroom.

Eli booed, and Braxton laughed. "Aw, c'mon! We're only teasing! Where are you going?"

"Got to shower and get some sleep so I can save some more people tomorrow. That's what we do, isn't it?"

"Amen!" Eli called, and Brax groaned.

"Addicts."

Maybe Brax was right. Maybe I was addicted. Nothing made me more present and alert than the sound of gurney wheels clattering through the emergency doors, like they did at seven the next morning as I rushed into the bay.

"Guess that wish didn't last all the way through to today, huh?" I rushed with Shae to meet the EMT straddling a guy's body to perform chest compressions. It was near the end of my shift, another long twelve hours of repeated trauma cases.

"Didn't you say some shit about making your own luck?" Shae hissed at me, her stethoscope swinging as she jogged by my side.

"Guess I need more practice." I met the swift pace of the medic who rushed the gurney toward a cardiac room. "Details?"

"Male, twenties." The medic veered the cart left and we careened down a corridor, more nurses joining us as we went. "Plucked out of the Potomac River by the manager of a nearby convenience store who saw him fall in. Found unconscious, CPR immediately. Still not responding."

"Jumper?" It made my stomach sink every time we received an attempted suicide, which was way more common than I would have liked.

"Probably." The medic grimaced. "Found him just downstream from Arlington Memorial. That bridge is a killer."

"Well, not if we can help it. Vitals?"

"No pulse, no respiration, no shockable rhythm. Compressions and Epi in the field."

The other EMT kept working on the patient's chest as we got the gurney into a bay and nurses pushed electrodes from monitors onto his chest and sides.

"Let's get a rhythm." I nodded to Shae who was working with the other nurses to hook up ECG leads. Dammit. We couldn't shock the patient with the rhythm his heart was beating.

"Patient is asystole. Epinephrine administered?" I felt my own adrenaline kick in as I rushed to help the nurses fit a new bag to help with respiration.

The EMT giving compressions glanced up and smiled at me, sweat dripping from his brow. "One mil, given once, doc."

I did a double-take. It was Owen, my red-headed brother. Relief washed through me. I trusted him implicitly.

"Once more. Epinephrine, one milligram. Continue compressions."

"Roger that." He nodded and continued grunting and pumping his hand against the patient's sternum.

Shae administered the IV drug, and I held my breath. It was always touch and go from a flatline. But three quiet breaths later, the heart monitor picked up a single spike of contraction.

"There we go, we've got v-tach." I clapped my hands. "Administering single shock defib."

Shae put gel on the paddles and handed them to me while Owen leaped off the table. Everyone stood back as I moved forward with the defibrillator paddles in my hands. The shock snapped through the patient while I kept my eyes on the monitors. The line remained in v-tach. I cursed quietly. It could take two minutes, but I wanted it faster.

"Resume compressions." I handed the paddles back and then made way for nurses to restart CPR.

The tension of shocking someone always took me by surprise, but it was followed by something worse—the two minutes it could take to see if the single shock had worked to get the heart started again. There was a flurry of activity as we rushed to stabilize his temperature, look him over for any obvious injuries, and worked around the patient's neck brace.

"Take compressions?" Owen called, tagging out of the exhausting task.

"Here." I stepped in and pulsed pressure against the patient's chest until my arms and shoulders ached, burned, almost gave up, and kept going while sweat soaked through my shirt.

All eyes in the room were fixed on the monitors, still showing no sign of independent heartbeat.

"Fuck. C'mon." I whispered and pumped.

"Tag out?" Shae offered to take over the compressions, but I shook my head. I grunted as I kept up the steady pace. I'd bring him back. I knew I would.

Suddenly, the monitor spiked, and a wave of relief moved through the group, everyone so professional that the emotion was almost imperceptible. I let out a heavy breath and swiped the back of my arm over my sweaty brow and let my other hand rest on the patient's chest where a heart was beating all by itself.

Pulse and breathing back online, Owen slapped my back by way of goodbye as I rushed forward to continue my care of the patient, while he headed back out to work in the field.

"This guy have a name?" I asked the nurses as I helped them hook up more IV fluids.

Shae read from the paperwork the EMTs had left behind. "No ID on him."

I glanced down at the John Doe, now visible without the ambu-bag over his face, and stumbled backward. "Fuck."

"Doctor?"

I wiped my face against my shoulder and let out a shaky breath. "Sorry. I know him."

He wasn't a John Doe. I knew him as the young man who'd been in the ER only twenty-four hours earlier, full of life. Seb.

A heavy weight landed in my gut. Dammit, I'd had an intuition that his circumstances hadn't been the most peaceful. The abusive boyfriend or whoever was responsible for the bruises and sprained wrist was surely involved in what might have been a suicide.

It's not your concern. I could hear my brothers in my head, reprimanding me for getting too involved.

"Oh, shit… Sebastian, right?" Shae tutted her tongue like it was a shame.

I shook off the past and snapped into professional mode. I threw out orders for X-rays and notes on his chart then walked out of the room. I needed to pull it together. Seeing him had shaken me, literally, and my hands trembled. I couldn't risk anyone questioning me until I had answers for myself. The weight of my shift suddenly crushed me, and my legs went weak with fatigue. I threw my gloves in the trash and started toward the staff room but ended up slumped in a chair in the recovery ward. Something about Sebastian pulled me. I wanted to see his X-rays, the blood work-up, the monitor readouts. It had been touch and go in there, but the guy was breathing again. For now.

I planned to stay for no more than twenty minutes, just to make sure he was going to make it. My patient. My responsibility. So, half an hour wouldn't kill me...

Chapter 4 - Sebastian

Nauseous. Thirsty. Awake. I pried one eye open and quickly scrunched it shut again when blinding light smacked my retina. I didn't move but listened to the sounds around me. The beep-beep-blip of a heart rate monitor, the shuffle of soft-soled shoes on tile, the scrape of metal on metal curtain loops and rods. The smell of ammonia and bleach, and overboiled vegetables. A hospital.

I opened my eyes, and it all came rushing back. Ben's laptop, the missing funds he'd scooped up from his clients, the argument, the confrontation… I remembered him stalking toward me, and then…nothing. I blinked at the bright light and glided my hands over my arms, feeling for protruding bones or bumps and lumps under my skin, for pain I didn't feel right then. Was I hurt? What about Ben? Was he okay? I suffered the inertia of falling without moving, dizziness or some other phenomenon. Dehydration, maybe.

I grunted and pushed into the bed with my good hand to try and sit up, but pressure on my arm stopped me. My breath caught. Dr. Dish. Holding me. He'd patched me up once. When? How long had I been out?

"What happened?" My voice was beyond husky. Closer to gravelly. Deathly, one could say.

"Close call. But you're alive. Still need some rest though." He lifted the world's tiniest cup of water. "Thirsty?"

I cleared my throat and nodded. He unwrapped the straw and passed me the drink to my good hand, but I wasn't ready for the weight of the tiny cup, and spilled half of the water onto the bed. My other arm rested in a new sling, my wrist wrapped in a fresh bandage.

"Do you know where you are?"

Dr. Dish sat back in the chair beside the bed, and I stole a glance as he poured me a fresh cup of water from a pitcher on a small table. He looked damn good in his gray button-down shirt, not that his scrubs weren't nice, but what he did for street clothes was…shameful. I caught a glimpse of a tattoo under his short sleeves—a sideways figure eight on his bicep.

"Hospital." I dragged my eyes back to his to show him I was lucid and not just staring

"Do you know what day of the week it is?" He passed me the cup, and this time I was ready to use all my strength to hold it up.

"Uh…" My head was foggy. "Tuesday?" It was when last I saw Ben and we had the argument. But I'd been asleep, so it could've been Wednesday. Or later, for all I knew.

"Yeah, it is. How are you feeling? Do you have any nausea? Headache?" His voice was deep and soft, and I liked the way he looked at me, slow, thorough, like he was taking me all in.

I thought for a moment. I let the pain I'd been denying have its moment which immediately led to a churning in my stomach. "Bad. Both."

He nodded, but he didn't move to get me any medication. Instead, he leaned forward, elbows on his knees, hands folded in front of him.

"What happened?" Good question. Maybe a detail would slip through and I'd remember how I got here, but the more I tried to remember, the less I could focus.

"I don't know. What do you know about it?" Maybe something in what he could tell me would jog a memory free.

"You were brought into the ER." He sat up, and his full mouth thinned into a straight line, a little less soft, and his eyes were steely. He didn't look unkind, but more all-business.

I braced myself for whatever gnarly details he had to give.

"You were pulled out of the Potomac River near the Arlington Memorial Bridge, and resuscitated here. You've got a nasty concussion, so we're monitoring you. We had to shock your heart because you came in without a pulse or any breath sounds even, and you need to recover from that—probably just a few days since you're young and healthy. All things considered, you're one lucky kid."

I winced. "I'm not a *kid*." If I sounded vehement, angry even, it was because I got that a lot. And I wasn't a kid. Age was a number. Experience determined how old a person was. And I'd survived my share of experience.

His eyes went wide, but he smiled slowly. "Okay."

I didn't have the energy to flash him one in return, so I let the information sink in. My heart had stopped. I died? Shit... And I was found in the river? The Potomac was a block away from my apartment. How the hell had I ended up in the water? Did Ben know what had happened?

My stomach turned, and I closed my eyes as the room began to spin. I was in some kind of trouble. I certainly hadn't gone into the water on my own and the alternatives to that weren't much better.

The last thing I remembered was Ben coming for me, but he wouldn't dump me in the river. Of course, maybe he knew what really happened. I had to speak to him.

"Cool. Thanks for...saving me. I've got to get out of here." I needed to see my brother. Now. Waiting would only make things worse.

"Whoa, slow down, you'll get lightheaded." Dr. Dish put his hand on my arm again as I sat straight and went to swing my legs over the side of the bed.

Of course, he was right. The room swam in little blurry waves of color and motion. But no way could I lie here and wait for it to right itself. I fell back against the bed and huffed in frustration. "Seriously, doc. I've got to go."

Edging his chair closer to the bed, he frowned and pursed his lips. All concern, with no real reason.

"Listen, Sebastian—"

"*Seb.*"

"Right. Seb. We can talk in confidence here, with doctor-patient confidentiality." He nudged closer still and held my gaze. Intense. Delicious despite being so serious. "Aside from your medical issues, I want to make sure you're safe before you leave."

My guts went cold and a shudder ran up my back when I considered just how much danger I must have been in to end up with a lungful of Potomac slurry. "Yeah, me too, that's *why* I want to leave." I didn't want to believe this had anything to do with Ben. I didn't want to believe that my recent run of bad luck was his fault, either, but I needed to hear it from him, needed him to look at me and say he hadn't involved me and that my seeing his spreadsheet hadn't put my life at risk. But somehow, I'd ended up in the water. And I wasn't the kind who would've thrown myself off a bridge.

"What are you afraid of?" Concern deepened his voice and I almost fell for it. Almost gave in. "Are you afraid someone's going to do something if you speak to me?"

Through the foggy haze of my concussion, I bit back a gasp when I realized what was happening. He thought I was in an abusive relationship, and maybe even that I'd thrown myself off the bridge. Fine, I could let him think that. If I told him about Ben coming after me, he would immediately think I was here because my brother hurt me. And we didn't know that. *I* didn't know it. So, no, I couldn't tell him anything.

It was a struggle, but I managed to keep a straight face.

"I'm okay. Seriously. No one tried to hurt me, I didn't try to hurt myself, it was an accident. For real." I grimaced inside at how overly insistent I sounded. I wouldn't have believed a word if I was in his position.

But Dr. Dish nodded as though taking my word for it, while his eyes pinned me against the bed. My heart raced, and my chest tingled until I dragged my eyes away. He cleared his throat.

"Well, just in case you need them, I have some pamphlets here. Outpatient clinics for various conditions, such as depression, anxiety…suicidal ideation… And some local outreach for people in abusive situations." He sounded so genuinely kind and concerned, I couldn't maintain my flip attitude. It faded, and I nodded.

"I mean, I don't need them, really. But thanks, Dr.— uh…what's your real name?"

"My *real* name?" He cocked an eyebrow, but grinned. "Derek. Uh, Dr. Carlisle."

"Carlisle. Huh." It wasn't the porny doctor name that I'd expected, but it suited him. Handsome, well put together…and particularly gallant. But I couldn't lie around staring at him all day, I had to find out what happened, and there was only one person who could tell me. Ben.

Shit. If I'd fallen or been tossed off the bridge, maybe Ben had too. "Did I get brought in to the ER with anyone else?"

He tilted his head. "Not that I'm aware of."

"Right." I blew out a sigh.

I shook my head and held up the hand with the IV stuck in the back of it. "Can you take this out?"

He grimaced and shook his head.

I scoffed, annoyed. "Can't or won't?"

"Can't. You're not my patient." He cleared his throat and sat back, his gaze at a spot over my head. "Another doctor in the ward is taking care of your case, you'll have to talk to her about getting released."

I squinted, trying to make sense of the very recent twists and turns my life had taken and why, if Derek wasn't my doctor, he was at my bedside. "Then what are you doing here?"

With his eyes down, a twinge danced at the edge of his lips. "I was your ER doctor."

"Oh." It wasn't a shock I'd come through the emergency room, but the idea of Dr. Derek Carlisle bringing me back from the brink of death was kind of a head spin. I admired him while he wasn't looking at me. Handsome, stubbled jaw, shapely nose, insanely plump kissable lips… "So, you saved my life?"

He laughed and shook his head. "It was touch and go, but like I said, you're a lucky—"

"Adult."

He nodded and smiled. "I was going to say 'son of a gun.'"

"Ha! How old are you? Eighty?" Honestly. No one said *son of a gun* anymore.

He scoffed and ran a hand through his short brown hair, maybe a little self-consciously. "Thirties, so not quite ready for the old folks' home."

Thirties. And perfect. Hanging around in my room when he probably had other things to do. And he was a hero. "Well, thanks. For, you know. Bringing me back from the brink of death."

"Don't mention it." Our eyes met, something moved between us. He licked his lips, and shy-smiled before a gnawing in my gut reminded me I needed to skedaddle and figure out what the hell was going on.

"I really need to get out of here so…"

"Right. Yeah, of course." His smile dropped, and his bright eyes clouded over. "I'll get your doctor. For the record, I don't recommend leaving. You have a serious concussion, and you need rest. She'll likely say the same."

I nodded and pretended like the movement didn't make the room spin.

There was nothing left for either of us to say, and he rushed out of the room faster than I expected. I'd stung him. Hurt him somehow, but I didn't call him back. I had enough problems without worrying about Dr. Dish's feelings.

It was sticky-hot outside, even at sunset. A little after seven that evening, I sat hunched over on a bench by the hospital doors and breathed in the swampy air to the count of four…out to the count of six…in for four…out for six. Tingles of residual panic pricked at my lips and fingers, but my pulse wasn't racing any more. Lucky, since the doctor on duty had been worried about my heart after the shock I'd been given in the ER by none other than Dr. Derek Carlisle.

My mind was completely absorbed with thoughts of Dr. Dish performing emergency resuscitation on my nearly dead body. It was weird how he kept showing up. Serendipity maybe. Or maybe he worked at the hospital where I kept ending up.

It took all day to get discharged, thanks to the resistance of the ward doctor, the battery of tests they put me through, and a six-hour nap I accidentally took in the middle of the day. They made it damned clear I was discharging myself against medical advice, citing concussions and risks of brain damage, but I'd been adamant I was good to go and readily signed the stack of papers they handed me.

Right up to the moment I stepped outside, I was determined to find Ben and face him. He wasn't answering his cell, and without my own phone, I had no way of checking in on his Facebook or emailing him. My best plan was to get out and go over to his condo and confront him. But as I stepped outside with determination, my head spun, my chest tightened, and I had to sit down.

Fear bolted through me. I couldn't shake the memory of Ben coming at me, fists clenched. Maybe I did need more rest to shake off the heebie-jeebies. But where? I had nowhere to go. I couldn't very well go back to my apartment. Who knew what was waiting for me there? I couldn't remember what the hell had happened immediately before I had to be pulled from the Potomac, so I couldn't guess who or what was safe. Cue mild panic attack that had me on the bench in the sticky heat, counting my breaths.

I kept counting and tried to focus. My mind cleared. All I needed was information, some reassurance I was safe. But the only person who knew shit-all about what had happened to me would have to be Ben, but no guarantee he'd tell me the truth. Thanks to a ten-year age gap and major personality differences, we'd never been close. He'd never approved of me being out and proud, but at least he hadn't disowned me. Any morsel of approval I managed to wriggle out of him was just a scrap I was supposed to be thankful for, but I was grateful he hadn't cut me off completely, and deep down I think he really did still love his me. He just never said it…

Still, it was a mighty coincidence that I'd ended up on the wrong side of an emergency room again and only after I'd seen his spreadsheets… Although, before he'd ever arrived, I'd thought someone was watching me. Maybe my dip in the Potomac had something to do with that.

What I'd seen on Ben's laptop had set off alarm bells, but it was probably all a misunderstanding. He'd caught me snooping. And been mad. Maybe he'd tried to explain. Ran out, and I ran after him. Tripped. Fallen a block forward into the river. I wasn't that klutzy, but something. And that something couldn't have been Ben. We were different and sometimes it caused friction, but he wouldn't...try to kill me. But Someone had tried—and almost succeeded.

With my head in my hands, I rubbed my temples and tried to soothe the pain blooming there. A hand touched my shoulder and I jumped, and almost leaped again when I saw who it was. Dr. Dish's dark blue eyes flashed over mine, and I smiled despite myself.

"What are you doing out here?" His voice was tight, and his brow furrowed. And even that was adorable.

"Waiting for a ride. What're you doing here?"

"My shift starts soon." He motioned to the hospital with his chin. His thick, square jaw masculine and delicious from my vantage point. "But seriously, what are you doing? You should be in bed." He raised perfectly groomed, thick eyebrows and stared at me, like he was waiting for the truth. When I stared back, silent and guarding my secrets because I wasn't sure what they were, he sighed and took a seat, so close that our knees touched. "You can trust me, you know."

I scoffed. "Really? You know people who say, 'you can trust me,' are generally *not* trustworthy, right?"

"Should I say you can't trust me?"

"Probably closer to the truth."

He blinked and leaned back, and I grimaced at the tone of my own voice. Gruff. Angry. But…I'd just drowned and had no idea how it'd happened. Cranky didn't seem so big a stretch. But then again…this guy had saved my life.

"Sorry." I sniffed and looked at the ugly brown buildings at the other side of the parking lot.

"Look. If you need help—"

"I don't." The last thing I wanted to do was break down in front of him. And I was close enough without his soft gaze and his gentle voice.

"If you *want* help—"

Yeah. Another pamphlet maybe? "I'm good." The guy was a doctor, what was he going to do? I needed a private detective or a bodyguard. Someone who could find out who was involved in my swim in the Potomac. He was expert at the patch-up but I needed the guy who could stop whatever this was from happening again.

My heart raced at the thought of the danger that I was in, and I winced as I pressed the heel of my hand against my breastbone.

"Are you all right? Chest pain?" He moved closer and his voice softened so much I felt bad for being a shit.

"It's all good, Dr. Dish."

Oh, shit. Did I just say that? I clamped my mouth shut, and giggled when his jaw fell open, and he looked way less put together and intimidating.

"Uh…"

I kept laughing, and the pain in my chest relaxed.

When I finally calmed, he blew out a quiet breath and pointed those big blue eyes at me again. "Look. I have a lot of experience helping people, and not just in the hospital. I can't shake the feeling you might need a hand." Help people? Of course he would be some crusading hero. Probably had a cape at home. Maybe some tights. Oh, wow. That was a visual I couldn't—maybe didn't want to—shake.

I cleared my throat. "I appreciate it. And maybe you're right, I might need some kind of help, but there's really nothing you can do right now."

"You sure?" God, all this care and concern was killing me. Making me weak enough to want whatever help he could give.

"Yeah."

"If not right now, then…" He shoved his hand into his pants pocket and scuffed his knee against mine as he adjusted to gain access to his wallet. I caught a flash of the perfectly organized credit cards and thick wad of bills in there before I looked away. He cleared his throat, and when I looked back, he held out a business card.

"I got the pamphlets already—" Self-help, group help, one-on-one help. Yeah. I had the pamphlets.

"It's my card. My personal details are on there. If you ever need any help—"

"I won't." But my hand moved by itself to take the card. My fingers grazed his, and a shock of energy moved up my arm when we touched.

"Keep it. In case you need it."

I shook my head as I looked at the raised letters of his name. Dr. Derek Carlisle, PhD. There was no denying Dr. Dish was my type. Older, good-looking, kind, had his shit together. But what was I going to do? Ask him out on a date?

My life was in the shitter, and the last thing I needed was a complicated, but probably oh-so-steamy affair with Dr. Dish. I cleared my throat, gave him a single nod, and hauled myself up off the bench. I had to make tracks. The sun was setting and heading home wasn't going to get any less scary in the dark.

Chapter 5 - Derek

The only way to stop myself from calling Seb back was to bite my tongue. I was glad to see the social worker I'd contacted had dropped off some clothes for him, an oversized button-down with a faded pastel pattern that made him look like a skater from the '90s. Not that he would remember the '90s…I took a deep breath and shook my head. I needed to move on. Not only was he a kid, but he clearly didn't want my help. Time to let it go.

But halfway into the hospital doors, I found myself reaching for my phone. Eli had given me a ride to work, and I'd have bet anything that he was still sitting in his truck in the parking lot where I left him, playing games.

He answered with a grunt.

"Hey, are you busy?"

"I mean, yeah. This new Tetris is killer—"

I didn't particularly have time to stand around and listen to how easily he could spin his colored blocks. I had work to do, lives to save, traumas to heal. "I need a favor."

I could practically hear him sitting up to attention. "Anything."

"There's a kid, twenties, plaid shirt, heading out of the parking lot right now. I've got a really bad feeling. Can you tail him for me?" With every word, the feeling dug deeper into the lining of my stomach. He was in trouble.

"Is this the same kid with the wrist and the river you were telling me about?" Thank God he paid attention. Plus, I hadn't really talked about much else between bites of food and cuddle time with my pillow.

"Yeah." I braced for today's savior complex lecture, but all I could hear was the engine turning on.

"I'm on it. I'll keep you updated."

I smiled as I made my way through the sliding glass doors of the emergency room. I'd been telling Seb he was a lucky guy, but so was I. I had Eli and my other brothers at my back, I could deal with anything life could throw at me.

Or so I thought.

Hours into my shift, I hadn't been able to shake thoughts of Seb. I was worried, but also more than that. Something about those eyes and the way his lips twisted into a smirk when he was being cheeky... I'd been attracted to patients before, but never to the point where I couldn't get them off my mind or to where I was having my brother tail him. Shit.

I was thinking about him as I crossed the break room. Shae started thumping on the side of the vending machine, and I looked up.

"No luck today?" Today, the machine won.

"Hell no. Today is officially a bad luck day."

"I'm telling you." I shook my head at her and we both stared at the machine as if by angry thought alone we could make her candy bar fall. "You've got to stop gambling with this machine, Shae, and just go to the gift shop."

"Says you! Aren't you Mr. Make Your Own Luck? Well, make some luck for me, and get D-4 to cough up the goods!"

It took a lot of thumping, swearing, and sweating, but we finally shook the haunted vending machine at just the right angle so the candy bar dropped. Hmm. Five minutes passed where I wasn't thinking about Seb, but as soon as Shae tore into the wrapper, my head turned back to thoughts of the young man.

By midnight, I'd attended to three traumas, removed a shard of glass from a hand, gotten an asthma attack under control, and *still* Seb remained front and center in my head.

I had to admit my interest in him was more than protective, professional interest. Those intense green eyes were just the start of it. When he'd been scowling at me on the bench out in front of the hospital, I could barely stop myself from staring at his cupid's bow lips. The guy was gorgeous, but there was something even more alluring about him than what was on the surface. He was younger than the type I usually went for, but his independent streak reeled me in. Too bad I'd probably never see him again. He hadn't given any indication he'd be using my business card anytime soon, and I just hoped he had enough resources to get out of whatever bad situation he was in.

It was almost seven in the morning when that bad situation came waltzing right into the emergency room.

"Dr. Carlisle?" Shae waved me over to the intake desk where two big, brawny guys looked me over. I puffed out my chest. Something about this felt off.

"How can I help?" I handed a patient chart to Shae who took the file but continued to stare.

"These two gentleman are looking for information about a patient from earlier today." Her polite nurse tone didn't falter, and she tilted her head to hide her suspicious nod from them.

"We're looking' to talk to someone who knows about a guy who came in here today." This one was big and bulky, a rough-looking brawler with a scar over his eye who cracked his knuckles with his thumb as he spoke.

"Lot of folks come through here. I might not be able to help you." Especially without specifics. "Your guy have a name?"

"Sebastian Lane." The smaller of the two, but still a good-sized man, shoved his hands into his pockets.

Sebastian. Seb, shit. My stomach turned, but I kept my face neutral.

Big and burly poked his chest with a thumb then jerked it toward the man next to him. "I'm Pete. He's my boyfriend. This is his brother, Benjamin."

Benjamin was tall and muscled, the opposite of Seb dancer's frame, but his eyes were the same sparkling green. Enough of a family resemblance for me to buy that part of the story, but Sebastian with Pete? He looked more like a hired goon than the type of guy I'd imagined as Seb's type. No way he'd go for a shaved headed, tattooed, full-on thug. God, I hoped not anyway.

Seb came in by ambulance. No ID. No one with him. Far as I knew, he hadn't even made a call while he was here. Something fishy about this. My gut feeling gave a sharper tug. "What makes you think he's been here?"

"We're worried about him, is all." Ben rubbed the back of his neck nervously. "We heard about a kid coming in with no ID, and we thought it might have been him."

Strange. There wouldn't have been any press about a John Doe since he wasn't one. I'd identified him almost immediately. "How'd you hear about something like that, exactly?"

Pete moved forward, and Shae gasped behind me. I stood my ground even though he reeked of cigarette smoke. "C'mon, man, we're worried about him. Is he here or not?" Pete looked over my shoulder, and I followed his gaze to the security guard staring him down.

Maybe I was just jealous, because I didn't want to think about Seb with the guy at all, but putting two and two together...this guy was big enough to have twisted Seb's wrist, to have knocked him out and thrown him into the river, to... *Whoa. Backpedal.* There was no evidence anyone had "thrown" Seb into the river. And if this was the kind of machismo idiot Seb liked, it was none of my business. But I still wanted to smash my fist into his face. I took a deep breath and reminded myself, yet again, that it wasn't any of my business. I'd offered the patient help and provided him with information about crisis centers and outpatient programs. My duty of care was done. I could let it go.

If only it was that easy.

"You're going to have to contact the authorities if your brother has gone missing."

Ben nodded, but Pete wasn't hearing it. He clenched his fists at his side and leaned in so we were nose to nose. "Fucking bullshit, man. I'm his boyfriend, keeping him away from me is homophobic." He spat the word. With actual spit.

I hardened my tone, my stance, and my resolve. This guy might be able to intimidate Seb, might take his aggressions out on someone half his size, but today, he wasn't dealing with Seb. He was in my face. His bad luck, too. "Sorry." The hell I was. "I'm bound by doctor-patient confidentiality, I couldn't tell you anything about someone who may have been here, even if I wanted to." Which I didn't.

"Yeah, yeah, yeah. It's a load of a shit." He poked his finger into my chest and Ben pulled him back.

"C'mon, Pete. We'll find him." Ben mumbled as he urged Pete away by the collar, the thug keeping his eyes on me as they swaggered out of the emergency room.

Something was definitely off. My instincts were screaming at me, but I couldn't hear what they were trying to say. It was late, but maybe Eli would be up. The last update I had from him came hours ago and all it said was he was following Sebastian downtown. I was about to call, when I noticed a text from Eli. Shit. I'd missed an update.

No. A single string of numbers that made my blood go cold.

911

My heart jumped into my throat. What if Eli was hurt? Or Seb? I wanted to run out. Sprint home if I had to and find out what the hell was going on.

"Shae... How long until my shift is done?"

She looked at the clock then at me. "Half hour, Derek."

Thirty-minutes. Too long. "Shit."

I chewed my bottom lip raw, and my stomach tightened as I dialed then listened to Eli's phone ring. But before the call could connect, a little girl with a broken toe came into the emergency room screaming bloody murder and my worry faded to the background. Taping her up kept me occupied until I was able to get out of there.

Eli still wasn't answering his phone when I sprinted out of the hospital and headed for my car— except Eli had given me a ride to work. No car.

"Shit, shit, *shit*."

It was a short sprint to the taxi rank, but my pulse was thundering by the time I threw myself into the backseat and told the driver the address of the Vanguard Tower. If something happened to my brother—or Seb—I would never forgive myself.

Chapter 6 - Sebastian

Derek's business card was dry and crisp. I dug the corner into my thumb and rubbed my skin raw with the edges of the card as I wandered around Georgetown, vaguely making my way toward my apartment. I felt like shit, my wrist burned without any painkillers in my system, and my head wasn't doing much better. I took a bunch of twists and turns down streets I barely recognized, and I found myself half-lost as the sunset cast a golden light over the buildings and the monuments here. But when I caught a glimpse of the top of my building through rooftops, I turned around, determined to get even more lost. I walked the labyrinth of DC streets away from anything familiar, away from memories just barely in my head.

Maybe I shouldn't have checked myself out of hospital so early. Maybe I wasn't brave enough to face whatever was waiting for me at home. My feet just didn't want to go back to my apartment, and I didn't blame them. I was groggy, but clear enough to recognize that returning home could be a life-ending mistake. I had no idea who was there, or if they'd chuck me off the Arlington Memorial Bridge again.

It was dark when I licked my lips and hissed from the sting of my chapped skin. The houses around me were suburban, some two-stories, with manicured gardens and sprinkler systems… Gardens doused in fresh, wet, hydrating water. I needed it. Like a man possessed, I pushed open an iron gate. A sprinkler hissed a stream of water, and I crouched at the edge of the lawn. I considered crawling, but I didn't want to get grass stains on my ugly— albeit most appreciated— new shirt, so I crept at a half-crouch and giggled quietly at the absurdity of my duck walk. Having a concussion with pain meds in my system was kind of like being drunk. I was desperate for water, acting like a weirdo, and finding it all absurdly funny.

With my mouth wide, I shoved my face under the water and got a mouthful before lights flashed and an alarm bleeped from the porch.

I hissed. "Let's go, feet. Go, go, go!"

But they were pinned to the grass, and the water continued spraying in my face while I stared at the lights coming on inside the house. The place was beautiful and *huge*. Transfixed, I couldn't pull myself away.

Maybe it's Dr. Dish's house.

"Hey!" a man shouted from the doorway; a man three times the size of Dr. Dish and looking eager to murder me…and starting toward me with a baseball bat in hand.

"Sorry!" I snapped out of my trance. I sprinted back through the gate and pounded down the suburban street as fast as I could, while the guy stopped at the edge of his property and raised the bat.

"I'm calling the cops!"

"*Sorry!*"

I kept running until I came to a more urban part of town, and then slowed to a jog. My wrist throbbed, and sprinting had made me even thirstier. I didn't recognize anything, but a convenience store called to me. I slid a bottle of water onto the counter and a man in an offensively bright green polo shirt rang me up.

"Two-fifty."

"Uh..."

The only thing in my pockets were my keys and, of course, the business card. I tapped it against the counter and considered what kind of help Dr. Dish might serve up to a concussed patient who discharged himself too early and wandered the streets for hours.

"I don't have two-fifty."

"Mm-hmm." He braced his hands on the counter on either side of an inlaid lottery dispenser. I liked the shiny colors of the tickets but refocused on the guy when he snapped his fingers on front of my face. "Two-fifty or get out."

I looked around and sighed. "Do you know where we are?"

He didn't so much as blink, but the annoyance was evident in his voice. "Yeah. There's the Potomac. My manager had to fish some asshat jumper out of there this morning."

I blinked. Okay, so maybe I needed to get that concussion tended to, because I was starting to feel like I was in a David Lynch movie. I followed his nod out of the window and there it was, right outside… The Arlington Memorial Bridge. And my apartment was barely a block away. I'd walked around in a huge circle and ended up back near where I'd started. The bridge. The one that I'd fallen from…

"Sir, do you want the water or—"

"Sorry!" I dashed outside and bounced through traffic across Constitution Avenue toward the bridge. The labyrinth had been leading me there all along. If I could remember *anything* about how I'd ended up in the water, maybe I could figure out whether I was still in danger or if it was safe to go home. I stopped at the middle of the bridge and leaned against the stone railing in the dark of a busted streetlight and waited for the memories to come flooding back. A steady stream of light traffic at my back made it sound like I was gazing down at roaring rapids, but the water was shining as it flowed gently.

Nothing came to me at first, so I stared harder, concentrated deeper.

Ben couldn't have chucked me over the edge of the river. There was no way. First of all, he was my brother. Even if that familial bond hadn't stopped him, he wasn't brave enough—or stupid enough—to throw someone off a bridge with traffic passing by, even at night…was he?

He'd left home when I was only eight. When Mom and Dad were alive, he'd visited plenty, but since the accident four years ago, there wasn't really any reason for us to see each other anymore. That was more on his side though—I'd always wanted a closer relationship with him, but I got a clear sense he didn't want to get any closer to me, his closest relative who also happened to be gay.

As a log floated by, a flashback hit me. I was aware the water was rushing up to meet me. My arms pinwheeled, and I stumbled back, gasped for air as a car horn blared and broke me out of the memory. I almost fell back onto the road.

I pushed my back against the pole of the burned-out streetlight and struggled to breathe. Panic. Chest tight. Hands digging in my pockets, desperate for something to hold onto. My fingers curled around the business card, and I dug the edges under my fingernails to give myself a sensation to focus on. I counted my breaths and laced the cardboard through my fingers then folded the corners like origami until I was calm again. Calm, and downright exhausted.

Shit. I needed to go home.

My apartment building was a block from the bridge, and my feet suddenly had no problem taking me there. But my hands were shaking when I reached for my keys, and I stopped at the front door of the building. Without a reason, I dashed into nearby bushes and crouched, waiting and watching…for what, I had no idea. Suspicious activity? It was the middle of the night, and the entire building was dark.

Jelly Belly, a neighborhood cat, yowled behind me and then rubbed against my hip. I hissed at her to be quiet. She must have taken offense because she flashed her butt at me and took off into the alley that ran beside the building.

Oh. Good idea.

I followed her with my new, weird crouch-crawl technique and hummed James Bond music in my head as I flattened myself against the wall. I was half being silly, but the other half of me thought it was smart to stick to the shadows and scout out the joint for signs of danger. I stood in the shadows at the back of the building and craned my neck to look up through the fire escape toward my bedroom window. The blinds were shut. Nothing to worry about.

Jelly Belly laced between my ankles and started purring, and I took that as an all-clear sign. But even cute tortoiseshell cats like Jelly could prove to be deceitful. For all I knew, she could have been working for the bad guys.

I crouch-crawled to the front door and opened it as quietly as I could, quickly shut it before Jelly Belly could sneak in behind me and listened for anything in the building. Aside from Jelly's irritated yowl, the place was silent. The stairs creaked under my lightest steps, and my chest tightened as I reached my floor.

It was dark. My hands shook so badly I had to steady my bad wrist with my good hand to get the key in the lock. As I opened the door, I braced myself for the worst, but I was still shocked by what I saw.

My apartment was a wreck. Coffee table upended. Favorite mug smashed against the floor. Couch shredded. Bookshelf toppled on top of a pile of torn apart paperbacks. I gasped and clutched my chest when I spotted my computers crushed under the weight of my broken desk. I rushed forward, a half-formed thought about saving the hard drives trying to bypass the images my mind couldn't process, but a hand on my shoulder stopped me and a sharp click popped in my ear. My breath caught when cold metal pressed against my temple, and I reflexively threw my hands up in surrender.

"Where is it?" a man's voice was deep and resonant.

"Wh-what?" Mine was barely a whisper.

"Don't play stupid, you fuck. Where's my money?" He shoved the gun harder against my head and my knees went weak. I screwed my eyes shut and focused on my breathing. He poked my temple with the barrel of the gun and growled. "Tell me where the fuck it is or you're dead."

I didn't question whether it was a real gun. When in doubt, I believed I would always assume it was real. Not that I planned to ever get entangled in another situation like this one. Although I didn't know how I'd managed to get involved in this one either. "Look, I don't know what you're talking about. I'm serious, I don't! Just tell me what you're looking for and I'll help you find it—"

"You have three seconds to tell me—" The menace in his voice was punctuated by the pounding of my heart in my ears.

"I would tell you, I swear—" He jabbed the barrel of the gun into my temple, and I winced. Saw pictures of my life pass through my mind.

"Three."

Oh, God. "Please don't do this."

"Two."

I did not want to die. "I promise, I'll do anything you want, I'll do anything, just please don't—"

"One."

I braced myself and just about pissed my pants in fear, before I heard a *thud* and the man let out a guttural cry. The gun slipped away and an even heavier thud echoed through the dark. I spun around. My attacker was on the floor and a handsome Latino guy leaned casually over the body. He picked up the gun, emptied the chamber, and rifled through the pockets of the guy's black suit while a beautiful, big black dog sat at his feet and cocked its head at me.

I took a shaky breath. Friend? Foe? I'd never seen him or the dog before in my life—the life almost been cut short *again*… But who the hell was this guy and what did he want with me? What the fuck did *any* of these thugs want with me?

He glanced up from the unconscious body and flashed me a grin that was, despite the circumstances, disarmingly charming. "Hey."

"Uh, hi."

"I'm Eli." As if that meant anything to me.

"Seb." I didn't move. Ted Bundy had been described as charming in his day, too. And I had enough on my plate without ending up in the obits for some rando who made it inside my place and saved my life from some other yahoo who wanted to end me.

"Pleasure." He nodded and reached a hand down to stroke the dog's head.

I didn't take my eyes off either of them as I stood plotting what to do if I heard the words "sic" or "him" pass between the lips still wearing that charming smile. "Yeah. Uh…how's that summer humidity, huh?" He seemed happy enough with the small talk. No point in going rogue just yet.

"Well, the city was built on a swamp. You work in politics?" He looked me up and down.

Politics? Me? Probably a joke in there somewhere but I didn't look too deep. Instead, I estimated how many feet between me and the door to the bedroom. Too many. The dog would probably get me before I made it that far. "Tech. You?"

He cocked his head as if he was measuring how quick he'd have to be to grab me or if I was as lithe as I looked—I wasn't. "Parks, actually."

"Cool. I'm just going to—" I motioned to the door he was standing in front of.

"Come with me." And there was no question he believed it.

But he was wrong. "Hell, no."

I backed up three steps, arms straight out at my sides like I was going to spin into a helicopter and propel my way out. He dropped the grin.

When I moved to my left, he moved to his right blocking me. "Seb, grab a bag and get moving. More could be coming."

"More *what*?"

He motioned to the man snoozing on the floor, and I backed up further. Should I run? No. My legs were trembling. I wouldn't make it two steps. Throw a lamp? Would've been okay had I owned a lamp, but my lights were overheads.

And who the hell died and made this guy the boss? Probably the same guy who gave him the big bad attack dog.

"You should know!"

"Me? Why would I know? I know shit about anything. My whole life has been turned upside down! But how did you know to come here? *You* tell *me* what the fuck is going on." My voice cracked with fear, but it felt good to get out some of my frustration.

Eli ran a hand over his face and motioned to the door. "Come with me and we can talk about it. We need to move *now*." There was an urgency as he checked the hallway then pulled himself back inside my place.

"No. You tell me how you knew to be here. *Then* we'll go."

I dodged, but he was quick and blocked my path. The dog's ears pricked up, and a chill ran up my spine. I backpedaled and dove behind the knocked-over couch. Eli grumbled and held up his hands. I faked right, dodged left, and he fell for it, chasing me from the wrong side. With more space between us, I almost had a clear shot to the door, but just as I was about to take my freedom run, he deftly leaped over the couch and grabbed me in a chokehold.

"Hey!" I croaked.

He yanked against my neck and almost cut off my air before he loosened his grip, like he was giving me a warning. "Get. A. Bag."

"Who put you up to this?" I coughed.

"Derek did."

"*Dr. Dish*?"

Eli laughed and loosened his grip more. "That's one for the old lab coat. I'll have to remember to call him that."

Still. WE weren't having a moment and I didn't trust him. My throat hurt as a reminder not to. "How do you know him?"

"I'm his brother. Will you get a bag so we can leave?" This time he checked out the window before he looked at me again.

"Brothers?" Tall dark and deadly didn't have a single sparkle compared to Derek. And it wasn't out of my realm to believe brothers didn't have to look exactly the same but come on. "You look nothing alike."

He cracked his neck and mumbled to himself. "Fucking hell, the things I do for him…"

Without warning, he hoisted me into a fireman's carry, and the dog barked, its tail thumping the floor. "Hey! What the fuck! Let me down! I need to get my—"

"Oh, what's that? You need to get something? Like, a fucking *bag*?"

I growled as he made his way to the door, but I kicked and almost managed to break free when I spotted a familiar shine under the pile of debris on the desk. "Wait! For real, I need my laptop."

Eli bent with me over his shoulder and yanked out the computer from the rubble. "This?"

I twisted to the side for a better view and grimaced as the dog licked my face. "Yeah. Be careful with it—"

"All right, nerd. Calm down. I've got it."

The little energy left drained out of my body, and I went limp with exhaustion. The dog licked my hand as it flopped near Eli's hip, and she followed at our heels as he carried me down the stairs and out to his truck. I was done fighting. Off my feet, and carried by fate and Eli, I was just *done*.

Chapter 7 - Derek

The sun rose over the top of Vanguard Tower, reflected off the smooth surface of the Potomac, and blinded me as I leaped out of the cab. Two steps toward home, I doubled back and gave the driver a tip.

"That was record time, Lyle."

"Hey, I pride myself on navigating the early hours." He tipped his hat and tucked the money into the breast pocket of his shirt.

The Tower was eerily quiet, and my footsteps reverberated off the walls as I sprinted through the foyer to my apartment and wrangled the keys out of my pocket. The door handle turned too easily, telling me it was unlocked from the inside. I held the knob and my breath, and listened. Silence… But that didn't mean the coast was clear. With a 911 message from Eli and now he wasn't answering his phone, I was worried. Anything could have been behind the door. Or anyone. It was a ridiculous thought–I'd been safe in the Vanguard Tower since we'd built it, but I steeled myself, took a step back, then threw my full weight shoulder-first into the door as I turned the knob, ready to fight.

Eli stared at me from the couch, his mouth a tense line, and his long hair sticking out of his bun at various angles. He held a bag of frozen peas against one eye and a bag of frozen corn to his groin. Owen stared too without his usual happy-go lucky grin, but he did shoot an amused smirk at our brother's plight. I blurted a loud laugh, and Owen chuckled until Eli stabbed him with an elbow to the ribs. Uno sat between their feet, wagging her tail and beaming at me. At least someone was happy to see me.

I shut the door behind me and put my hands on my hips, still catching my breath. "What's going on? 911? You look fine." Aside from his vegetables of choice.

"Oh, I look *fine*?" Eli scoffed and adjusted the bag of corn with a wince.

"Is our brother fine?" I asked Owen, who nodded, and got another elbow to the ribs for it.

"What happened with Seb?" I dropped my bag and wiped the sweat from my brow with the back of my wrist, still catching my breath.

"Your little boyfriend is a wildcat, that's what happened. Next time you want a favor, ask one of the others." Eli pulled the peas away from his face just long enough for me to catch sight of a nasty black eye.

My head was spinning. "*Boyfriend*? He's absolutely not my boyfriend. Tell me what happened."

"I won't be able to have kids after what he did to my balls."

"Can one of you tell me what the *fuck* is going on? Please." I crossed my arms and shot my best stern look—eyes narrow, thin lips, nose flared—as my blood reached its boiling point.

I was about to blow, and Owen knew it. He lifted his head and widened his eyes. Spewed the facts in a monotone designed for information delivery without emotion. Per his usual. "I was recruited to lend some paramedic assistance for the black eye and the squashed balls...after we got the prisoner locked up in the main bathroom."

I froze. Oh, shit. They'd taken prisoners? My stomach rumbled. "What prisoner?"

"I did what you asked me to do." Eli cleared his throat and tilted his head from one side to the other, like he was loosening up for a fight. "Followed him home—"

"Sebastian." Owen nodded and smirked.

"Yeah, Seb." Eli's head bobbed agreement and the peas in the bag rustled with every move of his head.

"Seb is in my bathroom?" Oh, no. Oh, hell no.

"That's right."

"*Locked* in my bathroom?" The words kidnapping and abduction flashed like neon in my mind. I glared at Eli. "You have about two seconds to explain before I—"

He held up his free hand. "Calm down." Then he cleared his throat. Stalling. "Well, to be completely honest…I might have lost him for a few hours, but then I found him on the bridge and—"

My stomach dropped. "Fuck. He was going to jump."

"Unlike you with your quick conclusions, I don't think so." Eli scratched his nose with his pinky. "But he stumbled backwards into traffic, looking all freaked out. That's when I found him again, and I trailed him back to his apartment. He was acting weird, like he was in a Bond movie. Which, well, I guess he was kind of right to be cautious."

My throat tightened, and I squinted at Eli, waiting for more information on whether Seb was okay. When it didn't come, I walked closer and rolled my hand to encourage him to hurry the fuck up and be more forthcoming. "He was right to be cautious? What does that mean?"

"When I walked into the dude's apartment, some guy had a gun pointed to his head."

I steadied myself with a tight grip on the back of an armchair and closed my eyes. "Okay. A boyfriend? Big guy? Shaved head, tattoos? Named Pete?"

I ignored Owen's wide eyes and open mouth, already well aware I knew way too much about my patient's backstory. Instead, I focused on Eli who scratched his nose again as he thought about it.

"I don't think so, bro. The guy with the gun wasn't acting like a jilted boyfriend. More like hired muscle working a hit. I got there as he was about to pull the trigger. I knocked him out. No ID, nothing on him, seemed pretty professional. The apartment was trashed, and clearly unsafe for Seb to stay there, so I had to get him out of there. But he put up a little bit of a fight. Just a teensy little tantrum."

"A *tantrum*?" I tightened my grip, and my jaw clenched.

"Eli took him against his will." Owen smirked as he spoke then got an elbow for it.

I tried to remain calm. Tried. Didn't exactly succeed and my voice was louder than normal as I spoke. "Define 'took,' please."

Eli's twitchy grin betrayed the solemnity of his voice. "Kidnapped. Hauled him over my shoulder. Caveman style."

"What—! What the *fuck*, Eli?" A life of dedicated "first do no harm" service shot to hell. I had a quick vision of prison bars and orange jumpsuits.

"You see what he did to me once I got him back here? He's a little demon, went after the family jewels—" Eli lifted the bag of now melting frozen corn, then gingerly returned it to its spot.

"He's a kid!" Oh, God. Kidnapping in the most literal sense. Even if the kid is of legal age. Mostly.

"What'd you want me to do? Leave him there? With the armed gunman? Chill! He's fine!"

"Except he's *locked* in the fucking bathroom, probably terrified for his life." I blew air out from pursed lips, ran a hand over my face, and paced. This poor guy had been through so much today. "At least he's safe."

Eli let out an annoyed groan. "I was *joking* about the boyfriend thing, but the look on your face tells me there's some truth to it." He looked me over with half-lidded eyes and a pinched mouth. "I thought this was just going to be another stray, but there's more to it, huh?" Such a know-it-all.

"Shut up. I met him at work. He's just like the others we've helped, okay? It's always a unique situation, and I'm the one who found him. I'm invested." That was my story and I was sticking to it.

"Mm-hmm."

"You met him at work," Owen echoed, like I needed reminding I'd not just stepped but rushed like my ass was on fire into an ethical gray area.

"Fucking hell, don't start on me." I needed to see Seb. I needed to apologize for how Eli had manhandled him—and I needed to *not* call it "manhandling" if I had any chance of getting that unsavory image out of my mind.

"Where's the gratitude?" Eli called after me as I made my way to the bathroom, and I gave him the finger as a thank you.

The door to the bathroom was locked from the outside with a chair shoved under the knob. I knocked gently.

"Let me the fuck out, you psychopathic fuck!" Seb's voice boomed off the bathroom tile and through the heavy wood door. Laughter erupted from behind me, and I did my best to ignore the peanut gallery in the living room.

"Hey, it's me. Derek." I wasn't a hundred percent sure he'd remember, but I took a chance.

"*Fuck you.*" Enraged didn't quite cover the sound of his voice. Probably closer to homicidal.

"I'm here to help—"

"I don't fucking believe you! You're all fucking insane. You had me kidnapped! The other one did the kidnapping. And now there's a third one trying to be my friend. I've got friends!"

I couldn't blame him for his anger. When he phrased it that way, it sounded bad. "I promise you, we're just trying to help. My brothers and I help out young guys in need—"

"Jesus! Do you hear yourself? That's sketchy as *fuck*!"

I probably could've phrased it better, but I pressed on. "We help out *lots of guys* who need a safe place to stay, and I don't know why Eli had to use such extreme force to get you out of that situation at your apartment, but all I want to do is make sure you're okay now. Do you think I could come in?" I glanced back to where Owen and Eli were turned the wrong way on the sofa to get a better look at me groveling at my own bathroom door. I shot a glare and turned back to talk to Seb. I pressed my palm against the wood and spoke softly. "Seb, I'm sorry. We're really just trying to help."

Silence. Then, "Okay. You can come in."

His trembling voice caught on something in my chest and made my heart ache. I slid the chair away and wiped my suddenly sweaty palms on my pants before I eased open the door. I wasn't sure what I expected to see—maybe a roughed-up and traumatized Seb crouching in a corner or, best-case scenario, those bright green eyes twinkling like he was happy to see me. But I sure wasn't expecting an empty bathroom.

"What the—Ah! *Fuck*!"

The heavy wooden toilet seat flew at me, barely missed my head and only because I ducked. Seb bolted out behind me, and I spun to chase him, but didn't get far because he came to an abrupt halt, and I smashed against his back. It took me a moment to get my bearings.

Then I saw it. All seven of my brothers standing in a row and blocking our path.

Chapter 8 - Sebastian

I stopped and barely felt Dr. Dish slam into my back, because what was in front of me was so unbelievable I thought I must have been hallucinating. Maybe the concussion was nastier than I'd thought because a solid wall of testosterone had popped up out of nowhere and blocked my path to the door. A semicircle of hot men closed in and I took in the diversity of handsomeness surrounding me while they looked me over in turn. Black, white, brown, tall, short, bodybuilders and lean queens—it was a smorgasbord of masculine perfection, and I literally rubbed my eyes. *Oh, please do not let this be a dream.*

"This would usually be my ideal type of fantasy, but I really have to get going…" The fiesta of fabulousness didn't budge. And I didn't have much chance of getting around a single one, and much less a chance of taking on…seven.

An insanely tall, built black man in a tight t-shirt with a DC Fire Service emblem on the sleeve cracked a smile, and a young Asian guy in hand-painted pajamas gave me a kind laugh. Eli, the Latino man I'd hit with a one-two punch-kick combo—the only badass move in my bag of tricks—scoffed and then passed a soggy bag of defrosted peas to the hot redhead who'd helped lock me in the bathroom and was now smiling kindly at me. But no one so much as inched to the left to let me pass, and all eyes were suddenly focused somewhere behind me.

I turned to find the good doctor smoothing his hands through his hair—probably checking for cuts—and for a moment, I regretted trying to knock him out with the surprisingly heavy toilet seat, until I remembered I was the one who had been kidnapped against my will.

"Can I just get through…here…" I moved toward two identical white guys who looked straight out of a military recruitment video. Shoulder to shoulder, they looked from me to Derek and back again without the slightest sign of an expression on their stubbled, damn handsome faces.

"Seb." Derek looked at me imploringly. "We're here to help."

Help? Like I was going to believe that after having a gun pressed to my head, then being dragged out of my own home and into the middle of a…what? A crime ring of gorgeous hotties? But in my mind, their imaginary knuckle dusters disappeared, and they were suddenly dressed in hero costumes and capes, because no way could these beautiful brawny men be bad guys…

But I still didn't know what I was running from, who had put a gun to my head, or how the hell the good doctor was involved. I was more confused than ever. The laptop, the guy with the gun… What I saw on the laptop. Where was Ben? Why was my apartment ransacked and why had the doctor sent Eli there?

"Why are you *all* here at once?" Derek asked, his tone gruff. He moved to stand beside me then glared at each of the guys staring at us.

"Your lucky day." Eli smirked.

The glare deepened. Derek wasn't feeling the luck. With all their attention on him, this was my chance. I dodged to the side, ducked around the guy in colorful pajamas, and almost made it two feet before the redhead came back to the group with a pack of frozen blueberries and almost collided with me. I huffed in frustration, and my chest started to tighten. Why wouldn't they let me leave?

"Everyone get out. Leave us alone." Derek motioned for the wall of men to scatter.

Not even a blink.

"Leave!" His voice boomed and the commanding tone went straight to my cock. It stirred, despite days of exhaustion and panic. Interesting.

The twins glanced at each other, then peeled away from the group. Eli rolled his eyes, grabbed the bag of blueberries from the redhead, and slapped it against his eye as the two of them headed out followed by the rest of the crowd.

A guy in a tank top who looked like a surfer bro pointed at Derek on his way to the door. "You've got some explaining to do."

Dr. Dish grunted.

I made to follow the crowd, but Dr. Dish dropped a hand on my shoulder, and I stopped to look at him as he smiled and squeezed it affectionately. "*You* have some explaining to do, too."

"Me? I don't know why I'm here or who thought it was a good idea to lock me in the bathroom or how your"—air quotes—"brother managed to find me."

"And save your life." There was nothing smug in the way he said it, but I knew the words for what they were. A reminder. Probably a quid pro quo. Bullshit.

Suddenly aware I really was free to go if I chose to, I took a proper look at the place. High ceilings with exposed beams crossed overhead and would have made the open-plan layout feel like a sterile museum if it weren't for the cozy, oversized couches and armchairs, the thick pile rugs, and sculptural knick-knacks on every flat surface. It felt like a home…like a real *grown-up* home. Not at all like my rundown depressing shithole of an apartment.

Derek took his hand off my shoulder and swept his arm in a small arc. "This is the Vanguard Tower. I had my brother follow you, and given the whole armed gunman thing, he thought it was best to bring you back here."

That cleared up some of it. "Your *brother,* huh?" I raised my eyebrows. "I told him I didn't believe it. You look nothing alike."

He shrugged. "None of us do. Except for the twins."

"Wait, what? That wall of muscle… They're *all* your brothers?"

"That's right." He pinched his lips tight, so his thick pout turned white, then flooded pink when he parted them again. "We've been through a lot together, and we pay it forward, which is why I *thought* it would be a good idea for Eli to keep an eye on you."

I scoffed and ran my hand over the tight weave of the nearby armchair. I didn't need rescuing…but I also liked having someone looking out for me, rather than just tolerating me. I wondered if that kind of watchdog dynamic existed between Derek and his brothers, too—so different to how Big Ben related to me, and a little bubble of jealousy popped in my stomach. Derek had seven brothers who seemed to care about him.

He lowered his voice in that caring doctor-y way again that made my belly feel warm. "I'm sorry if Eli hurt you. I just want to offer to help, and it seems like you could use some."

I picked at a piece of lint caught in the fibers of the chair. He sounded genuine, and when I looked up and caught his eye, he reminded me of a Labrador—earnest, sweet, and stubborn.

But I wanted nothing to do with it. My mind was in chaos, and I didn't trust myself enough to trust him. Exhausted, probably still concussed, and spinning—I couldn't tell what was real or fake, a lie from the truth, if I was in any real danger, or if my own brother had tried to kill me.

I slumped against the back of the chair and let out a low sigh, pinched the bridge of my nose, and my wrist pulsed with pain. Ben was related to all of this. Had to be. But I couldn't figure out how. I didn't think he'd try to *hurt* me or send anyone after me, but all the threads of every piece of information I had led back to him. He was the last person I'd seen before I woke up in the hospital, half-drowned and almost dead, *and* he was the last person in my apartment before it was ransacked.

Half of me was worried Ben was in just as much trouble as I was, and it was all a huge mistake. But there was no mistaking what I'd seen on his laptop, or the way he'd reacted. At best, he was guilty of embezzlement, so I had to wonder what else he was capable of. Hurting me? Throwing me off a bridge? Sending a goon with a gun to my apartment?

"Hey. You're okay."

Derek squeezed my shoulder, and I realized I was breathing heavily.

"Shit. Sorry."

He pointed a soft, concerned gaze into mine. "It's okay, it's fine. You get panic attacks?"

My eyes rested on the open button of his shirt and the chest hair poking through the fold of fabric. I counted my breaths. "Yeah. Sometimes."

I let his touch ground me, but I couldn't shake the confusion. Why the hell would someone like Derek—an accomplished and respected doctor—want to help me, a recent graduate with no real job, who was suddenly effectively homeless?

I could hear Ben's laughter in my head. All of his prophecies about me being worthless were coming true. Maybe they'd always been true.

My breath caught again. Rasped out.

"Do you want to sit down?" He guided me toward the sofa.

My head throbbed, my stomach churned, and my whole body ached. I needed more than to sit down. I needed to sleep for about three solid days. "I should…go."

"Wait." His hands fluttered as he reached towards my arm, then dropped his hand to his side. "Stay for the rest of the day. You need rest, and a hell of a lot of water."

He eyed my chapped lips, and I chuckled nervously as I pulled the lower one between my teeth. "Why do you care?" It wasn't like he knew me. I could've been a thief or a murderer.

The thick cord of his throat bobbed as he swallowed. "Personal history. All you need to know is that I just *do*." He took my hand with a warm, firm squeeze. "You're free to go anytime you want. But you're also free to stay. Speaking as a doctor *and* as someone's who's dealt with a lot of shit in his life, I think you should." He smiled as his cheeks pinked all the way to the tips of his ears. "Stay, I mean."

My lip stung from the pressure of my teeth as I sized him up. My head was abuzz with conflicting ideas, but under all the noise, I knew the answer deep in my gut. This guy was safe, and he wanted the best for me. Despite having seven nosy brothers, he seemed like a fairly regular, successful, well-put-together guy.

"Are you sure?"

He chuckled and nodded, like it was no big thing. "Yeah. I'm sure."

Chapter 9 - Derek

I heated up the sautéed spinach and mushrooms Eli had left in the fridge from yesterday's omelets, while butter melted in a skillet and I whisked together four eggs and a dash of milk.

Seb sniffed from his place at the table where I'd set him up with a glass of electrolytes. "Damn, that smells good. You're a cook *and* a doctor?" When he spoke like that—with such hero worship—my dick twitched.

"Hardly. Eli's the chef, I know the bare minimum to get by." The egg mixture sizzled when I poured it into the pan, and I broke it up with quick flicks of my wrist until it resembled scrambled eggs.

He sniffed the air and leaned back in his at the dining table. "This is way beyond my diet of instant noodles and microwave pizzas, though."

"I took a semester on basic human nutrition, and *that* kind of diet is way below the bare minimum." No wonder Seb's frame was lithe. Maybe it was more malnutrition than ballet classes giving him his dancer's figure. I felt his eyes following me as I brought the pan to the table and scooped food onto our plates.

"And yet, I live." He sounded sarcastic, and I chuckled and scooped an extra helping of spinach and mushrooms onto his plate for good measure. "Got hot sauce?"

Seb pushed to his feet, and I pointed at him. "Sit. I'll get it."

He grunted, but he obeyed and sat. "You always boss your guests around like a drill sergeant?"

"Yes." But I smiled. "Of course, most of them like it."

The hint of a smirk twitched at the edge of his lips, and I ignored it as I set the pan back in the kitchen and came back with a bottle of hot sauce, and then handed him cutlery. Sitting across from him, I was shocked into silence by those bright green eyes again.

"Thanks." He piled a forkful of scrambled eggs onto a corner of toast, bit into it with a deep moan, and his eyelids fluttered shut.

My lower belly rumbled, and my cock jerked to life as he licked a wayward crumb from his lips. He opened his eyes, and I looked away, shoved a forkful of food into my mouth, and silently admonished myself. I wasn't the kind of guy who went after someone else's boyfriend.

"You said your brother's cooking is even better than *this*?" Fuck. Even appreciation on this guy was hot.

The meal was okay but could have used more seasoning; there was always something missing when I cooked that never was when Eli prepared our meals. "This is nothing compared to Eli's food." I couldn't resist. "You remember Eli? He's the one with the black eye."

And if appreciation was hot, contrition was an accelerant. "Ah... Sorry about that."

"He's had worse." I glanced at Seb and he stared back with one cocked eyebrow. "Um, I mean, he works for search and rescue." It wasn't the full story of what I'd meant, but it wasn't my place to reveal Eli's entire back catalog of near misses, broken bones, street brawls, and run-ins with the cops.

"And your other brothers? They all seem, uh..." He twirled his fork in the air, as though trying to catch the word. "Fighting fit."

I chuckled. Perfect choice of words to describe the boys. "We're all first responders. Except Braxton is an artist."

"The colorful pajamas?"

Cute, funny, and he paid attention. I was screwed. I swallowed a lumpy bite and nodded. "Mm. That's him. But the rest of us are on the frontlines."

"Frontlines?" He finished the last of his electrolytes and poured himself a huge glass of orange juice from the pitcher on the table.

"Owen—the redhead—"

"The co-kidnapper." He pursed his lips and I almost moaned out loud, like I'd never seen a beautiful man before.

Talking about my brothers should keep my hormones in check. I hoped. "Right. He's an EMT. Brought you in that night…with the bridge…" Only an idiot would have brought that up now.

He took a deep breath and sat back, his face the color of ash, his eyes lowered. "Huh."

I moved on, voice low and even, soothing. I wanted him to feel safe here. "Sean and Matthew are Marine and ex-Marine, respectively."

"The hunky twins?"

Hunky was an apt word for Sean and Matt. Of course, it fit the rest of them with equal truth. "That's them. Hunter, the one in the tank top?"

"Wait, let me guess. Beach rescue?"

I couldn't wait to tell him he'd been pegged as the Baywatch babe of the family. I chuckled and wiped my mouth with a napkin. "FBI."

"No way!" Seb snorted, and I laughed as I threw him my napkin. "My second guess was a swimsuit model. Never in a million years does that guy look like he belongs in the FBI."

"Is it the long blond hair? The ultra-relaxed posture?" I did my best impression of Hunter by slinging an arm over the back of my chair and slumping into my seat. Seb let out a laugh and pointed at me as he nodded.

"Yeah. I've never seen a fed look so…at peace."

"Sure, sure." He passed back the soggy, sticky napkin, and for some reason, I accepted it, simply because he met my eye while he did it. "And you're all…"

"Gay?"

His eyes went wide, and his cheeks turned a deep, dark—utterly adorable—red. Even blushing this guy was better than anything I'd seen in a while. "Uh, I was going to say *close*."

"Sure, you were." I chuckled, and waited until he joined in before I cleared my throat. "Yeah, we're as close as it gets. And we're mostly gay. Richie, the fireman, and Sean…we don't know for sure, but I have my suspicions." Neither of them had come out as being into men, but I'd spotted a familiar longing on Sean's face whenever the other brothers talked about their homoerotic encounters, and Richie never spoke a word about anyone he hooked up with to the point where he'd refuse to refer to his lovers as anything except 'this person I met.'

"Huh." Seb stared at me and the silence lingered heavy between us. "A lot in common for brothers from different mothers."

"Mm. We're all big on making a difference and helping people out of tough spots. We've all been through…our own bits of heartache and pain." I bit into my toast to stop myself from spilling seven life stories I wasn't authorized to share with strangers. I wasn't prone to oversharing, and I didn't like that this gorgeous young man had made me feel comfortable enough my tongue couldn't stop flapping when I was around him. The line between wanting him to stay for *his* sake and wanting him to stay for mine blurred. His company put me at ease in a way I hadn't been in years. Damnedest thing.

His breakfast annihilated, he leaned back in his chair and looked me over with those eyes that seemed to sparkle even brighter in the morning light beaming through the high windows. "And you're the doctor… That's a lot of school. Why doctor?"

I didn't want to sound trite or practiced, but I got this question a lot. Especially when I was making the decision. "That part was easy. I always wanted to be able to save lives. Being a doctor made obvious sense, and I made sure it happened."

"That all"—he flapped his hand at me—"sounds a little white knight to me, Lancelot."

I raised my eyebrows and sat back, insulted. My cheeks burned. I didn't have a savior complex, if that was what he was insinuating. And even if I did, I was one of the good guys with the power to save lives because I worked at my craft, studied, learned. But why the hell did I care what Seb thought of me? He was a stranger with a boyfriend. Off-limits. I shrugged and stacked his plate on top of mine. "I just like to help people and I care about my patients."

His lips turned down and he sounded insolent. "Sure thing, doc."

I bit back the hurt and reminded myself not to care so much as I reached over to collect his empty plate. He pulled away, like he was worried I was going to accidentally touch him. That's right. He was hurt. Of course, he was moody. I could be patient with that.

"Speaking of caring about my patients…" I paused halfway to the sink. "Before you take a nap, I'd like to check your wrist. We might need to re-bandage it."

He looked me over and wet his lips. "Playing doctor is one of my favorite fantasies."

My cheeks burned, and heat prickled up my arms before I pulled myself together and snapped out of it. I didn't usually date guys who were so much younger than me, not by virtue of age, but because of the differences in values, and we didn't exactly hang around the same places so opportunities to meet up were limited. Kids like Sebastian just wanted to party. Plus, Seb was in trouble, and given the way he'd accused me of being a "white knight," he was also immature.

But my attraction knew no such restriction and pulsed straight to my cock.

I grabbed my bag from where I'd dumped it by the front door and motioned for Seb to join me in the living room. He got up without complaint, but he moved slowly, and I had my equipment unpacked on the coffee table before he made it over. He yawned loudly and drowned out the sound of his heart through my stethoscope. I gave him a look and he grinned apologetically, then pressed a finger against his lips like he was sealing them shut. His pulse was a little quick and grew quicker when I double-checked the timing with two fingers pressed against his wrist, but nothing pathological beyond a moderate anxiety.

"Your vitals are fine, no injuries but the sprain, and I believe a good night's sleep will take care of any residual effects of your concussion. How does your head feel?" I palpated his skull gently but couldn't feel any bumps or injuries.

"Sore, but better for the food."

"Good. I'd like to check your lungs, in case those breathing issues aren't solely relative to your panic attacks. Could you lift your shirt?"

He paused and grinned slyly before yanking his shirt over his head. My breath snagged. His body was beautiful, with a soft layer of flesh over his tapering ribcage and prominent collarbones. There was a dip just below his xiphoid process—the bottom edge of his sternum—and I badly wanted to press my thumb to the divot there, sure it would be a perfect fit. Tiny tacky bits of stickiness from the ECG pads still clung to his chest, but otherwise his skin was flawless and pale, like raw porcelain before it hit the kiln. I blew a hot breath of air onto the cold pad of the stethoscope while he watched my mouth from behind heavy eyelids.

He has a boyfriend.

I bit back the desire to touch his torso and pressed the pad against it instead. He flinched, and I caught his eye.

"Cold? Sorry."

"S'okay." He wet his lips and dipped his head so that he could catch my eyes and drag them up from his collarbone. I let my gaze be led. I was completely in his control. He lowered his voice, and it rumbled through his chest. I felt the sound deep in my belly. "What do you want me to do? Just, like, breathe?"

I took a shaky breath and pulled the stethoscope away. I needed to be professional. "Turn around for me."

"Yes, doctor!" He spun away and sat straight. His back was just as beautiful as his front, and I quickly pressed the stethoscope to stop myself from touching him. My lips tingled, and I wanted to kiss the freckles splattered across his shoulders and the curve of his thoracic spine that projected out just below his neck.

Boyfriend!

I pulled back and cleared my throat.

"All good?" He looked over his shoulder and his long, doe-length eyelashes caught the light.

"All good." I took the earpieces out. "I almost forgot to tell you, but your brother and your boyfriend were at the hospital last night, asking about you."

He stiffened and then faced away again. "I don't have a boyfriend."

"They were looking for you, said you'd gone missing." He slumped forward and stayed silent. "Seb?"

He shook his head, and I moved around to face him. His brow was furrowed, and his breathing was short and quick again. I knelt in front of him and put a hand on his knee.

"Was the accident in the river a domestic dispute?" I searched his face for a tell, but he was as blank as a stone wall. "Has Pete threatened you before?"

"Pete?" He reeled back and frowned.

Uncertainty pinged in my chest. Maybe I got the name wrong. "Your boyfriend—"

"I told you, I don't have a boyfriend!" Seb raised his voice and it pinched into a high pitch at the end of his words, echoing the sudden panic in his eyes.

"But your brother? Ben?" I hoped mentioning his family would remind him he had people looking out for him. "He seemed worried, and I'm sure he'd like to know you're safe. Have you called him? You can use my phone—"

"Can I take a shower?" His jaw muscles popped, and his nostrils flared. My heart stung when I caught tears welling in his eyes.

"Of course. There are extra towels in the bathroom. It's just down there, the room with the broken toilet seat."

He managed a half-hearted scoff, and relieved me of the tension in my chest until he bunched the oversized, pastel shirt into his fist and made his way out of the room silently, and I was left alone with a painful hollowness and a sense something was deeply wrong and about to get even more complicated.

Chapter 10 - Sebastian

I basked under the warm spray of the showerhead, feeling like I was being bathed beneath a tropical waterfall. Everything about Dr. Dish's apartment was luxe. The whole place smelled like wood, and something fresh like lemon or grapefruit—but not the sickly fake kind from a cheap air freshener. Did the guy burn scented candles every night or something? Probably. He had his life so put together that he could afford to do something like that.

And all seven of his brothers had their lives together, too. Each of them the total opposite of my own brother—who was apparently a thief, but he was still alive, and looking for me with some guy named Pete, and maybe he wanted to kill me. The dichotomy between Derek's family and my own was painful to think about, and I felt empty inside when I imagined about how nice it would be to have a team behind me.

I turned my back to the shower and let the hot water ease the tension out of my shoulder muscles. I was rattled by the information that Ben and this 'boyfriend' had shown up at the hospital looking for me. And this *Pete* was masquerading as my so-called boyfriend? *With* Ben? Who hated everything about the fact I was gay. None of it made sense. Ben was homophobic to the core, and I couldn't imagine him keeping a straight face around a man claiming to be my lover.

I soaped under my arms with a body wash that smelled like sandalwood and heaven, and I wondered if one of my exes could have been involved in this. Had one of them changed his name to *Pete*? Ew. I highly doubted it. None of them were that tasteless. Besides, it had been a long time since I'd seen any of them. Years since I'd even had a steady thing with anyone. Thanks to school and work, and it was hard meeting my *type*. I was interested in older guys but *not* interested in being their arm candy—a hard to find delicate balance. I just hadn't met the right guy.

I worked the suds into the sticky residue on my chest and remembered Derek's gentle touch as he'd placed the stethoscope there. Dr. Dish was my *type*, at least on paper. Intelligent, quick on the uptake, stable…and fucking hot. Damn, he looked good even after a twelve-hour shift, ducking a flying toilet seat, tending to my injuries.

My cock tingled as I soaped its base and thought about Derek's hands. My poor dick was tired, but the minute I started to think about Derek's stubbled jaw, it stiffened.

"I thought you were exhausted." I stroked it twice, and then hissed as my wrist twinged. My other hand wasn't nearly as good, but it was good enough. I moaned and leaned back against the warm tiles as I gripped my cock tightly at the base and watched as it reached its full length. Just like magic. Maybe a little release would do me good. A world of it. Get some endorphins pumping, pick up my mood, and pull my mind off the fucked-up events of the last forty-eight hours. Yeah. Quick release was exactly what I needed. Probably what the doctor would order.

But my coordination was pathetic, and I became increasingly frustrated when *quick* didn't seem to be on the menu. I flicked through my mental back catalog of fantasies but kept coming back to an old favorite. Dirty doctor.

"Ugh…" My cock bucked in my hand when I remembered the way Derek looked with the stethoscope around his strong neck. "Okay, fine."

Those thick hands of his had felt so good on me, comforting, caressing, kneading. What else could they do?

"Dirty doctor gets handsy?" My voice was raspy as I spoke to my cock.

My dick was hard but didn't swell with excitement at the suggestion.

"Dirty doctor does a naughty examination?"

Nothing.

I grunted in frustration and I was about to give up on the whole thing when a vision flashed through my mind.

My cock swelled, and I moaned and shuddered as pleasure washed through me, but I could barely believe how mundane the idea was. Derek, on his knees, taking me into his mouth. There wasn't a stethoscope in sight, yet my thighs were quaking with the thought of it.

"Oh, fuck." I squeezed my eyes tight. "Fuck, yes."

The lines by his eyes crinkled as he smiled up at me as he pressed a soft kiss to the underside of my cock.

"Too romantic," I hissed, but the image remained, and my balls pulsed with urgency.

Imaginary Derek swallowed my young cock in his mouth and moved with experienced, expert grace up and down my length, slurping and popping the head off his bottom lip until I was trembling, whimpering, ready to blow all over his tongue.

I gasped as my dick swelled, and I barely held myself back from the edge of orgasm. One more jerk and—

"Oh, fuck! Derek!" Fire rocked through me and shot after shot of cum erupted. I was high and buzzing with endorphins as the final shot burst from my cock, when the door flew open and Dr. Dish rushed in.

"Are you okay—whoa!" He had his eyes on my hand and what was in it. And watching him watch me kept my cock hard.

I gaped at him. "I uh—"

"Stress relief?" Oh, God. The smile. My dick twitched again.

"Ha. Yeah…" I slowly uncurled my fingers and expected my cock to flop, but it was still rock hard under his gaze.

Did he just lick his lips? Oh, fuck, he licked his *lips.*

His eyes met mine, pinned me in place. My pulse rocked and I met his gaze with just as much intensity. Energy buzzed in the mist from the shower, and I moved toward him as he stepped closer to me. He hovered at the edge of the spray, and if he came just an inch closer, I'd be able to taste his mouth. Just one…inch… He closed the gap, stepped into the water, and my head spun as he kissed me gently.

"Mm." I fell forward, chasing his lips as he pulled away, and he put a hand on my waist to steady me while his eyes searched mine for something—consent? Arousal? Both were in abundance, and I pushed my mouth against his, hungry. I threw my arms around his neck and climbed him like a tree, until he held me up with an arm under my ass. He moaned into my mouth and slammed us back against the shower wall, and I pulled his wet shirt until the buttons snapped and I could explore his pecs. His hands were all over my sides, my shoulders, my hips and my chest, greedily feeling me up and moaning desperately like he'd been wanting to do it for days. He grabbed my ass, pulled me closer and moaned when my hard cock pressed into his abs.

This couldn't be real. Had to be a fantasy.

With a sharp inhale, I pulled back and looked at him, searching for those crinkled lines by his eyes and the romantic smile I'd pictured so I could come just before he'd burst in.

He froze for a moment. I opened my mouth to beg him not to stop, but he was already putting me down, and he pulled away. He stepped out of the shower, his hair soaked and dark, and he shook himself off like he'd just taken a swim in the Potomac, like his body was heavy with sludge from the river instead of alive with my touch.

"Fuck." He paced the bathroom with a deep scowl and rubbed his mouth like he was smearing away my kiss as his clothes dripped a trail across the tile floor. "I'm so sorry. I shouldn't have—"

"It's okay." My voice was small, and I didn't feel okay. I felt empty again.

He stopped and a puddle of water pooled below him. He dragged his eyes up to meet mine, and his throat bobbed before he spoke in a terse voice. Doctor mode. "It never should have happened, and it won't happen again. Fuck. I'm so sorry. It was an accident."

The hollowness swallowed me, and I snorted. "Right. You *accidentally* shoved your tongue down my throat. Sure, that happens all the time."

Of course, someone like Dr. Dish with his perfect home and his scented-candle lifestyle would regret kissing someone like me.

"Seb. I… Fuck. I'm sorry." He left as quickly as he'd burst in, a slosh of water on the floor and an emptiness that seemed to echo around me the only indication it hadn't been a vivid fantasy conjured by my imagination. I switched off the shower and threw a couple of his excessively soft towels on the floor to soak up the evidence of my unfinished dream come true.

The reflection in the bathroom mirror was foggy, but I could make out a weedy little guy with a dour expression and a still rock-hard cock, despite the humiliation it had just caused.

I took my dick in my hand and gave it a disciplinary shake. "You need to just *chill* from now on. Okay?"

No answer. Just a dull, unsatisfied throbbing in my balls and, if I was being honest, deep in my chest too.

Chapter 11 - Derek

The sensation of wet socks in leather boots wasn't as bad as the feeling of betraying the confidence of a young man in my care, so I threw on the footwear and raced out of the apartment. I made it about three paces into the foyer before I collided, headfirst, with the twins coming out of their apartment.

"Well." Matt looked me over like he wasn't surprised to see me soaked and dripping my way across the tile.

"Showering in your clothes?" Sean raised his eyebrows and crossed his arms over his huge chest.

"I'm cutting out that laundry middleman." I couldn't manage a smile so I sounded like an asshole.

Matt stared me up and down. When his eyes landed on my face, he blinked and his mouth curled into a knowing smile. Intuitive prick. "He fucked the twink. Already."

I growled and held my ground without taking the step back I wanted, as my head hadn't quite stopped spinning since my bathroom foray into taking advantage of someone who needed more from me than anything my dick could provide. "He's not a *twink,* and I did not fuck him." Close didn't count here.

They shared a look.

"Then what's going on with him? We were just on our way over to get answers from you." Sean looked over my shoulder towards the door of my apartment, always ready for information.

Matt's frown deepened and his voice took on a gruff edge that had always made me feel like I was the youngest person in the room. "What's this about Eli kidnapping him?"

"I don't know much more than you do." Except what he looked like naked, what his mouth tasted like, and that his pale skin was as soft as it looked. My dick strained against my zipper. "He came into the ER for a wrist sprain, then the next night he showed up as a John Doe Owen's team pulled out of the Potomac near Arlington Memorial."

"Jumper." Matt sounded like he'd already decided. He didn't turn to Sean, didn't do more than nod.

"John Doe? ID lost in the jump?" Sean watched me, never wavering in his inspection of my reactions. He didn't look without leaping, act without thinking. I probably could've taken a quick lesson from him.

"Maybe. But he had his keys on him. Wallet would have survived the fall if his keys did, right?"

"Hm. Maybe. Depends on the pocket he had each one in, how he landed." He shrugged. "There are variables."

Sean glanced at Matt, as though his twin brother might know something I didn't. Now that Matt had discharged from the Marines, none of us really knew what he did for cash—just that he had plenty of it, that he was using the spare apartment as an office. Even Sean didn't know for sure, which said a lot because they normally shared everything. But there were benefits to working in the dark—maybe he'd have connections or access to information the rest of us couldn't get.

"Actually...could you look into someone for me, Matt?"

"What's the kid's name?" He got his phone from his back pocket and pulled up an app I didn't recognize.

It seemed that it was a mystery to Sean too, and he poked at the screen. "What's that app?"

Matt grunted and smoothly pulled the phone away from his twin's reach. "What's his name?"

"Sebastian Lane. But it's his brother I want you to look into." The two of them looked at me with raised eyebrows. "Benjamin, or I guess 'Ben'."

"Brother?" Sean sounded surprised. "So, Sebastian's not a lost boy."

"Maybe. I don't know, maybe the brother's involved in all this shit." The thought made me uneasy, more worried about Seb.

"Involved in the bridge fall?" Matt didn't look up. Just typed into his app.

"Maybe." A sinking feeling gripped at my guts as I remembered how stiff Seb had become when I mentioned his brother. "Ben came into the hospital looking for him, with a boyfriend Seb denies having…"

"His brother came in to see him?" Sean crossed his arms again.

"Yeah, but Seb had checked himself out of recovery, and he was on his way back to his apartment."

"Where Eli kidnaped him." The tiny twitch of an amused grin on Sean's lips made me growl.

"After he found him with a gun pointed to his head." I sounded gruffer than I meant to, but Sean dropped the grin.

"Jesus… So the kid is in *big* trouble." He tightened his arms over his chest.

Matt looked up from his phone. "What else do you know about the jumper?"

"Nothing." My tongue felt heavy in my mouth. I knew very little about Sebastian and his problems at home. The twins stared at me like I'd let them down somehow, and I clenched my jaw. I hated feeling like the weak link in a conversation. "I'll find out what happened."

Matt shoved his phone back in his pocket and the two of them moved, as though they were sharing a single brain, to squeeze my shoulders. They turned, and headed back to their apartment without another word, leaving me to continue dripping in the foyer, with the tingling in my crotch that wouldn't let me forget what had just happened in the bathroom.

"Fuck." I ran my hands over my face and tried to scrub the memory from my mind. I'd practically molested the kid, taken advantage of him when he was hurt, and confused, and relying on me for help. He was so young, he was probably overwhelmed by my tongue and my hands and my body forcing itself on him. Probably had just gone along so it would end sooner. Damn it. I knew better, but seeing him naked and wet with his hand on his dick short-circuited my brain.

I walked back to the apartment. Leaving didn't suddenly seem as important as making this right. Seb was on the couch dressed in the clothes I'd been leaving out for him when I'd heard him cry out in the bathroom; a tank top and jeans, left behind by one of the guys who'd crashed with us before. One I hadn't molested, by the way.

"Thanks for the threads. More flattering than the hospital garb, huh?" He was swimming in the oversized tank top, but the skinny jeans fit, tightly hugging his thighs…

I caught a towel he chucked my way, and I snapped my eyes onto his. "I'm so sorry."

"What for?" His voice had an air of casualness, like he was prepared to give me an out. But I wasn't a fan of living under unspoken resentments. Owning my mistakes was important to me.

I lowered myself into the leather armchair opposite him and met his gaze, his eyes wide and full of forced naivety, like he was still pretending it hadn't occurred. "What happened in the shower never should have happened."

He flinched, and guilt surged up from my gut and into my throat. Guilt tasted a lot like bile. "I shouldn't have taken advantage of you—"

"Is that what you think happened?" He huffed and shifted on the couch, then threw his hands up in the air. "You think you took *advantage* of me?"

I was filled with the compulsion to assuage my guilt with some kind of explanation, and I gripped the towel in my lap tightly. "I'm older—"

"Oh, please! I'm an adult, doc." His arms flopped to his sides and he shook his head at me, as if I were a lost cause. "Not sure if you're aware of this, but I know my own mind and my own body, and I'm responsible for my own choices. I can act on my desires and no one needs to freak out about it. I don't need you to be a martyr. In fact, it's a total turn-off." He slumped against the couch and scowled.

I opened my mouth then snapped it shut again. Where I'd pictured him as a vulnerable, impressionable kid, he was instead a self-assured young man adamant nothing we'd done—my intrusion during his shower, the kisses, the touching—had been a violation.

I sounded desperate. "Seb—"

He held up a hand and shook his head, shaking off the moment. "Now that we've cleared that up, thanks again for your help, but I'm gonna head out and figure out what the fuck is going on with my life." He ran his hands over his thighs and my greedy gaze followed the path. I was out of control.

"Whoa, wait." I reached out reflexively, curled my fingers around his arm and waited for him to look at me. Instead, he stared at my hand where it touched his bare skin. Or maybe smoldered was a better word.

"For what?"

I lowered my hand and picked at the towel. "You said you'd stay the day."

He sat back down, glanced around, then looked me over skeptically. His obvious distrust felt like an uncomfortable itch at the back of my neck. "Plans change."

I spoke quickly and implored him with my eyes to stay. "The twins are looking into what went down at your apartment, so why don't you hold tight here, get some rest, and then we can make a new plan with the info they dig up."

He scratched the back of his head, and I did my best not to look at the blush of nipple that was peeking out from sleeve of the tank top.

"Look. You've got no phone, no wallet, no money, and your apartment was ransacked. Where are you going to go? To your brother?" He had to see reason and I was prepared to argue this for as long as I needed. To help him. To show him he was safe. To remind him of the danger waiting for him when he stepped out of Vanguard Tower.

He nodded, petulant and pouting. "Thanks for reminding me that my life has gone to shit."

I chuckled at his sharp sarcasm, and relaxed when he smiled a little. If he was so desperate to leave, the least I could do was help him figure some things out. Plus, any information I could get would help Matt. "Why *has* your life gone to shit? What's all this about?"

He gave an agonized groan into his hands and leaned back on the couch. "I wish I knew!" But he dropped his hands and turned his head to gaze at me.

I glanced away because looking at him still stirred heat in my belly and I was apparently ill-equipped to handle it without letting it get the better of my good intentions. "No idea? Really? There has to be something." Concentrating on his issues was a good distraction.

"Yeah. There's something." He sighed and sat forward, dropped his hands onto his thighs and rubbed his legs again. I absolutely didn't notice the rasp of friction where his hands ran over the denim hugging him so well. Didn't pay any attention to the way his fingers curled around his knee for just a second before he slid them back. And no way did I focus on the intensity of his sigh as he prepared whatever he was about to say. I was an adult, not ruled by my dick. I could have a conversation and be fine. "I think I saw something I shouldn't have. Next minute, everything is upside now, I died in the river, I'm basically homeless...and now I don't know who to trust."

"Me. You can trust me." I put a hand on my chest, swearing a silent oath. It was the right answer.

I caught his gaze and my breath snagged.

"Yeah." His voice was barely a whisperer, and he wet his lips nervously. Inched closer. "Maybe I can."

I held his eye and a painful magnetic pull urged me to move closer to him. But if I did...things would happen. I couldn't just hold him and tell him everything was going to be okay. I was too desperate to touch him. To claim his mouth with mine. Again.

He cleared his throat with a fist in front of his mouth, and I sat back, my eyelids heavy and threatening to close mid-conversation as the weight of the day landed on me.

"Now you're the one who looks dead." His voice moved through me like it had when I'd been listening to his lungs and it reverberated in my belly.

"Long day." I laughed lightly and ran a hand through my hair as I looked at him. "I don't usually follow my all-nighters by ducking a flying toilet seat and, uh, half-showering."

He snorted, and his smirk looked so pretty I wanted nothing more than to kiss it. Age aside, he was the type of guy I went for, when I went for anyone. Sweet, smart, and sassy, with a jaw that looked like it was carved from granite, and the soft curve of his lower lip that gave even his snarkiest smirks an air of kissable sensuality. He didn't seem like he wanted to stay at all, which was really hot because sometimes it took an act of God and two or three brothers to get some of my one-night stands to go home. But not so much when I was trying to *help* him.

"Will you stay until I wake up?" I swallowed the pride that almost stopped me from asking.

He pursed his lips and hummed, just long enough for me to take it as a yes. I didn't want to leave him alone, but the Tower was secure and effectively guarded by my brothers. Safest place he could be right now, and it would be easier to sleep knowing he was taken care of and had a roof over his head. Tomorrow would have to worry about itself.

"Do you want one of the brothers to come and keep you company?"

"Ha. Which one, which one…" He tapped his finger against his chin. "How could I choose between the fireman and the Marine?" He smirked, then nodded at me seriously. "I'm good. You sleep."

I wasn't sure if I could trust myself around him. I rose slowly and gave him the nickel tour of the apartment pointing out the various areas of interest, ignoring the rest. "Coffee. Spare bedroom. And you know where the main bathroom is."

His snicker was equal parts adorable and endearing, and I took a long look at him before I headed to my bedroom, unsure if I'd ever see him again.

After a much-needed hot shower in my en suite bathroom, I slipped into bed, ready to pass out. But my mind wouldn't shut down. I wanted Seb to still be there when I woke up almost as much as I wanted to close my eyes and let sleep take me. There was no denying my body craved Seb, and my mind was intrigued, too. But craving and wanting for one night was different than what was happening. Foreign. Mysterious and odd.

I bunched up a pillow and shoved it under my head, comforted by the fact I just needed to get him out of my system. He was a whimsy. Once I got to know Seb, his baggage would start to feel really heavy on my shoulders. That was the way it always went, and Seb's baggage seemed chunkier than most.

Chapter 12 - Sebastian

I slumped against the back of the couch and let a day's worth of stress leave my body in one long, heavy sigh. The Dish's hot and cold flip-flopping was doing my head in—kissing me one minute, regret the next, begging me to stay, treating me like a kid. And the struggle was real. My crotch hadn't stopped aching since he first kissed me, and I wished I'd taken Eli's advice and packed a bag, if only to be wearing some pants that weren't as tight as the hand-me-down jeans from the last of Derek's charity cases.

I yawned, fatigued and wary, but the throbbing in my jeans wasn't going to let me doze off anytime soon, and I couldn't jerk off *again*. I had to figure out if my brother had tried to kill me.

I needed my laptop. If I could log onto a secure network, I had a chance of monitoring police reports and seeing if Big Ben had blundered across their radar, or if there was any talk of an armed hitman found unconscious at my apartment building. Or maybe I could just check Ben's Facebook…

I sat up too quickly, and my head spun. Concussion maybe. Exhaustion, more likely.

If I had any hope of staying awake long enough to find out if Eli had stashed my laptop in Derek's apartment, then I'd need a cup of Earl Grey. Unfortunately, Dr. Dish's pantry was stocked with seven different types of coffee beans but not a single box of tea. No black, no green, and certainly no matcha. Not even the wimpy herbal stuff. What kind of doctor didn't have a single bag of not coffee? His nervous system had to be shot. Or maybe he'd sold out to big coffee along with big pharma.

I brewed what I figured was a weak cup of joe and looked around while it cooled. The large open-plan area and eat-in kitchen could have been ripped straight from the pages of an architectural magazine. Sleek lines, polished cement countertops, and designer lighting of a modern architectural design. Most of the apartment was dark navy and tan, with pops of white that made the place look fresh.

The fridge was gorged with vegetables, but wedged behind a gigantic cabbage, I found a carton of caramel hazelnut nondairy creamer that turned my coffee into something sweet and divine, rich and decadent. No wonder Derek liked this stuff. The mug was heavy and satisfying to drink from, and I couldn't believe that even Derek's crockery was *comfortable*. With a tentative sip, I felt my brain cells coming back online, so I started poking around the apartment for my laptop.

No sign of it on the dining table, down the back of the couch, under the coffee table, or under the cushions of his many armchairs. I'd never seen so many comfortable places to sit down in one home. But then, the dude did have *seven* brothers. Did they come over to watch *sports*? They looked like the type to yell at the television as if the players could hear them.

In the bathroom, I found the bandage that had been around my wrist, and strapped it back on with clumsy, untrained hands. My efforts weren't nearly so neat and professional as my delicious caretaker's and made me appreciate Dr Dish's skills. It'd have to do, at least until he woke up.

I picked up the broken toilet seat and did my best to reattach it to the bowl with one hand. It had been a challenge to get it off in the first place and was even more of a pain to get back on. Lucky I'd been too weak to manage more than a feeble throw earlier, because I might have knocked the doc out cold and then his army of brothers waiting just outside probably would have kicked my ass.

Back in the main living area, I ventured over to a study nook set deep into the wall when I caught a glimpse of silver on the desk there, but my heart sank when I got close. Not my laptop. His. It was hooked up to a large monitor that lit up when I flicked open the laptop. I sipped my coffee as I tried a few predictable passwords to see if I could get in without running a workaround, the kind of key phrases a doctor in his mid-thirties would remember. *123456, hospital, qwerty, blink182, 1111111.*

On the fifth attempt, the screen flashed with intruder detection software, warning me it would wipe the drive and alert authorities if I kept trying to get in. Huh. Impressive. Derek was more conscious of cybersecurity than I would have thought, or maybe it was one of his brothers that had set up the gatekeeping software. Either way, it made me curious about exactly what it was he was trying to hide. Patient files? Or something more...sensual? My fingers hovered over the keys, ready to reset to a boot screen and hack my way in, but guilt got the better of my curiosity, and I closed the laptop. If Derek didn't want people poking around, then I'd respect that. My laptop had to be around here somewhere, so I turned my attention to the rest of the cozy nook.

Like the rest of the apartment, it felt lived in. By which I meant...safe. The safety of money, of family, of a future clearly laid out and planned. I let myself imagine what it would be like to live somewhere like that. My heart twinged. My lips buzzed with the memory of our kiss, but it made me sad. I wasn't good enough for someone like Derek. Sad, but true.

I set down my coffee on a slab of slate surely meant to be used as a coaster, and pulled open his drawers. Pens, so many pens, branded notepads, and a collection of scented candles with charred wicks. He really did live that scented candle lifestyle. I scoffed but took a deep sniff before I slammed the drawers shut and carried on with my search.

Maybe it was the coffee or my lack of sleep, but I was getting antsy. Where the fuck had they hidden my shit? I gritted my teeth and let out a frustrated growl when my second look under the couch turned up nothing but dust bunnies. I could press charges for kidnapping *and* robbery at this rate.

By the time I shuffled past the closed door of Derek's bedroom, my coffee had run dry. It had tasted damn good, I had to admit. A second cup would be my reward when I found my laptop. Or a consolation if I couldn't locate my stuff. I stuck my head into a spare bedroom at the end of the short hallway. It had bright azure walls covered in what had to be custom art, plush dark gray carpet that melted under my toes, and another scented candle on the bedside table. And at the foot of the double bed, shining on the quilted bedspread, there she was. My baby. My laptop. Laid out like she'd been waiting for me the whole time.

But it wasn't my laptop as I knew it... The hardy case has been crunched and cracked on the edges into a disfigured shape. I threw it open and found the edges of the body were crushed in at the corners and a portion of the screen was peeling away where a piece of metal was poking through. My heart sank as I smoothed my fingers lovingly across her wounds. It looked like something had smashed against her from above, and I shuddered to think about a baseball bat hitting my most prized possession.

Something didn't add up. Why had they smashed her, but left her there? The laptop was worth over a grand, even second-hand, and the only thing worth a damn in my whole apartment. I hated seeing her beat up and busted, but I had to tend to her wounds. I sat cross-legged against the wooden headboard as I booted her up. She groaned from the violence that had been bestowed upon her but came to life with a heart-lifting *ding*. I almost collapsed with relief. My baby! She lived! I thanked my lucky stars and the manufacturers of my hardy case for the miracle.

My fingers raced across the keyboard faster than usual as I hacked into Derek's Wi-Fi network. Holy shit. I was quick. Probably needed to drink coffee more often. It seemed to do wonders for my manual dexterity. But I remembered why I kept away from the stuff when I opened my email and found a big, fat, unread message from Ben. My blood pressure spiked and my hands shook as I struggled to take a full breath. The edge of a freak-out. An unreasonable one. This email might have the answers I needed. Oh. Panic attacks. Coffee. Bad combo.

I slammed the laptop shut and counted my exhales as I stared at the artwork on the opposite wall. It was a gay adaptation of Klimt's *The Kiss*, all gold and shining with two men embracing. It was kind of gaudy, but I liked it, and examining the fine details kept my mind off the fear roaring just below my ribs.

"What are you even afraid of at this point?" I spoke in a hoarse whisper, but even that was so loud my own voice startled my jittery, caffeinated nerves. With a deep breath, I considered the email and what could be in it. Maybe Ben admitted trying to kill me. Or maybe he was finally set to sever our relationship since my gayness bothered him so. Or maybe he'd finally typed out his homophobic manifesto.

Of course, any of those would have been better than the cloud of confusion I was currently living under. With my gaze on the shining gold leaf of the painting, I peeled the laptop open again. With quick flicks of my eyes to the screen, I opened the email and braced myself.

Seb,

Call me. I'm worried. I know you're freaked out by the file you saw. I never would've showed you, but I needed help and you're the computer nerd. But I can explain what you saw. What happened. Just need you to call. We need to talk. Love you, man.

Ben

"What the fuck?" My eyes stung, and I swiped the tears out of them with the back of my good hand. That asshole was the only family I had left, and he had the audacity to tell me that he *loved* me at a time like this? Clearly emotional manipulation, and damn, was it working. I so badly wanted to believe him that what had happened was all just a weird but completely explainable miscommunication. Why was I scared of my brother in the first place? Did I overreact to what happened? My head said no, but my heart wanted to give Ben a chance.

And at the very least, I deserve an explanation, to know what the fuck was going on, and it looked like that explanation was going to have to come from him.

With coffee-fueled fingers, I dashed out a reply.

Ben,
One chance. Your place tonight.

As soon as I hit send, I lay back and passed out. My body had put up with a lot, and with some potential answers finally on their way, I took the opportunity to nap. I dreamed of Dr. Dish rebandaging my wrist with slow, sensual touches that kept moving higher and higher up my arm until he'd wrapped me up in a deep embrace.

I must have slept deep. When I woke up, it was a little after four, and to my surprise, Google Maps told me I wasn't far from Ben's apartment—or mine. It was too early to go meet him, but I had to bust out of the Vanguard Tower before Derek woke up and tried to talk me out of meeting my brother and interrogating him until I was satisfied with the answers.

The small closet in the spare room was stuffed with clothes, presumably from past kidnapees, and I shoved my laptop and any clothes that looked like my size into a Hershel backpack I found on the back of the door. There was a pair of boots a size too big but close enough I could wear them, and I tucked them under my arm before making my way out of the room. I paused at Derek's bedroom door and pressed my ear to the wood but couldn't hear a thing. Just one last look...

I held back a groan when I opened the door. Dr. Dish, half-naked, sprawled across his bed, face-down and ass up, his thick thighs tangled in the sheets as he snored softly. How easy it would be to forget Ben and crawl into bed with Dr. Dish. I swallowed and tried to tear my gaze away, but I couldn't stop staring at the rise and fall of his muscled back, his stubbled jaw, and his parted lips. Fuck, he was the whole package. Handsome, smart, kind, an out-of-this-world kisser. Too bad I had no shot at someone like him. Not yet, anyway. Maybe after a decade of career progress and real estate investment, if he didn't find an eligible husband before then, I'd be able to, at least, earn his respect.

Shit, for all I knew, he already had some uber-respectable, insanely hot boyfriend waiting for him to get rid of his latest charity case. Maybe that was why he'd freaked out and acted like kissing me had given him a roaring case of the herps or some plague kind of thing that would attack his appendages.

I headed to the kitchen for a sandwich and shoved a bottle of sparkling water into my backpack. I felt a little sad as I pushed my feet into the boots at the front door, knowing it would be the last time I'd see the place. But who knew? Maybe I'd come back for his help one day.

Tying laces sure wasn't easy with just one hand and a backpack on, so I shuffled over to the living room area and plopped onto the couch so I could prop a foot on the coffee table and lace the boots from there. I was almost all set when the door rattled. I held my breath. Surely it was locked…

No, of course it wasn't, or if it had been, then Eli most certainly had a key. The Latino cutie stood in the doorway with his hellhound at his feet, and raised his eyebrows at me in surprise.

"You look like you're ready for an adventure." He tilted his head to the side and sized me up.

The dog rushed over and dove onto the couch beside me, and I tried to disguise my feeling of being *caught* by patting it.

"This is Uno. You haven't been introduced properly. She's a search and rescue dog. Good at finding people when they go missing." His last word was pointed, and I looked up as he slid the door shut behind himself without taking his eyes off me.

"I'm not your prisoner, you know." But I sure was starting to feel like I was.

Eli tilted his head to the side and wandered over to the ottoman near the couch, while Uno nudged my hand for more pats.

"Of course. How's your concussion? And your wrist?" He sat down on the ottoman with a heavy thud and craned forward to look at my poorly bandaged wrist, and I self-consciously tucked the end into the wrapping.

"I'm fine." I sounded petulant but whatever, this guy wasn't going to be in my life for much longer. "How are your balls?"

He sighed and pulled his hair back, then held up his hands in surrender. "We got off on the wrong foot."

"Right." I finished tying one boot and quickly moved to the next. "Kidnapping someone tends to sour the relationship."

He gave a short chuckle and smoothed his hands over his knees while he searched for my gaze, but I wasn't giving it to him. I kept my eyes locked on my laces. "Look, I know it doesn't seem like we're on your side, but we are. We're looking out for you. The best thing you can do for us, and for Derek, and for *yourself* is to stay here and get some more rest. Maybe get a doctor to bandage that wrist properly." Eli winked at me with his black eye. The gesture was not unkind, but it made me angry.

"Hey, what I need *help* with right now is to get to an important appointment, so if you don't mind—" I was cut off when he slapped my hand away from my boot. I recoiled, but he held my foot in place while rage throbbed in my belly and I frowned in confusion.

He grinned at me as he yanked at my laces and tightened the boot around my foot.

"These used to be mine, you know?" He smiled proudly and slapped the underside of the sole. "First pair that Derek ever bought me."

It wasn't news that Derek was a good guy, and I didn't get what Eli was getting at. He was making fast work on lacing up the boot though. "This place is called the Vanguard Tower, did Derek tell you that?"

I nodded like the name of a building mattered. The Sears Tower had a nice name, as did the White House, but I wouldn't like being held captive at one of those, either.

"Good. But I don't think you really *get* what that means. Not yet, anyway." Eli put a mysterious edge to his voice, and finished tying a bow and motioned for me to lift my other boot.

I reluctantly presented my poorly laced footwear, then slumped back into the sofa, ready to hear about the weird cult they ran under the guise of being good and helpful souls. I could spare five minutes for story time if it meant getting a little help…

Eli spoke towards his fingers as he tightened the boot, while Uno rested her head in my lap and I smoothed her ears back as I listened. "All of us work on the frontlines, we're all dedicated to helping people. In our jobs, we save and heal, find and rescue…but our real work is with guys like you, the ones we meet who need the kind of help the system can't or won't provide."

I flicked my eyes up, indignant. He must have the wrong idea about me. "I'm not in foster care, you know." I immediately felt ashamed by how I sounded, like foster care was something to be ashamed of.

But Eli met my gaze and smiled, not seeming offended, his fingers paused on the knot he was halfway through tying. "I mean *any* system. Law and order, healthcare, education, military—those systems let people down." His voice shook with emotion and I was surprised by how sincere he sounded. "We all went through a time when no one was there for us until we found each other. So, we have to pay that back. Pay it forward, I mean—to people like you."

I swallowed down a rising uncertainty about my plan to get out of there, and Eli tied off my laces.

"And if *people like me* don't want your help?" But did I? I put my feet on the floor, and Uno put a paw on my thigh like she was urging me to stay put.

Eli shrugged and then leaned back. "Then you probably would have left already. You said it yourself, you're not a prisoner here."

I glanced at the door. Boots laced, but I wasn't rushing out there to get my answers. Maybe I felt safer in the Vanguard Tower than I wanted to admit.

Eli slicked a hand over his hair and lowered his voice again. He seemed to have the knack of sounding like he was completely casual and confiding a secret at the same time, and despite myself, it made me feel special, like he was letting me in on something important. "Look, we're not saints, just a bunch of guys who came together to help others. We're all fucked up in our own ways. We've seen a lot of shit. But Derek... Man." Eli tucked a piece of stray hair back and tightened his bun. "If you're anything like me, you're trying to run because you're worried about getting hurt. You want to be the one to get out first, so when it all goes south like we're conditioned to believe it will, you can protect yourself from the sting."

I popped my jaw and shrugged. Okay. So maybe he knew stuff.

"Derek's the type of guy who you can depend on. He won't let you down. He's trustworthy and dependable. Most dependable one of us." He reached over and scuffed up Uno's fur on the back of her neck. "And that's saying a lot, because we are eight dependable sons of bitches."

My bottom lip was raw from how much I'd chewed it, and my chest tightened when I thought about what it might be like to be able to depend on someone. I cleared my throat, but my voice still came out weak and croaky. "I appreciate what you're saying, but I can't afford to trust anyone right now. Not even someone like Derek."

Eli seemed to look right inside me. "Why not someone like Derek?"

Good question.

"I don't need a hero. I need a...friend. A companion. Someone to share my life, not take it over." I had Ben for that. "Heroes need someone to save. I'm not that guy." I still had some pride left. And I was going to save myself. Come hell or more hell.

Eli pulled back and frowned, sounding confused. "Yeah, but we all need some saving sometimes... What's the problem with that?"

I shrugged, but a surge of emotions pinched my insides and tears pricked at my eyes. "I don't want to be just another victim to him. Someone he can save. I want his respect." What I wanted was for him to adore me the way I'd come to see him.

"I'm sure he respects you or you wouldn't be here." He smiled, a flash of smugness in his eyes. "He wouldn't have *brought* you here, I mean." Sure. Maybe not kissed me. Because he brought all his poor little charity cases home from what I could see.

Eli's nodded to a point over my shoulder, and I turned. Derek stood behind me, ruffled with sleep, in nothing but thigh-hugging sweats. My jaw dropped because this was a whole lot of man and I could see a fair amount of him. He was close enough that he could have clearly heard a lot, if not everything I'd said and I felt a blush creep into my cheeks.

Eli chuckled and with a click of his fingers, Uno jumped off the couch. "We'll, uh, be going now. Excuse us." Eli squeezed my shoulder on the way past and the two of them slinked out of the apartment together. Leaving us alone. Just me, my stupid emotions, and the delectable Dr. Dish.

Chapter 13 - Derek

"You tried to leave." Disappointment welled in my chest and I wished I didn't sound so…desperate.

"Yeah. And?" Seb's voice was quiet but unapologetic, and the tone annoyed me.

I stepped closer and crossed my arms, more holding in my vulnerable feelings than trying to look tough. My voice was stronger now. "Even after you told me you wouldn't."

He frowned at me over the back of the couch. "Why do you care so fucking much? You're not my boss."

I ran my hands over my stubble and groaned as I looked up at the ceiling and tried to get my head in the game. I was pissed he'd essentially lied to me, but it was more. This was why I didn't do relationships—I couldn't rely on anyone but my brothers, and someone always *left*. Not that what I had with Seb was anything more than a fleeting sexual attraction.

"I'm not your boss, and you're not some victim to me, but it's fucked up to tell someone you'll stay and then sneak out." I sounded like a jilted lover, as if I'd woken up in an empty bed after a one-night stand. As if that wasn't what I usually wanted.

Seb flinched but set his jaw defiantly. "Yeah."

Shit. He had no idea where I was coming from. How could he? We knew next to nothing about each other and there was only one way that was going to change.

I came around to the couch and slid down next to him while I searched for the right words in my sleep-hazy head. "I…had a pretty shitty childhood. I know everyone did in one way or another, but I need to be able to take people at their word. I get a bit…angsty…about honesty."

He lowered his eyes and nodded. "Yeah… Fuck, yeah, I'm sorry. That was shitty of me. I'm not normally a do-and-dash kind of guy."

I laughed, and he smiled at his knees.

"I can arrange for you to stay with one of my brothers, if you're uncomfortable here because of what happened—"

"No. I told you, that wasn't a problem…for me." He shot his green eyes at me before staring down at the bag in his lap. "This is the most comfortable place I've ever been. I just need to go and see my brother."

My heart faltered. His brother? The guy was trouble, I was sure of it. His presence in the hospital had been sketchy at best, and I got a nasty feeling when I thought about him being involved in the trashed apartment in some way. "Ben?"

Seb shrugged. "Yeah, I got an email from him. I'm meeting him tonight to get some answers."

Absolutely not. I couldn't let it happen. But Seb seemed determined, and I'd meant what I said–I wasn't his boss or his keeper. I cleared my throat and shook my head. "Then I'm coming with you."

"No." He snapped his head up as a panicked look flashed across his face.

A knot rolled in my stomach, and I slumped back as though slapped. Another rejection. More mistrust. Not that he owed me. I'd built my life around being someone people could rely on—a doctor, a patriarch of my mish-mashed family, the *dependable* one.

Seb shook his head. "It's not about you—"

"It's fine." The hell it was. This shit hurt.

His voice pleaded. "Really, it's not."

"Then what's it about?" I waited for his answer, but he opened his mouth and nothing came out. "Fine. I'm going for a run."

Twenty minutes ago, he was hell-bent on leaving. He could damned well see himself out. I was acting like a dick, but I couldn't listen to his shit. I couldn't sit in a chair and pretend like he wasn't tearing my heart out. Neither could I understand why I felt so hurt. Instead, I went straight for my gym gear in my bedroom. A run would help me burn through my emotions and clear my head.

"Hey." I looked at Seb, framed by the doorway like a perfect picture. "I'm serious. It's not about you. You're the best person I could have in my corner. I'm just not sure I can trust Ben, and I don't want to drag you into my mess."

I sighed and slumped onto the bed, relieved. He leaned in the doorway with his bag on the floor, and his wrist so poorly wrapped it was probably cutting off circulation to his fingers.

"Can I fix that?" I nodded to the injury.

The loose bandage trailed down his forearm as he held it up. "This? You don't like my handiwork? Artistic, no?"

I chuckled. He could lift my mood with just one playful comment. "Maybe expressive, but not effective."

"Ha. I like that." His grin grew into a smile, and my irritation slipped off my shoulders.

The bed sank as he sat beside me, and I unraveled the twisted bandage. "So, you don't want to drag me into your mess?"

"Yeah." It hurt me to hear the shame in his voice.

I pulled the last of the wrapping from his arm and wound it into a workable coil. "I was born into a complicated scene, you know. Spent most of my early life in one, too. I'm familiar with mess."

He let out an amused breath and gave me more of his wrist as I began to strap it up. "Even the really messy mess?"

"Oh, yeah." I gently turned his forearm for a better angle. "I've had my share of it, in my life and my brothers' too. I know how to climb out of the shit. My brothers and I are real experts at shit-climbing."

"Ha!" I loved seeing him relaxed and happy, a glimpse of the 'real' Seb without the arrogant smirk or the annoyed pout. It made me want to share more, an unusual feeling for me. I spoke softly and spiraled the bandage up his arm. "I grew up in foster homes, maybe you got that already. My mom died when I was eight, which is an awful time to go into the system."

Seb hummed and I met his gaze. "Orphan club."

"Huh?"

He grimaced and shrugged. "My parents died when I was fourteen. Car accident. Both of them, just suddenly…gone."

"Shit." I sat back, surprised that we had this in common, and my heart aching for his loss. "I'm sorry."

I expected him to give me a fake smile or a glib response, but I was touched when he held my gaze and nodded as he spoke softly. "I'm sorry for you, too. You get by though, right?"

"Yeah. You do what you can." To keep the grief from pulling me deep into a flashback, I tried to focus on caring for his wrist but I'd messed up and had to redo a section. "You didn't go into foster care?"

He grunted, and I caught a hint of disappointment in his voice. "Nah, my big brother was old enough to become my guardian."

"Hm." Ben. The scary older brother. I wondered if the bruises had anything to do with him.

The wobble in Seb's voice told me I might be right, and my heart surged. I wanted to protect him. To build walls around him and keep him safe. "He's never been my greatest fan but I'm having a really hard time with the idea that he'd want me dead."

My fingers refused to tie off the bandage, and Seb glanced at me sheepishly.

"Too heavy?" He grimaced like he'd made a faux pas and I was quick to put a reassuring hand on his shoulder.

"No. Tell me more." I held my breath and hoped he'd take the invitation. I wanted nothing more than to know everything that was going on with him, and how I could help.

He pinched the bridge of his nose and squeezed his eyes shut in frustration. "I don't want to say it out loud because it sounds insane."

"Hey, I'm the doctor here. I'll be the judge of that." I tried to sound light-hearted but my chest was heaving. Seb was in danger.

He laughed and then shot me a warm smile. Warm and beautiful. "You're a really nice guy, huh?"

Every time, he made it sound like an insult almost. Something mired by the intention to show off my goodness which was never the case. "Is that such a bad thing?"

"What? No. Shit, no. It's…nice."

I bit back a smile, but I couldn't help but beam at him. My fingers started to work again, and I tied off the bandage and tucked the ends in.

"Thanks. About being insane…well, after you bandaged me up"–he held up the wrist and admired the new wrapping with a satisfied nod–"the first time at the hospital, I went home and Ben asked me to fix his computer. I saw something I shouldn't have, evidence of him stealing money from some big power players."

"Ah. And he knows what you saw?" The pieces were starting to fit together, and I was glad I'd listened to my gut when Ben had been asking after Seb.

"Yeah, he was *pissed*. And then…" His eyes glazed, and he stared into middle space. I put a hand on his knee and he snapped back to look at me.

"The river?" I spoke quietly.

His bottom lip trembled, and he gave me a stoic shrug that made me want to take care of him even more. "I don't know, I *guess* so. All I can remember is Ben coming at me, and then…you."

I let out a long, strained breath. So he didn't have an abusive boyfriend, but he might have a psychopathic brother. Great.

He picked at my sheets and mumbled quietly. "Pretty big mess, right?"

"Not the worst." I squeezed his knee again and cleared my throat, desperate for him to really listen to me. "But I'm worried. Don't go to meet him alone."

He glanced at my hand, and his eyes lingered there. "Don't you have work? Save some lives?"

I slowly lifted my hand, but only got an inch above his knee before I felt compelled to put it back and squeezed him harder. I spoke with confidence, hoping to instill some of it into him. "I've got three days off. Plenty of time to spare. And you're welcome to stay here as long as you want."

His eyes dragged up from my hand, over my shoulders, and up to my face. He looked at me and blinked slowly, my heart rattling in my chest with excitement as he wet his lips. "Okay. I'll stay."

I could barely believe it. "Really?"

His smile was so sweet I almost melted, and before I knew it, we were kissing. It was softer and sweeter than the rushed passion in the shower, but the moment his tongue skated across my bottom lip, my dick got hard.

With a sharp breath, he pulled back and fluttered his lashes, making me swoon.

"Mm." I touched my lips as my heart pounded heavy. "Sorry for apologizing about the kiss before."

"You're apologizing for apologizing?" He laughed and kissed me again but pulled away quickly when a bolt of worry ran through me, and I didn't kiss back.

He searched my face for an explanation, and I shakily found my words. "I'm sorry but we probably shouldn't. Just for now, while all this is going on."

He ran his fingers through his blond hair and nodded. "Yeah. Don't want to make more mess, right?"

He was right, I didn't want to make a mess of this. Whatever *this* was. I'd never been so attracted to a guy I'd helped out before, but keeping out of the ethical gray areas was a good way to proceed when someone needed my care…if only I could keep my hands off him. I traced the palm of his hand where the bandage wrapped around his thumb. "You okay with that?"

"Yeah, for sure. It's cool. I'm not really your type anyway." He laughed and I did a double-take. Aside from the age gap, he couldn't have been more wrong, but he pulled away and motioned to my gym socks before I had a chance to correct him. "You going for a run?"

"Got a better idea?" I sounded more casual than I felt, and almost reached out to touch his knee again.

But he stood and wiped his palms on his sides. "You ever been to Zuconi's?"

"Zuc-who?"

Seb laughed and headed back towards the living area, calling back to me over his shoulder. "Oh, geez. Get dressed, old man. We're going to dinner."

Seb emailed Ben to reschedule his visit, then met me at the front door wearing a turquoise button-down I thought I recognized but couldn't quite place. He caught me looking and grinned. "Found it in the closet in the spare room. Thought it was my color."

"It is. You look good. Should I wear something smarter? Is this place fine dining?"

He snorted and walked through the door. I followed him out of the foyer in my gym gear, wondering what I'd said that was so funny.

He took us between the warehouses of the Southwest Waterfront, half of which were converted to residential blocks like the Vanguard Tower, or had been transformed into fine restaurants, while the rest retained their primary function of storage, manufacturing, and sea shepherding.

It was still hot and muggy as the sun slid down in the sky, and the smells of the wharf neighborhood mingled into a thick mix of fresh fish from the seafood market, rubber and dust from storage warehouses Seb buzzed past with me on his heels. I admired how good he looked. For a guy who was deep in a serious mess, he walked with confidence, shoulders back and a cute swagger in his hips. He turned heads, but I didn't think he noticed.

He made a quick turn and took us off the main thoroughfare, led me down laneways that skirted the river and deep into the industrial lanes back from the water.

"Uh, what kind of place is this restaurant?" I was a little breathless trying to keep up with him, and from the way my heart kept leaping whenever I glanced at his finely angled profile.

He looked ahead and didn't turn his head to meet my eye. "It's an institution. Five minutes from here. Can't believe you've never been. Your generation…"

I stopped short. "My *generation*? How old do you think I am?"

"Old as time." He didn't break his stride, and I had to jog to catch up before we turned a corner into a particularly dirty laneway.

"Ouch. I'm only as old as *Lethal Weapon*." I was amused by the talk of our age gap, but I was glad we were approaching it lightly.

"Huh?" He finally looked at me and squinted, confused. I loved his attention, and I dragged out the moment for as long as I could.

I spiraled my hand as if by motion alone I could jog his memory. "The movie?"

He rolled his eyes and looked over my shoulder. "Sure thing, Pops. Uh…hang on, let's try turning left here."

I glanced up and down a tight alley I'd certainly never been in before, and tried to sound nonplussed. "Are we lost?"

Seb smirked and winked, then elbowed my ribs and started walking again. "You know us kids these days, we need our phones to navigate."

"Oh, yeah, we've got to get you one of those. Remind me after dinner, I'll set you up with a kit."

"A kit?"

"Phone, cash, an excuse to call out from work."

He smiled, and my knees almost buckled. "A shit-climbing kit."

I laughed, the sound escaping so quickly and loudly it shocked me when it echoed off the high walls on either side of the laneway. "Yeah. Almost everything you need to climb out of the shit. Got to make your own luck, though."

He came to a sudden stop beside a graffitied wall topped with a barbed wire and motioned with his chin toward the half-broken wooden gate. "Zuconi's."

I looked over the top of my sunglasses and sized up the crumbling brick wall and the ramshackle warehouse attached. "Well, now, I feel *overdressed*."

Yanked in by my arm, I was shocked to find a gorgeous courtyard restaurant packed with teens and twenty-somethings, sprawling on couches and benches. Seb led me through a winding path of built-up decks covered in cushions, plants, and hipsters, toward the indoor space where a DJ spun early '90s hip hop, and a bar served bright-colored cocktails. We skirted the full dance floor, bumped through the crowd, and wove around a gigantic wood-fired pizza oven and cooking station, to find our way to a quiet spot near the rear of the garden. We sat by an ivy-covered wall, beside a water feature with lily pads and a gentle fountain, lit by huge rose-colored lanterns hanging overhead among blooming wisteria.

He spread his arms and smirked. "Good?"

I turned in my chair to take it in. I was impressed, both by the beautiful space hiding in the back streets of my neighborhood, and that he'd led me there. "I can't believe this is here. It's huge, and I've never heard of it."

That smirk flashed again, and my heart raced. "Yeah, cool kids only."

I scoffed and glared at him, but I was secretly starting to like the way he ribbed me about our age, like every playful jab rubbed the sharp edges off the topic.

Seb leaned back in his chair and caught the attention of a waiter with bright pink hair, who practically screamed with delight as she rushed over and threw her arms around Seb.

"Bas-man!" She sounded as excited as I was about him.

"Julie, oh, how I have missed you." He squeezed her back with his good arm.

My skin prickled with an undeserved jealousy, and I forced my politest smile.

"This is Derek, he's kidnapped me." Seb pointed to me, but kept his eyes on her.

I held up my hands in defense. "I—that's not—"

"Lucky *you*." Julie beamed at me and untangled herself from around Seb. "Thanks for keeping him out of society at large, he's a menace."

"Hey! I'm a good citizen!" He pouted. Kissable. So damned kissable.

Julie grabbed his jaw and squeezed his cheeks. "Are you kidding me? Walking around with this face? *So* cute that it should be illegal! Keep it off the streets. Right?" She turned to me and I managed a smile and a nod to play along while I was literally reminding myself to breathe, and scolding myself for thinking about what a cute couple they'd make.

Julie released Seb's face with a gentle slap and grabbed her order pad from the back pocket of her ultra-tight jeans, while he rubbed his jaw and grinned at me.

"What can I get you, Bastian?" Julie clicked her pen.

He leaned back and cracked his neck, speaking casually. "You still doing those special margs with the red wine sauce—"

"And the rosemary mozzarella? Hell, yes, we are." She nodded and made a note.

"Yes! Bring us a big one." He turned that million-watt smile on me and I basked in the light from it. "You good to share?"

"Of course." I nodded, and he upped the wattage. I could've melted.

"And two iced teas." He spoke without breaking eye contact, and I was pinned to my seat, completely under his control. I loved how he shone under the attention of others, and I was getting a glimpse of the carefree guy he was when he wasn't under siege. And I wanted to see more of it. "Great. Gotta stay hydrated and caffeinated to keep up with this one." Julie shot me a wink and pointed to Seb with her pen. "Pizza and two iced teas coming' up, boys."

"She's great." He cracked his neck and watched her walk away.

"You two are friends?" I tried to hide my suspicious jealousy, but it leaked into my voice.

But maybe he couldn't tell, because he shifted in his seat and shrugged. "Yeah, I guess."

"Oh. More than that?" I sounded way more like a shocked old man than I'd wanted and hoped Seb hadn't noticed, but he burst out laughing.

He leaned forward and took both my hands in his reassuringly. "No. I only swing one way and it's not in Julie's direction. I just mean that I *guess* she's a friend, but she was always more of a workmate. I used to do the coffees here."

"Ah. Right." I hated how much it relieved me. "What else don't I know about you?"

He paused for a moment, as though considering, then quickly shook his head. "Nuh-uh. No way. You already know some deep dark shit about what I'm going through, and I know next to nothing about *you*. Imbalance of power."

"What do you want to know?" I set my sunglasses down and opened my hands like I was a book to be read, but I hoped he wouldn't pry too deeply.

"Hm… What's this about?" Seb slapped his bicep.

"Ah. Easy." I rolled the sleeve of my t-shirt up to reveal the thick figure eight tattooed on my upper arm and a surge of pride made me smile as I looked at it. "All the brothers have one."

"Ha! Eight of you. Right. Cool. Why is it on its side, though?" He tilted his head as though to see it upright. "Oh, wait. Looks like an infinity symbol…"

"Exactly. Never-ending bond. And it's a perfectly balanced symbol, and we balance each other out." I watched him watching me, and a tingle ran up my spine as he wet his lips.

"Nice." He smiled at my arm and tilted his head again. "You know, it's also kind of a Mobius strip."

I was about to ask what he thought about it, when Julie reappeared with our iced teas and pizza, and a bonus basket of garlic bread. "Compliments of the chef, to keep Seb's mouth full."

He shoved a piece in his mouth and gave her a bready smile before she left. I hadn't realized how hungry I was until a waft of the pizza hit me and my stomach grumbled.

"Mobius strip?" I asked as I took a slice onto my plate.

"Oh, yeah. It's a nice allegory." He spoke around a mouthful of pizza, then held up a hand while he washed it down with iced tea. "You know, a twisted piece of paper or whatever, to create a shape like that figure eight. If an ant was going to run around the sides of it, the ant would touch *both* sides without ever having to cross the edge. It's like, you can all go through shit, without ever having to 'cross the edge' or leave your brotherhood, or whatever you call it."

I took a long gulp of my tea, alarmed by how touched I was at his reading of the tattoo, and cleared my throat. "Yeah. That sounds right."

"Cool. As you may have gathered, I don't have that kind of relationship with my brother. He's kind of a dick." He grinned like it was no big deal, but I caught the pain in his voice.

I smoothed down the sleeve of my shirt. "Yeah, it doesn't sound good."

"He's a homophobic asshole." Seb turned his plate and kept his eyes on his pizza, but I swore there was a tear in his eye.

"Shit. I'm sorry." I wanted to say more but he shrugged and stuffed his mouth with an oversized bite of pizza, as though putting a stop to the conversation. We ate and conversed in satisfied moans, until I couldn't hold back my curiosity anymore.

"Do you have any?" I looked him over as though searching for tattoos and enjoyed letting my eyes take in the porcelain, smooth flesh of his exposed arms.

"Huh?" He gnawed on a crust and tilted his head.

"Tattoos." I'd only seen him from the front and my eyes hadn't exactly been lingering anywhere other than his crotch and his bright red lips. The memory made me hard, and I shifted to stop my cock from jamming too hard against the seam of my pants.

He kept chewing but his eyes dragged down my body like he knew. "Mm-hmm."

I wet my lips. "You do have tattoos?"

"Mm." He nodded and met my eyes again, making my heart stir and my cock swell when I tried to imagine where he was hiding them. Or it.

"How many?" I sounded raspy and desperate, so I took a big gulp of tea.

He held up his forefinger and took another bite of pizza while I swallowed thickly and tried to keep my dick under control. Not so easy with my brain working double-time. Imagining. Wanting.

"One?"

"Mm."

"Where?" I was desperate for a visual.

His green eyes seemed to flash even brighter than usual as he smirked cheekily and shrugged.

I flicked my napkin at him. "You're not going to tell me?"

He grinned so smug I wanted to wipe it right off his face. Wanted to kiss it. Wanted it to go slack so I could push right into his beautiful mouth…

I inhaled sharply and put my attention back on my meal. I was supposed to be keeping things platonic. Out of the ethical gray area. I mumbled. "You're impossible."

"Impossibly good at ordering pizza." He kicked me under the table and shot me a smile as he pushed my plate closer to me. "Eat up, it's not as good when it's cold."

We finished off the food, and Seb grimaced when he reached for a wallet that wasn't there.

"Hey, I've got it." I slid the bill toward me, and he feigned to grab it back, but quickly let it go.

"I'll pay you back."

"Please, it's on me. Let's not keep a tab."

He flushed as I paid the bill, but maybe it was just the pink of the sunset pouring off the brown brick walls making his cheeks red as we stood up to leave.

"Besides, you showed me this place. Now I know where Zackori's is."

"Ugh! It's called *Zuconi's*! Oh my god!"

I winked, and his horrified expression turned into a playful scowl as he shoved me all the way out to the back lane.

The lights of the commercial wharf district glowed off the Potomac as I wandered back to the Vanguard Tower, full of pizza and happy with Sebastian by my side. We walked in silence and I appreciated how comfortable it was to be with him.

Back at the apartment, I made myself a coffee and turned. Seb was watching me, his lips twisted and eyebrows narrowed.

"What? What's wrong?" I panicked and hovered the spoon over the mug.

"*That's* how much coffee you use?" His eyes widened, and he came close to me to look in my cup, so close that I could smell his scent mixed with my soap.

"Yeah…why?" I dropped the spoon into the cup and stirred slowly as I searched his face for an answer and took a deep, greedy breath of his scent.

"Yikes." He looked up and blinked his eyelashes. Adorable. Beyond tempting. "I put *way* more coffee in mine. No wonder I was, uh…wide awake."

I chuckled and took a sip, then stepped away to give myself a break from temptation, Being so close to him was a test of my will. My strength. My ability to control myself. "You want another?"

"Absolutely not. I wouldn't sleep for a week."

I leaned against the counter and took him in as he poured himself a glass of water from the filtered faucet. "You look like you could use some more sleep."

"Is that your professional or personal opinion, doctor? Either way, you're right. I'm zonked. Mind if I go to bed?" He switched off the faucet and looked over his shoulder.

I wanted to keep him up all night. I wanted to get to know everything about him, ask him questions that only got asked in the darkest parts of the night. But I just took a sip of coffee and nodded. "Make yourself at home. I sleep late, and you're welcome to as well. You'll need your energy to see Ben tomorrow."

Seb's face fell. Tomorrow was going to be a tough day. "Yeah. I suppose I will."

He paused at the hallway leading to the bedrooms and turned to face me as I took a seat on the couch and grabbed the remote. I waited for him to speak, and he cleared his throat.

"Thanks. For everything."

Sincere, he sounded wounded, scared, and genuinely grateful. I nodded, and waited for him to say more, but he simply rubbed his wrist and made his way to the bedroom.

Chapter 14 - Sebastian

"Veer left at the fork. Your destination will be on the right."

Derek's navigation technology didn't know the first thing about Ben's condominium. I nodded toward the far entrance at the back of the block of buildings. "Ignore her. Go straight, there's a parking lot—"

Matt, the scarier of the twins, leaned forward from the back of the car. "Can we get in the back?"

Sean craned forward too, and nudged Derek. "We should scout the back."

I shot them a look. "—a parking lot around the back."

"Turn left," the automated voice drawled.

Derek took a calming breath, ignored the navigation system, and drove through the intersection. I chewed my nails and ripped one down to the quick when I pointed at the back entrance. Derek yanked the wheel, Sean barely stayed upright, and Matt grunted as we turned into the lot, bounced over traffic humps, and pulled into a spot by the door.

"Okay, kids, we made it!" Derek slapped the wheel and shot a dirty look at the twins who didn't seem fazed by his irritation. He grumbled a bit louder. He was cute when he clenched his jaw.

Maybe he was reconsidering the wisdom of bringing 'some muscle' with us to my meeting with Ben, something I'd adamantly opposed. They'd barely acknowledged me in the car on the drive over, and I couldn't imagine them giving me backup out of the goodness of their hearts. Derek, on the other hand, was a good guy and maybe our chemistry compelled him to help me out. The twins, though, they had no reason to have my back, and that made me nervous.

I wasn't used to people offering help for no good reason, and frankly, I didn't want to get used to it either. If everything went well with Ben, I'd have my answers, be able to make a plan, and get back to my old life. Great... I was sad about the idea of losing Derek and going back to the way things were.

Matt and Sean got out of the car and scouted the back entrance, which seemed to mean looking around the half-empty parking lot, poking the spindly saplings struggling to grow by the back walkway, trying to peer into the basement apartments, and checking the garbage cans while Derek and I "stayed safe in the car." It didn't look like a very well-coordinated effort to me. I'd expected them to break down the door, whip out some guns, and charge into the building ready to fire.

"You said these guys are in the military?" My disbelief was audible.

"Marines. Sean's currently serving but he's off on an injury right now, and Matt got out a few years ago." Derek spoke with such pride for his brothers, and no one had ever taken up for me like that.

"Oh, right. What does he do now? Clearly not breaking and entering."

Derek chuckled at the two beefcakes as they rattled the back door—locked—and it didn't budge. "They know what they're doing. It might not look like it right now—"

"It doesn't." I raised my eyebrows as one of them tried to peer into the keyhole.

"—but they'll be useful. Trust me."

He was already staring at me when I glanced at him, and my cheeks flushed. "Trust you, huh?"

His bottom lip sucked between his teeth, and he nodded. He'd taken off his sunglasses, and his deep blue eyes studied me.

I cleared my throat, but my voice still came out hoarse. "Working on it."

A sharp whistle broke the tension. The twins gave a thumbs-up and waved us over, while my stomach turned when I realized what I was about to do.

"Fuck." I let out a shuddering breath.

Derek paused with his hand on his door handle and considered me over the top of his sunglasses. "Okay?"

"Just realized how unprepared I am for this. If it goes wrong… Even if it goes right." My brother wasn't going to tell me anything I wanted to hear. Probably things I *didn't* want to hear.

"Hey." He took my hand and squeezed, his grip gentle but steady. "That's why you've got us here."

It was more comforting than I would've ever thought.

With my backup of handsome, muscled men behind me, I buzzed Ben's apartment from the locked back door. And we waited. When I buzzed again, I glanced at Derek as worry nipped at my chest.

"I'll try calling him, maybe the buzzer's busted." My stomach clenched. The buzzer wasn't busted. We all knew it, could hear it sounding when I rang. Oh, God. Ben. My stomach churned as I pictured Ben, injured, in need of help.

"Good idea."

While I listened to Ben's phone ring, the twins crowded around the security door, and before I ever hung up, it popped open.

"What—?"

Ben's voicemail droned in the background while Matt slinked into the back foyer and headed straight up the stairs, Derek gave me a grin, and I stood slack-jawed. They'd broken in. Jimmied a lock. Broke and entered.

"After you, princess." Sean held the door and swept an arm as an invitation.

Shocked and pleased, I ended the call and hurried inside, shooting Derek a look as I scuttled past. He laughed and matched my quick pace as I jogged up the concrete stairs. "I told you they'd come in handy."

"Breaking and entering!" I gasped and shot him a look. "Not what I expected from you. You're a doctor."

"Hey, I wasn't here. My prints are not on that door. And besides"—he pushed past me and spoke over his shoulder—"I could have popped that lock quicker than they did."

A bolt of arousal shot through me. "Stop. You're turning me on." Angelic savior Derek had lock-picking skills?

"I'm a foster brat, remember?" He winked and picked up the pace, his divinely pert ass ascending away from me as my heart tumbled. Damn, a secret bad boy. The Dish was getting hotter by the day, and I wondered how many more sides he had. So far, I liked them all.

I was out of breath when we made it to the fourth floor, but his grin told me he was barely warming up.

"Here." I slapped his ass with the back of my hand and bit back a moan at the firmness of the rebound, then pointed to the fire exit door. "This way."

Heat climbed up my spine when I pushed past him, and his hand grazed over my hip, dangerously close to my crotch. I led the way to Ben's apartment, but Matt had gotten there first and stood outside the open door.

"No one's home."

His huge frame took up most of the door opening, and Derek held my shoulder as I tried to peer around the bulk.

"It's the same scene Eli reported about Sebastian's apartment," he said to Derek, as if I wasn't standing right there.

"*Excuse* me." I pried past Matt.

"It's not pretty." The twin's warning came too late. I was already inside, stunned by what I saw.

"Oh, man…" I turned in the middle of what used to be Ben's living room and took in the devastation.

The place had been destroyed, just like my apartment, only his apartment looked ten times worse because Ben had way more stuff than I did. His huge screen television was a busted bundle of wires and plastic, the legs of his dining table were snapped off, ugly leather couches were ripped to shreds, frames that once held sports jerseys were smashed, bookshelves were knocked over, and even the glass on the kitchen cabinets had been broken.

But where was Ben? I rushed into his bedroom, half expecting to see him face-down with a gunshot wound to the head, but let out a sigh of relief when I found it empty. The stuffing from his gutted mattress coated every surface like a blanket of fake snow, but no sign of Ben. But even without a body, none of this was good. If he wasn't here, where was he? From the looks of things, he was in as much trouble as I was, but he sure didn't have a team of hot homos helping him out. I crouched down and clutched my stomach, urging to cramps to leave and my lungs to take a decent breath.

Dr. Dish came to stand at my side and dropped a hand on my shoulder. "How are you doing?"

"I'm okay." I sounded calmer than I expected, and I wiped my hands together and was surprised to find they weren't sweaty. Maybe I really was okay.

"We found this." He held up a busted laptop with its hard drive and all the other innards hanging out of its warped case. "Think it's worth taking with us?"

It was almost definitely the laptop I'd 'thawed' for Ben when this whole shit had started, and a little bubble of hope floated up in my chest. "Nice. Yeah, take it. It could have the answers I need."

Derek smiled. "I sure hope so."

I poked around the debris for a few minutes while the last strains of panic settled down, but found nothing else of interest. I prayed that the laptop would have *something* on it that would lead me toward Ben, wherever he was.

Back in the car, I tried to boot it up, but it wasn't looking good.

"We should do a thorough sweep of Sebastian's apartment." Sean slid into the backseat from where he'd been keeping lookout in the parking lot. "Maybe your thugs left something behind telling us where we can find them."

"A calling card?" I watched crime TV. I knew the lingo.

Sean nodded and smiled. "Something like that."

Derek nodded to him in the rearview mirror. "Good idea."

"Terrible idea." The last thing I wanted was to face that mess again, especially with Derek. What would he think about the poky little apartment I lived in? Shabby furniture. Bare walls. Nary a scent of candle. It was embarrassing as hell.

"We need clues. And you need clothes." Matt spoke gruffly, but at least he spoke directly to me. And he had a point. My own clothes would be nice.

"Maybe being home will jog your memory about what happened before you ended up in the Potomac." Derek spoke softly enough I could ignore it or acknowledge. I gave a slight nod then focused on reassembling the computer to keep my mind off the anxiety trickling behind my breastbone.

"Any luck?" Sean leaned over the seat, his breath on my shoulder.

I looked at the laptop, lost cause it was. But maybe I could salvage the files. "Nah, I think the hardware must be busted."

"Hm. Can we take a look?"

I glanced at him, and while he wasn't anywhere close to cracking a smile, his voice was calm. It was the nicest he'd been to me, so I passed him the laptop.

"Be my guest."

"Thanks." A barely there upward twitch of his lips felt like a grand gesture, and I wondered if he was feeling sorry for me. Pathetic score ticked up a notch.

And then I opened the door to my tiny, shitty apartment with the three of them behind me, and the meter shot off the chart. The place was crummier than I remembered. Smaller, too. Now that I knew what a good life looked like, going back would feel all the worse. Not to mention losing Dr. Dish. His support. His friendship. The kisses. I could've cried.

"Where should we look?"

Derek's voice made me jump, and I shook my head. I didn't know and I sure as hell didn't want him to see the extent of the place, unless there was a chance he'd believe the intruders had stolen all the food from my fridge and cabinets, had taken the fluffy towels and bed linens and left me threadbare shreds of fabric in their place, had taken my bedframe and left the mattress on the floor. I didn't want him nosing around.

"Uh, just look through this room, I'll check the bedroom." God. I wanted to shrivel into a ball and hide.

But if he noticed, he didn't mention. Instead, he nodded. "Sure thing."

Smashed mirror glass crunched under my boots when I stepped into what had been my bedroom. The closet door hung by one hinge, and I shouldered it shut so I could squeeze past and stuff a bag full of the clothes that had been dumped onto the floor. I flung it onto my back then shoved my shaking hands deep into my pockets as I bit back the stupid, weird emotion welling up in my throat. It wasn't as viscerally satisfying as anger, not quite as devastating as sadness. This was loneliness. This place had once been my sanctuary but was now a dump.

A gentle knock on the doorframe jolted me, and I held a hand to my heart in shock. "Fuck."

Derek grimaced. "Sorry, I didn't mean to scare you. Anything missing in here?"

"Not that I can tell." I swept my hand across the room as though presenting the slashed mattress, broken blinds, and smashed lamp as a prize combo on a gameshow.

Derek took it in without expression, and then slumped against the doorframe, as though the devastation hit him as hard as it hit me. "This sucks."

"Whatever, right? Shit happens." With my hands stuffed in my pockets, I made fists so tight my nails bit into my palms, and my sprained wrist burned with pain.

He stared at me with that same gentle look he'd given me the first day in the ER, and I felt my chin tremble. I quickly turned to face the window, to focus on the ugly view of the neighboring building's stucco.

Derek lowered his voice to a gentle hum. "You scared?"

I bit my bottom lip to stop it from quivering and gave a quick nod, still not looking at him.

"You want to come with me to get some ice cream?"

"What?" Ice cream? Like he could ply me with a children's treat. Maybe if I was good, he would order me extra sprinkles. I shot him a narrow glare.

"I sent Sean and Matt home, so we're done here, unless you want more time to go through your stuff?" Oh, so accommodating. Probably because they were too old, too mature for a cone at the local froyo shop.

"Ice cream? Really? I'm legal, you know. Old enough to drink real alcoholic beverages. Going for a scotch seems more appropriate, don't you think? Jesus."

He frowned and rubbed the back of his neck as his cheeks burned bright red, seeming sheepish and annoyingly adorable.

"Shit, sorry, that's not…" He mumbled the words, and I cocked my head, trying to catch it, until he repeated himself. "*I* want ice cream. My inner child has cravings. A couple scoops of Chunky Monkey with a Milla Vanilla in the middle." He kissed the tips of his fingers and flicked them through the air.

This age barrier was a conundrum. I threw my head back and laughed. "Are you serious?" Protest as I might, ice cream didn't sound half bad. Scotch was better, but a dip cone would be a good starter.

"There's a place near here that does a bunch of cool flavors."

I shook my head in disbelief. Too cute to be true. "No need to defend your cravings, doctor."

He caught my bag when I tossed it at him, and I squeezed out of the small space between the bed and the closet before I took a long look at the trashed living area and bit down a swelling tide of loneliness that rumbled in my chest. Derek waited by my side, holding my bag at his hip like it was a child, until I'd surveyed the damage, found it way more than I'd be able to afford to repair for a while then decided I was ready to go.

He checked the hallways and then the front entrance of the building and led me out to the street with a protective arm around my shoulders. By the time we were outside, the loneliness and fear had faded a little. Relying on him was getting easier. Every time I accepted his help.

"Perfect day for ice cream." He lowered his sunglasses and smiled, dimples deep into his cheeks as the midday sun glowed against his skin.

I leaned against him to stop myself from completely collapsing into a puddle in the street. Damn, he looked good. But I couldn't get wrapped up in his life any more than he'd want to get snagged into mine. It wasn't good timing. But it could…no, couldn't happen. *Don't get your hopes up, idiot.*

"Where's this place with all the flavors?" I unwrapped myself from his arm and offered to take my bag, but he waved me off and adjusted it higher on his back. He looked relaxed, cute, young even with the backpack and his white, short-sleeved button-up. I smiled to myself as I imagined what he would have looked like as a teenager on his way to school.

"Oh, so you *are* interested in ice cream? It's not just me and my inner child?"

"Bring on the Milla Vanilla." I could go with it.

He chuckled and started crooning some '90s song about blaming it on the rain. He nudged me with his elbow to navigate us around the back of my building. I followed him through the dirty streets and wrestled with embarrassment at the overflowing dumpsters, broken bottles, syringes and trash that decorated my neighborhood, but Derek didn't take even a second glance. He'd seen his fair share of shit as a kid, and probably as an ER doctor too; hopefully nothing in my trash town 'hood would shock him or make him think less of me.

We turned a corner onto the remains of a commercial district that had escaped gentrification, which meant in this instance half the storefronts were empty and boarded up, or smashed to pieces.

A homeless man stumbled out of an alcove with his cupped hand outstretched. "Help for a veteran?"

"Sorry, man—"

I kept walking until Derek stopped short.

"Sure thing, sir." He handed a shockingly thick wad of cash to the guy whose hands were dirty and trembled.

"Thank you. Thank you so much." The man bowed his head to both of us. Every time he thanked me, I grew an inch smaller. Why hadn't I stopped in the first place? Well, I had shit-all to give him, for one. But was that all?

I was wracked with guilt as we walked away.

"White knight." I shot Derek a wink to let him know I was joking, and he pushed me playfully with a growl. "Are you worried he's going to spend it on booze?" I didn't mean to sound accusatory, but genuinely curious.

Derek smiled. "So, what if he does? Don't you spend cash on alcohol?"

"Yeah but…" I didn't have an alcohol problem, a weakness that left me on the street. Of course, it didn't matter. Once my time with Derek was finished and the "help" dried up, I would be as homeless as that guy.

"But what?" His tilted his head and stared like I was supposed to be able to put it into words, to make him understand.

"I don't know. It's different…" I groaned and rubbed my face. "Shit, maybe it's not. But if he's an alcoholic, and if his alcohol use keeps him on the streets, then it's unethical to support that, right?" And since when was I spouting ethics? Since when was a bend or a slight fracture of the rules too much for my righteous soul? Since never. I was a hacker. I took information I needed whether it was mine or not and sold it to clients based on what they needed. I should've been no judge.

"First of all, he's an adult, he makes his own choices. And *if* he's an alcoholic, then his body could go into shock if he doesn't drink, and then he ends up in my ER, I patch him up, but there's nothing I can do about his addiction or his homelessness, and the emergency housing system is bullshit, so once he's stabilized, there's nothing else but to send him on his way to make room for gunshot victims and heart attack patients. Except this guy doesn't have a home, so he's back on the streets, still addicted to booze, nothing changed for him because he couldn't get enough cash together today but buy the alcohol he needed to prevent it."

Hmm. His words made sense. Maybe. "So…you're basically paying him to *not* end up in your ER?" If that was the case, if he planned to keep the ER empty by paying off the homeless in DC, he was going to go broke.

He laughed and slapped my back. "You make it sound like I'm lazy!"

"Efficient, I guess." And tonight, he'd saved one.

He stopped again, his smile aimed and potent, and my heart leaped as I turned to him. Was he about to kiss me? Right here in the middle of the street? No, he pointed with his chin over my shoulder.

"We're here."

The hole in the wall behind me was covered in Turkish lettering and it was impossible to identify its name, let alone recognize it was an ice cream parlor. I did a double-take and Derek beamed as he pocketed his sunglasses. "Trust me, it's great."

He was right, the place was incredible. We sat by the window in the front of the small cafe-style space, my heavy backpack between us on the bench. He jumped up and gave my shoulder a squeeze.

"I'll order for us." He looked at the words on the menu board then turned back to me. "Any allergies?"

"Yeah, I'm allergic to not making my own choices. I'm an adult, remember?" Jesus, this guy.

But he smiled, braced his hands on the edge of the table in front of me. "An adult who doesn't like fun surprises?"

I could grumble and pout, be way too aware of how petulant and stubborn I sounded, but I waved him off to go order for me. Whatever. But he leaned over and held my shoulder tightly as he reassured me, and my resistance melted. "I've been coming here for fifteen years, and I want to impress you with the flavors. But you can come order with me if you want."

I sighed and shook my head. "You order. I'm a *fun* adult who is into *fun* surprises and having *fun*."

He left, and I leaned back to watch as he walked up to the counter and greeted a guy in a turban like they were best friends. He motioned toward me, and I quickly spun around and looked out of the grimy window as trucks rumbled past and blew dust onto the struggling plants in flower boxes across the street.

"Chocolate tahini." Derek slid a scoop in a cup in front of me, and then another, and then another. "Rosewater and orange. And my favorite, Turkish cherry. I recommend you try them in that order, too."

"This is…actually super cute." I smiled at the bright colors and then back at him as he took a seat beside me.

He brushed my hand as he reached over to take a spoonful of the chocolate tahini flavor and moaned loudly as he rolled the ice cream around his mouth. So loudly I stopped breathing and my cock sprang to life, until the old man behind the counter coughed and wheezed, and Derek shot us both a happy grin.

"I'll have what he's having," I mumbled, and dove in to take a bite of the stretchy, mastic ice cream. As promised, the taste and texture sensation forced an involuntary moan out of my throat, and Derek burst out laughing.

"Not just for kids, right?"

"Mm-mm. Kids shouldn't be allowed in here, with how loudly we're enjoying this." I took another spoonful and my knees went weak. This stuff was so good.

"I used to come here with Matt and Sean, right after we met."

I shot him a sideways glance and practically held my breath, waiting for him to tell me more. But just like every time he started to talk about his past and how his brothers came together, Derek shut down and quickly changed the topic.

"Try the rosewater and orange." He motioned to the bright pink and orange swirls. "It'll blow your mind."

I almost asked for more details about his history, but who was I to pry into his past? Even though this sojourn to get ice cream was starting to feel like an actual date, I reminded myself it absolutely, definitely wasn't. He licked his lips, and I told myself it was just the flavor of the ice cream that was making him grin at me sweetly. He'd made it clear he didn't want anything to grow between us. I was some kid he was giving a place to crash, and that was *it*. He was helping me, and what he'd done for me was already way too much. He didn't owe me shit. And I needed to remember that.

Chapter 15 - Derek

Seb settled into my apartment over the next week, and my routine returned to normal. And having a gorgeous young man around did great things for my mood. I whistled now. I wasn't really a whistler before, but now, happy tunes blew through my lips when I cooked, when I worked, during the drive home. And I looked forward to seeing his tousled hair in the mornings, his fingers around his favorite mug, and the way his face scrunched up as he grew accustomed to drinking coffee with breakfast. There was nothing particularly *hot* about those little things, but even his most domestic moments seemed incredibly sexy. It was a struggle to keep from telling him as much, and even more difficult to keep from acting on my urges.

But my nosy brothers did a good job of killing the mood and keeping things PG. Every day, a new brother barged in during dinner or watching a movie—or Seb's absurd favorites, infomercials. My brothers acted innocent, but it was clear to me they were playing games, and the excuses were always the same—help, or a search for updates on Seb's situation. By the next Saturday, I was so fed up, I called a roundtable discussion to get everything out in the open.

"So, this is the roundtable, huh?" Seb poked my coffee table with a toe from his place on an ottoman, and Richie laughed beside me and elbowed my side.

"I like this guy!"

Seb struggled to stop at Richie, our resident firefighter, but a glance at Matt quickly made his face fall to mimic the twin's stoic expression. Eli handed out tiny plates of cheese and cracker snacks then took his place in an oversized armchair and kicked his legs over the arm, while Uno lay down beside him, within Seb's reach. She pushed her snout into Seb's hand, and he smoothed her ears back affectionately while I clapped loudly for attention, and the gentle chatter died down.

"Thanks for coming, everyone."

"Of course," Braxton said through a mouthful of crackers, dropping crumbs down the front of his paint-splattered smock.

"No news from your brother?" Sean stared down Seb. Aside from the little games my brothers were playing, some of them had trust issues with Seb. Matt and Sean, to be specific.

"No." Seb shot him a frown. "I was hoping *you'd* have news on Ben."

"Nothing yet." Sean's tone was brusque. Hard. But he'd spent a lot of time in the desert and he'd seen things that made his voice that way.

Hunter sat so close to me I could hear every pop when he cracked his knuckles. "I've got some contacts at the headquarters looking into the details about your missing brother."

We all stared at him, and I waited for more information, but he was busy slicking his blond hair back behind his ears to notice. When he looked up, he almost jumped from all the eyes on him. "What?"

"Says the FBI agent..." Matt mumbled, and Seb snickered.

I rolled my hand at Hunter, and he finally got the message. "Oh, right, yeah...there's no info. Ben is in the wind."

We let out a collective sigh.

"No missing persons reports?" I asked.

"No. No injury accidents involving a DC man in his thirties or any identified man in his thirties who can be traced to Seb. No John Does who fit his description." Hunter shrugged. "In the wind."

Sean grunted and crossed his arms over his chest, and Hunter shot him a look.

"Oh, you think the *Marines* would have a better time tracking Ben down?"

While they bickered about the finer details of state surveillance, I kept my eyes on Seb. After a week of settling in, he looked relaxed here now, sitting cross-legged on the low ottoman in a bright-patterned button-down and jean shorts, and stark white ankle socks that made him look somehow even more adorable.

"How's your wrist?" Owen nudged Seb and spoke quietly, as if he didn't want to draw attention to it.

"It's almost good, I think." Seb rotated his wrist then rubbed it. "Hey, I've been meaning to thank you…for saving my life."

"Ah, don't mention it. Besides, you were dead when I was around. It was the talented Dr. Carlisle who brought you back." Owen winked at me, and I looked away, caught eavesdropping.

"So, what do we do? Keep looking for this guy through the official channels?" Matt's voice lifted an octave.

Seb sat up and set his jaw as he spoke to Sam. "What's going on with the laptop we got from Ben's house? Any luck recovering data from the hard drive? That's got to be our best lead…"

"Waiting for our computer technician." Sean didn't bat an eyelid. And he had answers, even if they weren't ones I particularly liked.

"Reaching out to some other underground contacts, too," Matt said. Ah, the power of teamwork, of having a group of guys who wanted to do their part to help

"Nothing we can do until then."

Seb opened his mouth to speak but shut it. Richie started instead. "So, until then, what can we do to *help*?"

"Yeah, I keep barging in here ready for action, and you just get me to do the dishes while you two watch those weird-ass commercials for those knives that cut through pennies." Eli pointed at me, then Seb, and back again. Braxton cackled and Richie howled.

"Who needs their pennies cut up? Anyone here? Need a smaller penny? I'm your man, your boy's got a knife for the job." Braxton mimed sawing through a tiny penny which set the rest of us off.

"Hey! They're *info*mercials, and they're super fun to watch!" Seb huffed as his face turned red, which just made them laugh harder.

"Okay, honey. This isn't a hill worth dying on, but you do you." Richie patted his shoulder, and Seb laughed.

"Can we focus?" I wrapped my knuckles against my empty cheese plate and continued when the group gave me their attention. "Seb's apartment is still trashed. Matt, you've been staking it out, right? Any sign of anyone poking around?"

He nodded. "All clear."

"I can help clean it out." Eli raised his hand, and I was relieved that the brothers understood the situation. It wasn't safe for Seb to go back there yet, let alone to spend days clearing out the trash.

Owen, Braxton, Hunter, and Richie followed Eli's lead and volunteered to help, while Seb did a double-take.

"Wait, what?" Seb sat up straight and waved his hands. "No way. You really don't have to. It's my mess, don't bother—"

"It's cool, dude. We've got it." The argument from Braxton was almost enough to placate Seb, but he looked at me, eyes pleading. I shrugged and grinned—the apartment needed clearing out and the idea of him doing it alone broke my heart, let alone the security risk.

"Why are you so worried, Seb?" Eli sized him up. "We gonna find your secret stash of infomercial products?"

Seb burst out laughing and reached over Uno to shove his knee, while the dog excitedly licked his face. "At least let me help!"

"Nope." Matt and Sean shook their heads.

Hunter joined in. "Security risks galore, dude."

"Plus, it's, like, fun for *us* to help." Braxton poked Seb with his toe. "It'd just be depressing as fuck for *you* to do it, and the security risk is too big right now."

I watched Seb. He lowered his eyes and nodded. This wasn't easy for him. Letting someone root through his stuff. Knowing he wasn't safe. And God help me, I wanted him to feel better. "Thanks, guys."

I wrapped things up. "Okay so we're waiting for any intel from the FBI." Hunter gave a thumbs-up. "The twins have a computer guy looking at Ben's busted laptop." They nodded. "And you four—five, sorry, Uno—are going to clean up the apartment. Right?"

"Right." Eli nodded.

Uno barked in agreement.

"Great. So, everyone has a way to help Seb." I got to my feet and urged everyone to do the same. "And now, you can all get out of my apartment and stop poking around every day."

A collective groan went through the crowd, but they said their goodbyes and filed out without too much more cajoling. With the door shut behind Uno, always the last to leave, I turned back to Seb and found him picking lint from his socks.

"Feeling okay?"

"Yeah… Just a little shaken up thinking about the apartment." He had the same quiver in his voice and tremble in his hands he'd had when we'd been at his place together.

I crouched down beside him and resisted the urge to take his hand or hold his shoulder. I wanted to comfort him, but boundaries were more important than my own desires, so I kept my fingers laced. "You want to go back there? We can go check it out with Sean or Matt again, take a bit of extra muscle with us in case things get dangerous."

"Nah, it's not that, I don't need to see it again." He sighed and ran a hand through his hair, shiny and soft from using my shampoo. "Did you ever feel lonely when you had to move from one house to another?"

Foster kids always moved. Often. Eighteen months in a single place was a lifetime and I'd never made it so long. A surge of memories smacked against my heart, and I reflexively swatted them away and cleared my throat. "Yeah. Sure. Homesick?"

"I guess. It feels different, though. Like…I'm not really *sad*. Just, alone." I could empathize. I'd been alone, so sad I couldn't breathe, so desperate I didn't want to move.

"Hm." I knew exactly what he meant, but this was about him, not me. He glanced up, eyes wide, but I just nodded and then cursed myself when he looked away, disappointed. "You're not alone."

"Yeah…" He gave me a forced smile that hit me in the gut. "Not alone at all."

That night, I awoke to a sudden shout. Disoriented, I thought I was in the lounge at the hospital, startled by an emergency patient crying out in pain. I threw myself out of bed, and still confused, stumbled into the light of my hallway. Another cry pulled me toward the spare room where Seb was writhing in the bed, kicking sheets, and gasping for air.

I rushed to his side and took him by the shoulders, then gently shook him while he struggled in my grip. "Seb! Hey. Sebastian. Wake up, Seb."

He gasped, and his eyes blinked and opened a second before he became fully conscious. As his gaze focused on mine, his expression softened from horror to relief.

"Oh, fuck." He covered his face and shuddered.

"Nightmare?" I remembered the nights after my mom had died, the way my mind processed my trauma with horrific flashback dreams that felt more real than reality, and my guts ached with concern for Seb. He was going through the same thing.

He pulled me closer so I was on the bed beside him, his bare skin warm against mine, under my hands, as he trembled and let out a soft whine. I hated seeing him scared and a surge of protective energy tightened my arms around him. I pressed my lips to his temple as he dug his fingers into my arm and kept his eyes squeezed shut.

He blew out a shaky breath and glanced at me. "I was drowning. It wasn't like a dream. It was like a memory."

"Shit." I yanked him closer to me without thinking, until we were flush against each other. I smoothed the hair back from his forehead and tutted. "Sounds fucking terrifying."

"Don't go." He held me tighter, and the desperation in his voice made my chest ache. "Please stay."

I moved to pull him onto me so he lay beside me with the back of his head resting against my chest. He took my arm again and wrapped it around himself, holding it pinned against his chest. I could feel his heart pounding through his breastbone and his skin was so soft I could barely stand it. My hands itched to feel him, to enjoy every inch of his body. To satisfy my urges. I rubbed my thumb over the tight muscles of his forearm while I murmured comforting sounds until his pulse slowed and his grip loosened.

"Thank you for this. Thank you for *everything*." Seb sighed and craned his neck to look up at me. "Thank you for the ice cream, and the movies we've been watching. And the infomercials you watched with me."

I chuckled and tried to keep my breath steady. I was so excited to hold him, to feel his warmth. "Some of them were cinematically *excellent*."

He laughed, the sound hollow and tight. "It's been nice here with you. It's been kind of like…dating."

My breath snagged, and maybe it was the rush of pleasure surging through my cock as he pressed tighter against my body, but my head spun, and being together suddenly seemed like a realistic possibility. "Is that what you'd like this to be? Dating?"

After a deep silence, he moved to face me and parted his perfect, pink lips. "Yes."

I couldn't resist. My mouth met his with two weeks' worth of pent-up tension, and memories of him smiling when I got home from work flowed through my kiss.

He moaned and melted in me like mastic ice cream, before I pulled away and looked at him again.

"Is this definitely what you want?"

"Yes. Yes, fuck, *yes*." He straddled me before I could ask again and kissed me, hard.

My breath snagged when I met his tongue with mine, but even while I greedily stroked that soft skin I'd so badly wanted to touch, I was torn. He was a grown adult and he'd made it clear that he could make his own choices when it came to sex, but I didn't want to lead him on. Dating and fooling around was one thing, but I didn't *do* relationships, and if that was what he was looking for, then this was a big step toward inevitable heartbreak.

He leaned back and gave me a sour pout. "Hey. For the millionth time, I'm not a kid. I know my own mind, and I'm old enough to know exactly what I want. I want *this*."

He grabbed me and kissed me hard enough I got the message, then he pulled back and looked at me seriously. "Okay?"

The huskiness of his voice pushed me. My dick was rock hard, and my hesitation was all but forgotten, if only for right now. I grinned and grabbed his ass. "Mm. Trust me, I know you're all man."

He moaned at my firm squeeze of his small, round ass, and kissed me again. The passion we'd had when I'd pinned him against the shower wall was still there as I shoved my tongue deeper into his mouth, but there was more familiarity between us now. I didn't just want to get off; I wanted to make him happy, too.

With his warm thighs on either side of my body and his pajama shorts riding up to his hip creases, Seb slid down my body and moaned when his perfect little ass pressed against my full erection. I grunted and thrust up to meet him as I treated myself to cupping his pert pecs. He whimpered as my dick jammed against him, and he rocked back and forth on it, working it through my sweatpants as I felt him up, his tiny pink nipples hardening under my palms.

When he pinned me with his eyes, I almost lost control. A surge of lust bolted through me, and I wanted nothing more than to bury myself deep inside him. He was wide open to me, and even though I knew it could end up with one of us heartbroken, I wanted to fill him up, wanted to see how his mouth looked when he came, wanted to hear him moan when I buried myself inside him.

I wrapped him in my arms and his hands felt small but strong as he grabbed my waist and leveraged forward to kiss me. I moaned and shoved my tongue deep inside him, then thrust up against his ass over and over until we were practically fucking through the fabric, the head of my cock jamming right against his tight hole.

Seb whimpered and pulled away. I cursed myself for letting go of control and pushing him too hard, too fast, too sudden; but he moved just as quickly and slid down my body, yanking down my sweatpants.

I steadied myself on my elbows and watched as he took the head of my cock between his lips. My head fell back as he gazed up at me, and my breath came out in shaky moans. His lips were bright pink and wet even in the dim light streaming in from the hall.

"Oh, fuck, you're good." I groaned and pressed up into the heat of his mouth, urging him to take more. To take it all.

The resistance at the back of his throat made my balls jump, and he moved with the same urgency I felt, slurping and sucking my entire length as though he was hungry for my cum. My eyes fluttered shut as I enjoyed the young man struggling to take more and more of my dick.

Fuck, he is young. For once, the thought thrilled me and my cock swelled. The sweet taboo of a younger lover. And oh, how sweet he looked working my dick with his big doe-eyes on mine.

With a *pop*, Seb sat up and my eyes flew open. His eyes were glazed over with lust and his mouth was shining wet with spit, and he slowly prowled up the bed on all fours.

"You were close, weren't you?" he whispered between kisses.

"Mm. You could tell?" I was still close. Couldn't breathe or think. Couldn't stand the thought of walking away now.

"You got so big in my mouth." He ran his tongue over my lips, and my body jolted with arousal.

"Come here." I grabbed for his hips, but he pulled away.

"You want me?" With his bottom lip between his teeth, he fluttered his eyelashes and arched his back. The perfect curve of his buttocks and waist made my head spin as he shoved his ass high in the air and moaned seductively. "You want this?"

"Yes, fuck, yes." I sounded hoarse and desperate, and he dove toward me for a deep kiss. *I want to fuck him. Twenty-two or not. I want him to never forget being with a real man.*

He jumped back and practically wagged his tail until I leaped up behind him and slapped his butt with an open palm.

"Oh! *Mean.*"

I massaged his tight balls from behind, cupping them in one hand, tugging at them just enough to make him groan, then held his cock and stroked the long, curved length with adoration.

"Derek...fuck me. Please? Please fuck me." Over and over, he begged until my dick ached so badly I couldn't hold back. I left him only long enough to grab a bottle of lube and condoms from the bathroom, then came back to find him face-down and ass-up, his head turned to the side to smile at me sweetly.

"Do you see it?" He fluttered his eyelids. I looked him over until my eyes landed on a small red love heart tattooed on the plump of his ass, barely bigger than a beauty mark, and I laughed.

"How did I miss that?" I growled excitedly and pressed a soft kiss against it, making him moan. I pulled back and looked at him. "It should be illegal how good you look like that."

He smirked and wagged his ass again. "I'd look even better with you behind me."

Oh, God. He wasn't wrong. I jumped onto the bed and lubed his ass with generous squirts and two thick fingers. The moment I slid my digits into his tight hole, I was overtaken with the *need* to put my cock inside him. I'd do anything, say anything, be anything to feel the head of my cock pop into that tight ass.

Seb whined when I pulled my fingers out but smiled when he looked back because I was sliding the condom onto my dick. I couldn't wait to feel him around me, but something nipped at my heart again.

With the head of my cock pressed against his wet hole, I paused. "You're sure this is what you want?"

Seb let out an exasperated breath and slapped my thigh. "Fuck me!"

I was happy to, and quickly eased the first third of my cock into Seb, pushing a long, happy moan out of him. I loved how he took me so easily, his tight ass stretching obediently around my dick.

"Fuck, you feel *good*." He turned his head to gaze at me and smiled so brightly I could practically see the stars in his eyes. "More."

I gave him more, and more again, until he cried out, and I groaned with satisfaction at being up to my balls inside him. With deep thrusts, I found the pace, panting, and a warm tension grew in my belly. Seb met my rhythm, and soon we were moving as one, until he suddenly gasped, grabbed at the sheets, and cried out.

"Shit! Ah!"

I didn't know what was happening, until his ass tightened around me and he bucked his hips. He was coming—*already*. I gave gentle thrusts while he bounced on my cock. He bit into the pillow as he came. I reached under him and jerked out the last of his orgasm, and he whined as shot after shot of cum emptied onto the bed.

I pressed a gentle kiss to his neck and spoke softly as his cock grew limp in my hand. "Do you want to take a break?"

His eyes flew open, and he gave me a dirty look. "Don't you dare stop."

Like magic, his cock sprung to life in my hand as soon as I started fucking him again. By the fifth thrust, he was rock hard again, and he slapped my hand away.

"Just fuck me, give it to me, take it out on me." He panted and slid up and down my cock until I slapped his ass and took hold of his hips.

"I love that fucking mouth. I fucking love it."

He moaned in approval, cut off by my sudden thrust. I rammed hard and deep into his tight, young hole, and my dick stretched him wide. With my grip tighter on his hips, I yanked him against my cock until we were both crying on the desperate edge of orgasm.

He threw his head back, and I twisted my hand into his hair, yanked him onto me, and felt my balls pull tight against my body. The pleasure in my belly bubbled over, and I could barely catch my breath and keep my rhythm as my cock swelled with cum. He was so hot, and such a confident fuck. I could do anything I wanted, and he'd beg me to push the limits even harder. Oh, God. I moaned again. Wanted more. So much more.

"Come with me—" He gasped, and his ass clenched tight around my cock. "Harder!"

I slammed into him with all of two weeks of passion, unrequited want, ignored passion, and barked a cry as I started to come. He met my wail, and we rode each other over the edge as I unloaded inside him, my dick rammed hard inside him, and his neck arched.

We collapsed onto the bed with a heavy thud, and I pulled out with a sudden release. He hissed when I slipped out, and I quickly held him tight against my body. I needed him with me, needed to feel his hot skin against mine as we gasped for air. I'd never felt like that before after coming, but a lot of things were different with Seb.

When the tingles receded and I caught my breath, I expected to find the blank-minded peace I usually encountered after orgasm. But my heart was still pounding, my head spun with questions, and my stomach knotted in worry.

I'd fucked Seb. Or, we'd fucked each other. Oh, shit. That sweet taboo wasn't so sweet when I remembered being a twenty-year-old, when I realized he was living under my roof, relying on me for help… None of that seemed so important anymore, especially since he knew exactly what he wanted and how to get it.

But as he let out a content sigh and settled into my arms, something still nagged at me.

We'd hooked up… And I had no idea what he wanted out of it.

Fuck…For that matter…what did *I*?

Chapter 16 - Sebastian

Good morning, Dr. Dish!

My muscles ached in the best possible way, and I stretched before I realized with surprise that the warm, heavy weight pinning me to the bed was Derek's arm, wrapped tightly around my waist. I could remember the last time I'd woken up being spooned. It felt good… Really good. I smiled, and I rolled onto my back to say good morning, but he was still asleep. A shock of hair fell over his forehead and relaxed on the good doctor was as sexy as the excited or the passionate or the half-lidded, lips parted look he wore when my mouth was wrapped around his cock.

The night before had been better than I could have imagined. Good sex with a good man. Everything I hoped for.

But what now?

My private smile faded as the morning-after reality settled over me. I couldn't go back to where I was, or who I was. I didn't have a normal life anymore to go back to. Pre-Derek, I was scraping by. Barely. No prospects to make it better either. Derek wouldn't want anything to do with that version of me. Because that version didn't fit into this world. I'd only been here for a couple of weeks, but I liked it and how I felt when I was in it. I didn't want to leave, but the more I thought about it, no way could I stay. I had nothing to offer.

"Good morning." Derek sounded croaky but happy until he saw my expression. "Or…is it a not-so-good morning?"

"No, it's good." I kissed him and pulled my face into a bright smile. "It's so good."

He rolled onto his back and stretched as he yawned, and I stared at his gorgeous body, his thick hairy chest with his pecs popping, and biceps like a pro wrestler. Dishy.

"How do you do that?" I sighed and ran my hand over his chest, admiring his body.

"What? Yawn so loudly?" He smirked down at me, and I slapped his chest playfully.

"Ha! No, your arms…you look like you've just been to the gym. It's unfair."

"If I recall, you gave me quite a workout." He flexed, and I slapped his arms. He wrapped them around me and pulled me in for another sweet kiss. "Last night was good."

"The best?" I cocked an eyebrow, only half-teasing. I wanted to be everything to him. And I wanted to go away. I wanted to save us both the heartache of whatever happened when he realized I wasn't good enough to be here, but I couldn't walk out.

"Hey, I don't dish out superlatives…" He caught my exaggerated pout and kindly made an exception to his rule. "It was squarely in the top ten."

"Top ten!" I was shocked by how genuinely offended I was. "How many am I competing with here?"

He laughed and shook his head, then smoothed my hair back from my face. "I've got a lot of years on you, and if I tell you my number, it is going to sound high to you because you're young."

I grumbled and pulled his hands away. "I thought we were done with treating me like a kid."

"All right then. Let's talk about your sordid, adult history then." He poked me in the shoulder then touched my arm gently. I liked how he looked at me. I liked having his attention. "When did you start?"

"Ah, my first?" I smiled at the happy memory and shook my head. "The story is way too ridiculous, given the circumstances." I'd happily take it to my grave, no need for anyone to know it, but I wanted to share with him, wanted him to know.

He tilted his head and lowered his voice. "I'm intrigued. Now you have to tell me."

"You first."

"Absolutely not. Beauty before age."

I scoffed at his stupid compliment, but my cheeks heated all the same. "If you *must* know, it was with an older guy."

"It wasn't..." His eyes went wide, and his head cocked to the side as his mouth dropped open. He pointed a finger at his chest, and I laughed.

"Relax. You weren't my first time. *Obviously.* They don't teach those moves in porn, baby." I waggled my eyebrows and enjoyed a little rush of pride as I remembered how worked up I'd gotten him the night before.

He barely covered his snicker, and I jabbed his thigh with my knee under the blanket until he grew serious and rolled over onto his side, propped his head with his hand, and looked at me with kind eyes. "Was it a good experience? Your first time?"

"Not as good as last night, if that's what you're asking." Not even in my top ten.

"It wasn't, but thank you, that's good to know." His proud grin was so cute I had to kiss it.

"Arrogance looks good on you." I let my gaze linger, and then kissed him again, greedy for whatever I could get before this all inevitably fell apart.

"Mm. I guess there's something about you that brings it out in me."

I kissed him, sweet and gentle, until his hands slid under the blankets and grabbed my ass. He rolled onto his back and pulled me on top of him, then slipped his tongue deep into my mouth while my cock jabbed into his hip.

"Hang on." I accusingly jabbed his chest. "You don't get to smooch your way out of this. What was your first time like?"

He sighed and smiled, like I'd caught him at a devilish plan. "Fine… I was a late bloomer."

I leaned back and gasped theatrically. "It wasn't…"

"Ha-ha." He rolled his eyes. "No, you weren't my first time, Seb. *Obviously*."

I loved how playful he was. "*Obviously*." I pressed a hand against his cheek and enjoyed the prickle of his stubble. "Those moves of yours were not porn moves either."

"Is that a compliment?" He cocked an eyebrow suspiciously.

"Shit, yes, it is." More than impressive, his moves hadn't just gotten me off. They'd made me feel attractive, beautiful, treasured… If he could do that during a casual, one-time thing, I loved to think what he could do with someone he was in love with.

"Well, thanks." He brought my hand to his lips and kissed my palm gently, looking up at me with bedroom eyes that made my heart swell.

"So *how* late of a bloomer were you, Derek?" I wrenched my hand free and held his jaw, squeezing his cheeks so that his lips pouted.

"Twenties." He spoke through my grip, and I felt his muscles expand as he tried to smile.

"The 1920s?" He growled and tried to kiss me again, but I dodged him and gently slapped his cheek. "How old *exactly*?"

"Early twenties." He rubbed his jaw.

"I don't believe you."

"Twenty-four!"

"Ha! That's your *mid*-twenties!" I howled with laughter, and his face shot into an angry scowl which just made me laugh more.

"Are you seriously shaming me about this?" He barely kept the laughter from his voice, and I couldn't stop cackling.

"Yes!"

"I was having sex before you were! That's all you need to know."

I paused to do the math in my head, and he took the opportunity to pounce. Fingers dug into my armpits and sides, and shocks of tingles pulled loud giggles out of my belly and then it was a tickle war. A war I was losing. I kicked and scrambled, but Derek had the strength to keep tugging me back under his evil wriggling fingers, and he seemed to have some kind of medical knowledge about all of my tickle spots, even the weird one between my shoulder blades. I squealed and begged for him to stop, until I collapsed in his arms…and then he started all over again, laughing at me.

Nothing stopped him. Not kicks or slaps, pathetic efforts at tickling him, not even begging for mercy. He turned me into a spasming, giggling wreck. Like the night before, he wouldn't stop…and damn, if that didn't make me hard.

He wet his lips and watched my half-hard cock grow to full size. He let me fall onto my back and ran those evil fingers all over my length. I gasped for breath and moaned at the same time, creating a weird garbled sound that made him laugh. I loved his smile, but I wanted his moan. God, he was so unbelievably hot. I needed more of him.

I shoved him off me and clambered up until I was kneeling with my arms around his neck and my mouth on his.

"Shut up." I grabbed his jaw and kissed him again, desperate to make him feel good.

He moaned as he pulled me closer, and satisfaction rolled through me. But it was fleeting, and I wanted more. I grabbed his ass and went weak when my fingers sunk into tight, plump flesh. My dick jumped and the twitch pushed it against Derek's hard-on, which grew bigger with every kiss.

I pushed him back, so he sat against the headboard, and then straddled his lap. He moaned and moved me to push our erections flush against each other and a thrill ran through me as his hot flesh touched mine. His thick, chunky, solid rock of a dick was so hard I could rut up against it while precum dribbled down and smeared between us.

He yanked my head forward to kiss me with passion rivaling that from the night before, and I melted into a puddle of gooey, lusty putty in his hands as he moved me back and forth. Somewhere between shoving my tongue deep into his mouth and grunting as I fucked myself against him, he grabbed the lube and the next thing I knew, my dick was sliding back and forth over his like wild, slipping to the side, jabbing at his belly.

We laughed into our kiss, and he smiled as he took things in hand. He jerked us together, his fist stretched wide to grip both our dicks at once, and I helped him by holding the other side.

He looked down and moaned. "We look good together."

The sight of our cocks squeezed tight together made me groan, and I pumped my dick into our hands. He gripped tighter and started to fuck his hand, my hand, *and* my cock with urgent, sharp thrusts. It was almost too much, and I took a shuddering breath as I tried to keep myself from shooting too early.

But Derek grabbed the back of my head and pulled me forward to press my forehead against his as he panted and grunted. "I'm close."

"Oh, fuck. Me too." I let myself ride the sensation as sparks of pleasure swelled up from my balls and burst through my belly.

I breathed in time with him, and as he smashed my mouth against his, I was right on the edge of coming. He groaned loudly and slid his tongue into my mouth, and we kissed with awkward, sloppy coordination as our orgasms burst.

I grunted with every thrust as cum spurted from my cock and hit our bellies, and Derek growled low and deep when his dick kicked and shot out a hot, heavy load all over our fists. I bucked and jerked until the last of our pleasure was drained and the head of my cock grew too sensitive, and then I collapsed into Derek's arms.

He moaned happily and pressed his face into my neck as we gasped for air and I slowly came down. The euphoria was almost too much to comprehend, but I already wanted it again. I could blame my young libido, but the fact was I'd never felt this way before, like I couldn't get *enough* of someone.

My after-sex glow was severely dampened by the horrific idea that I might never get enough of Derek—in fact, I might never get any more of him at all. This could have been a one-time thing, as far as he was concerned.

Shut up, brain. Just ask him what he wants this to mean.

I pulled away and caught his eye. Those deep blues, sultry and sexy, and damned if they didn't shoot all thoughts from my mind.

"Mm? Want to go again?" He smirked with that arrogance I'd just discovered, and my heart swooned.

"Yes, but...I want to ask something." I resisted the urge to pounce on him and kiss away the worries mounting in the back of my mind, the questions about what he wanted this to be.

He wet his lips and nodded sagely, as though he knew where this was going. "Go for it."

"I just want to ask—" I was cut off by the sound of the front door sliding open. Footsteps. A cacophony of baritone voices, and the scampering of paws on floorboards.

"Yo, Derek? Where you at?" Richie's voice bellowed and grew louder as he came closer.

"Shit." Derek grabbed the blanket and pulled it up over us, but not in time.

Eli, Matt, and Richie stood in the doorway, and Uno burst through them to throw herself onto the bed. She barked and licked my face while Richie howled with laughter at the sight of us together, then pretended to gag, while Eli snickered. Matt was left in the doorway with his arms crossed and a frown.

"Get up." Matt motioned for us to follow him and turned toward the living room.

"And get *dressed*, you filthy animals!" Richie swatted at my naked shoulder and Uno barked again. My head spun as they filed out of the room—I'd never been walked in on by anyone before, let alone three hot men, and I was surprised I wasn't embarrassed. In fact, I was thrilled and highly entertained. Derek, on the other hand, blushed like a Disney princess who lost her tiara in a crazy game of poker. He sank down beneath the blankets with a mortified groan, equal parts adorable and worrying.

I gave him a moment, and then peeled the blanket back to get a good look at him. "Are you…regretting anything?"

"No, definitely not." He pulled me in for a sweet kiss and peppered my cheeks with them for good measure. "I'm just embarrassed about *them*."

"Your brothers?"

"Yeah. I'm so sorry. They just walk right in whenever they want. I really try to enforce some privacy, but it hasn't done any good. As you know."

"Hey, it's okay. I mean…I don't have anything to hide." I gave him a wink, threw back the covers to show him my best centerfold modeling poses. He laughed and trailed off into a moan when his hungry eyes caught sight of my erection.

"*Again*?"

"Why not? We need to shower, right?" I jumped up, grabbed a towel, and shook my ass on the way out while he laughed and chased it. It clearly wasn't the right time to ask about the nature of our relationship, but I wasn't going to miss the opportunity to have fun until I got some answers. Especially since they probably weren't going to be the answers I wanted to hear.

Chapter 17 - Derek

I did my best to come as quietly as I could when Seb jerked me off in the shower, but the way Matt looked at me when we joined them at the dining table told me I hadn't done such a good job. I could read his disappointment, and it weighed as much as any stress I'd ever suffered. But I liked Seb, and I wasn't going to stop seeing him until I wanted to. I bit back the urge to lecture Matt about minding his own business and was surprised at how badly I wanted to defend what I had with Seb. Which was…what exactly?

Seb clearly liked me, even the morning after, and I had absolutely no regrets about what happened. I'd been holding back when I said it had been in the top ten nights of my life. It was more like it was in the top three, and the fun we'd had in the morning had punted it into the top spot. I wasn't sure how we could go from where we were to more, but the afterglow was real. I had Seb holding my hand under the table, and that was all that mattered.

"Here we go, bacon is done." Eli brought over a tray heaped with scrambled eggs, bacon, and the pièce de résistance—his quintessential chicken waffles.

"Are you kidding me?" Seb's eyes practically bulged out of his head. "This looks gourmet as fuck."

Eli scoffed and took a seat. "It's not."

"It is." I handed Seb a plate. "Trust me, go hard on the chicken and waffles."

"But the eggs look so good."

Eli slapped Richie's hand when he reached for extra bacon. "Hey! Those two need the calories more than you do."

Richie recoiled like a wounded puppy. "Um, excuse me, but you don't know what *I* got up to last night!"

"*Do* tell." Eli challenged with raised eyebrows, and Richie immediately pursed his lips and shook his head. He was notorious for kissing and *never* telling, even when extra bacon was on the line.

Matt grunted and bit into a piece of chicken while I heaped my plate with all of the fixings and Eli sat down with Uno's head in his lap, looking up at him with sad, begging eyes. She got a piece of bacon for her trouble, and then moved around the group begging for more.

"So why the early morning wake-up?" I asked.

Eli chuckled around a bite of waffles. "Early? It's almost nine."

"You're kidding." I spun around and glimpsed at the clock. "I start work at ten."

"You do?" Seb asked.

"You won't have time to eat all of *that* then…" Richie snatched a piece of bacon from my plate and bit into it with a victorious smile until Uno shoved her snout onto his lap and successfully wrenched it from him with her most sorrowful look.

"You and Uno are still off work?" I passed Eli the maple syrup and tried not to panic.

"Mm-hmm. They don't need me back yet, and *I* need the break." Good. He deserved time off, and I appreciated having him around, especially now with Seb's safety was in question.

"What do you do?" Seb asked Eli.

"What *doesn't* he do?" Richie reached for a piece of bacon from Seb's plate, but I intervened and handed him one of mine.

Seb pointed his fork at Eli and squinted suspiciously. "Are you a chef?"

Eli grinned and retied his dark hair into a bun. "Very generous of you to assume. No, this is just a hobby."

"He's basically turned his hobbies into professions. Mountain climbing, cooking, piloting planes..." Richie counted them on his fingers while Eli tried to wave off the compliment and I beamed with pride. I was impressed by how well all the brothers had turned out, but Eli was especially talented.

He didn't let the compliments go to his head though, and he waved off the chatter before he grabbed another piece of toast. "We're search and rescue with the

National Parks Services based around Washington, DC, mostly in Virginia and West Virginia national parks."

"We?" Seb frowned.

Eli nodded to Uno, who was now on the couch and cleaning her paws. "She slips into domestic dog mode pretty quickly whenever we're home, but believe me, she's a bad-ass in the woods."

"What do you do?" Richie pointed to Seb with his fork.

"I sling glasses at a bar in the downtown area while I wait to crack into high-level cybersecurity. I just graduated." Seb shrugged, his voice quiet, like he was ashamed of his place in his career, and I turned to get a better look at him. His face was neutral, not its usual expressive. He was holding back. It worried me he might feel anything but proud of how far he'd come in life. It wasn't easy without parents. Harder still with a family who didn't support you.

Richie didn't seem to pick up on the subtleties of the moment, or maybe he just wanted to lighten the mood, because he clapped his hands together and beamed. "Oh! You want to be a government drone?"

"Maybe." Seb shrugged.

Richie rubbed his chin. "You should talk to Hunter, maybe he can hook you up with the FBI."

Matt glanced up from his food for the first time in forever, and looked Seb over with a curious expression. A twinge of possessiveness prickled in my chest, and I swallowed it with a gulp of orange juice. It wasn't like I owned Seb. We hadn't even spoken about our relationship.

"That'd be amazing. Yeah, I'll talk to him, I guess. Thanks for the tip." Seb smiled at Richie.

Richie saluted. "I mean, *I'd* hook you up with some work, but the fire department's technology is…well, it isn't near what you'd be doing at the FBI."

I glanced at the clock and flinched. Time got away from me again. "Shit. Sorry to cut this short, but I've got to get ready for work." I took a long gulp of juice to wash down my last bite, and squeezed Seb's hand. "You good here?"

"Yeah, of course."

I was aware of the six eyes pinned on us as Seb smiled sweetly at me, and I lingered a little longer than was *friendly*, but couldn't bring myself to dive right into a public display of affection, so I walked away and got myself ready for work.

With my bag packed, I stopped by the kitchen to grab some snacks on my way out. Seb and Richie were chatting on the couch with Uno at their feet, and I thought I was alone with my head stuck in the fridge when Matt's voice startled me from behind.

"You've got it bad."

I hit my head and almost dropped my tub of hummus as embarrassment flared color into my cheeks. "Do you know how scary you are?"

"You are a scary man." Eli patted Matt's back.

Matt just grunted, but a pleased grin tugged at his lips.

"But he's right. You"—Eli pointed at me—"do have it bad."

"Oh, c'mon." I glanced at Seb and lowered my voice as a niggling doubt wormed up into my chest. "He's way too young for me."

"Uh, whatever." Eli reached around me to put leftover bacon in the fridge. "You really like him."

"He fits with you." Matt coughed, as though clearing the sentiment from his throat.

What? Last thing I expected to hear him say. "What makes you say that?"

Eli stepped in. "He makes you smile. And…that's enough for me."

"That's enough for all of us." Matt gave me a meaningful look.

I braced myself against the fridge and looked back and forth between them. This wasn't a conversation I was ready to have. I didn't even really know how I felt about Seb, beyond being relentlessly attracted to him, fond of literally everything he did and said, and hating the idea of him being in danger…

Eli shrugged, then reached past me to put the maple syrup away. "Plus, he's a cool kid."

"He's not a *kid*." I surprised myself with the defensive veracity of my voice.

"What are we talking about?" I turned to find Seb, smirking with a stack of plates in his hands.

"Uh—" Oh, shit. No telling how much he'd heard.

"Just—" Eli spluttered, too, so I wasn't the only one concerned. But dammit. Some things I needed not to talk about because I was a shitty liar and I didn't think especially fast under stress.

Matt simply shrugged.

Seb rolled his eyes. "Me? Very subtle. Good things, I hope?"

I put an arm around his shoulders and pulled him in. "Good things."

"Well, don't stop on my account." He shoved the plates toward Matt. "I've got a question for you, though."

"Me?" Matt took the dirty dishes, which looked like tiny disks against his big frame.

"Yeah. Have you heard from your computer guy yet, or what? It's been weeks." Seb frowned and chewed his lip, a habit I'd noticed when he was worried or anxious.

Matt cleared his throat. "We had a small breakthrough. The hard drive is intact but we're still waiting on the pro to see if he can recover anything from it. Apparently, there's a firewall or something. But he's still AWOL."

Seb perked up. "Can I take a look?"

"Uh, *no*?" Matt scowled.

Seb threw up his hands like it was a no-brainer we weren't getting. "I just graduated with a degree in computer technology and cybersecurity, I can find my way into a busted hard drive."

I clenched my jaw and cursed at myself for being so stupid. Why hadn't I thought to get Seb to look at it in the first place?

"Oh. Right." Matt looked him over and then gave a decisive nod. "Sure, you can give it a crack. I'll bring it over today."

Something gnawed in my gut, an instinct telling me this was a bad idea. Seb was too close to the situation with Ben, and letting him poke around in the hard drive would be dangerous. Not that it was my call. But at least he'd be here with my brothers keeping an eye on him.

I glanced at Eli. He stared back, probably reading my face. He nodded like he was agreeing to keep tabs on Seb, and I gave him an appreciative grin.

"You're late." Matt motioned to the clock.

"Shit." I grabbed my bag, gave them quick hugs and waved to Richie and Uno on my way to the door with Seb at my side.

"Sorry we didn't get a chance to hang out alone this morning." I stopped at the door and slipped on my jacket.

"It's all right. Those waffles were worth it."

I grinned and grabbed my keys, then paused as worry nipped at me. "Take care, okay?"

"Um, *always*." Seb patted my chest and the touch helped soothe my concern. "Don't worry about me so much. I'm not—"

"In the middle of an unsolved mystery?" I raised my eyebrows. "Yes, you are."

"Ha. Yeah, okay. Point taken." He smirked, but softer than usual, and then turned his attention to picking lint off my shoulder and straightening my collar. I accepted the attention, then took his hands and held them warmly at my chest.

"The brothers will have your back. Ask them for anything you need." I looked at him, imploring him to take my advice. It worried me to think of him alone, or lonely, or worse—running out of there and putting himself in danger.

"Yeah, yeah. Okay." He sounded annoyed, but his grin suggested it pleased him just a little to have someone looking out for him.

I took in those bright green eyes and his perfect pout, and I wanted to kiss him. But not with all three of the brothers watching, and Uno, too. I moved back, and Seb's face fell so dramatically that my heart snapped. I couldn't bear to see the disappointment and resignation in his expression. *Fuck it.* I grabbed him, kissed him hard, and was relieved when he kissed me back. He pressed his body against mine and ran his fingers through my hair before pulling back and beaming at me.

It was a statement, and one that I was surprisingly happy to make.

"Take care of him today, all right?" I pointed to the brothers over his shoulder, who were all smiling at us. Even Matt.

Chapter 18 - Seb

Code streamed across the backs of my eyelids in the rare moments I remembered to blink. I pressed my thumbs into my stinging eyes, shook out the tension in my shoulders, and dove back into the code.

"More water?" Richie shoved me. No telling how long he'd been standing there with the pitcher in his hand probably repeatedly asking me if I needed a drink. I offered him my glass and an apologetic grin, and he pursed his full lips with sass.

"Thanks, man."

"Mm-hmm. Don't mention it…and don't *expect* it again."

"Wouldn't dream of it." I downed the glass in one gulp and smiled when he squeezed my shoulder and headed back into the living room. Despite his surly attitude, he'd been hanging out all day and keeping me company, while the other brothers slipped in and out in shifts.

Uno was the other consistent presence, sitting at my feet and sighing at regular intervals. Getting the data off Ben's computer was a long process. Way longer than I'd expected.

I'd hooked up the hard drive to my laptop and networked it through to Derek's computer so I could work on a larger screen. I'd expected to have accessed the data within the hour. But whatever Ben had hidden on the encrypted drive, he'd hidden well. It was the late afternoon now, and I'd run though the most common access keys I knew, and all of the brothers had stopped by to look over my shoulder and poke at the screen. I was surprised to find I liked all of them—though I still had a favorite. That, of course, was the unparalleled Dr. Dish.

In the more meditative moments of typing fresh code to try and crack a way through the encryption data, my mind jumped back to that morning, our shower, Derek's soapy, hot cock. I closed my eyes and inhaled deep, counting to ten before I exhaled. No need for a full-on erection. I needed all the blood in my brain, all my cognition to get into the hard drive, and I was glad when Matt pulled up a chair beside me. Even though he was a hottie in his own glowering way, his grumpy demeanor was the opposite of Derek's, and it kept my dick down.

"Huh. How's it going?" He'd come by earlier but left, probably unimpressed with my work then, but now he leaned in, curious.

"Yeah, I *think* I'm close, but I can't really tell yet. I've broken through the first wall of encryption, and it looks like most of the data on the hard drive is intact, but this partition was encrypted too, and that's proving to be harder than I thought."

"English, please!" Richie called from the living room.

I craned my neck toward him. "I'm still working on it."

"Thank you!" He sang out his words.

While the brothers' constant attention frustrated me at times, I actually liked that they were interested in knowing what I was up to. It didn't smack so much of being babied like it used to; now I felt like they were genuinely looking out for me as a member of their family.

I was getting way ahead of myself. Derek and I hadn't talked. I still had no idea where I stood with him, or if we'd just had a one-time, or three-time, thing. No way could I get attached. Not to Derek or his brothers.

Matt scratched his chin. "Huh. But you got through the first wall. Any chance that same technique works with the next layer?"

"Tried it, no way in with the standard decryption software on the market—and trust me, I've got it all—so I've written this code from scratch to go in through a backdoor."

"You wrote this?" Matt shifted closer and watched as my handwritten code ran through billions of variations on possible passcode combinations.

"Yeah, it's working...or close to it, anyway. I might need to make a few tweaks. But that's assuming there *is* a backdoor into the partition. If Ben got someone to create a custom code for his encryption, then it's possible they didn't leave any other way in." It wasn't complicated. I could either go in this way or not. But it was going to take a while to find out.

Matt grunted and sat back as he nodded at the screen. "Impressive. Mind if I watch?"

"Be my guest." I'd taken him for an overbulked jock who loved God and country but didn't have much else going on upstairs. Instead, he was nice in a gruff, big guy kind of way, smart too, and I appreciated his company.

Richie slipped out for his shift at the fire station and left us to it while Sean, Eli and Uno raided Derek's pantry. Matt and I sat in silence with just the patter of my typing keeping us company in the study nook. I was completely comfortable with him. He seemed to follow a little of what I was doing, and I found myself explaining things out loud in a way I hadn't done since practical exams at college. In return, he gave suggestions for how to apply codes I'd used previously to the new lines. I executed a long string, and we sat back to watch the progress as the program searched for a way into Ben's documents.

"How long have you been here? At the Tower, I mean."

Matt ignored my sidelong glance and continued staring at the screen. "Since the beginning."

"Oh, right—Derek said you and Sean helped him renovate the warehouse?" They'd created something so they could stay close, be a family. I missed having a family. Missed my parents. Missed being a part of something. Loving. Needing. Caring beyond myself.

"Yeah." A smile twitched at the corner of his straight-lined mouth. "You wouldn't believe the work it took to get this place looking this good. Sean and I put in a lot of muscle, but it was Derek who really pushed the project through. He's a good man, you know." No hidden message there. And I didn't disagree, but seven brothers along with me and Derek made for one crowded relationship. That was a lot to think about.

And in spite of my thoughts, I smiled as I leaned back in the chair and rubbed my wrist. "Yeah. I know."

His voice dropped to a near-whisper. "I don't know how much of his past he's told you. He keeps that close to his chest, mostly."

I was intrigued, and so desperate to hear more, I held my breath and silently willed him to continue.

"He saved all of us, one by one. More than that though, he gave us hope. Gave us a family. That's some kind of magic." The slight smile on his face made my heart surge with affection for Derek, and Matt, and the whole family of brothers. Derek meant so much to so many people, and it was dawning on me how lucky I was to be one of them.

I lowered my voice and nodded, sincerely. "He's really special."

"He is." Matt locked his gaze onto mine, and the darkness in his gray eyes sent a spike of fear from my stomach to my throat. I didn't want to get on the wrong side of Matt, which it seemed also meant staying on the *right* side of Derek. "Don't fuck with his feelings."

"Got it." Yeah. Not the news bulletin he thought. I could read a room and this one was pro-Derek's happiness. I would be welcome so long as I could maintain that happiness.

I wasn't sure whether to be appalled or pleased. I didn't know where this thing between Derek and me was going. Maybe it was the start of something...serious, but we hadn't talked about it. Even I knew a few morning kisses by dawn's early light did not a relationship make. And it wasn't like I had anything legitimate and long-term to compare it to.

It would have been nice to have spoken to him that morning, not that I'd normally trade shower sex for a deep and meaningful conversation... And maybe it was better than we hadn't had the time for him to straight-up dump me before work. And good sex or not, I still couldn't see why Derek would tie himself down to a runt like me. Hot guy like him could go anywhere and get laid.

"Good." Matt seemed satisfied, and turned back to the computer, but Sean whistled from the living room area and held up a pair of beers.

Matt looked at me. "Take a break?"

"Nah, you go." I turned back to the screen and focused on the lines of code while the three of them toasted something then switched on the television. Sports. Predictable.

"Is this too loud?" Eli called.

"Nah, it's cool. I like the ambient noise—"

"TOUCHDOWN!" Sean cried and Eli howled.

Amidst their yelling and cheering, betting and grousing at the screen, I slipped back into my meditative state and became *one* with the code. I collated the bits that I'd been working on and sat back biting my nails as the program ran.

And there it was. The file directory. I downloaded them all to my laptop. I just about cried out with as much excitement as the brothers had given the sports game when the download froze. My hard drive wasn't big enough. Fuck. I checked the files. Some were huge. No way would they all fit.

I tinkered with the networking and rerouted the download to save to Derek's computer, then held my breath and watched as the files poured in. I turned to call Matt over, but I wasn't sure what I was going to be looking at yet. Probably best to open the documents without anyone reading over my shoulder. Ben was in enough trouble and I wasn't sure how to keep it from spreading or dragging him so far under he'd never be able to get out. Asshole or not, he was still my brother.

I waited for the entire download to finish and took another glance to the living room area to confirm the three of them were still wrapped up in the game. And Uno had fallen asleep on the ottoman.

The first documents I found were the same ones I'd seen when Ben had…what? *Attacked* me? I still wasn't sure I could call it that, so I let the thought float away while I opened the rest of the haul from his encrypted partition. There were folders full of spreadsheets. The latest created file looked like a tally of gambling debts…I couldn't tell if they were Ben's or not, but it looked like it. I had no idea he was a gambler, and in so deep. There was a list of names of bookies and amounts, with little asterisks under a column titled '*Diversion.*' Did that mean something about someone else who was involved? A red herring?

It took all of five minutes and some borderline illegal hacking to get addresses for each of the names under the '*Bookies*' column, and by then, my skin was buzzing with excitement.

I thought about telling the brothers, but when I turned around, Sean was in the kitchen, Matt was on his way to the bathroom, Eli and Uno were nowhere in sight, and it was better if I took the rescue mission into my own hands. Because certainly, Ben needed to be rescued. That explained why I couldn't find him, why he hadn't answered any of my emails or calls, why he'd disappeared. Someone had him and he needed me to save him. I respected the eight brothers because they had saved themselves from the shitty hand life dealt them, and I wanted to be more like them. I wanted to be more like Derek. And following his example, I decided to man-up and find Ben on my own.

With the addresses in my phone, and my phone in my pocket, I slipped out through the front door. Easiest thing in the world since they trusted me now. I was going to track down the bookies, find out where Ben was, and get the answers I needed. Then maybe I'd be ready to figure out what the future held for me with Derek…and his brotherhood. Because it was clear now they were a package deal.

Chapter 19 - Derek

"Bay five, doctor." Shae shoved another file in my hand as I passed her in the corridor, running from one ER bay to the next.

"Get me a wish, Shae!"

"Yes, sir! I'm making a beeline to D-4. Candy bar coming up."

The shift had been a shitshow from the minute I stepped into the hospital and was getting worse by the hour. It started with three back-to-back overdoses, and now a multi-car pile-up on the highway had brought in a dozen more patients than we had space for. The last two hours had been nothing but blood and broken bones with no sign of a break before my shift ended.

And if that wasn't bad enough, I wasn't entirely focused. I knew this morning before I left that I shouldn't go, Like I knew Seb shouldn't be the one poking around the hard drive. But instead of checking in at home, I'd been too busy to check my personal phone, so I had to trust my brothers were keeping an eye on him. We'd come this far. Surely things would be fine for one more day.

Shae leaned against the wall while I finished the end of my shift. She wagged her eyebrows at me. I lifted mine in response, and she bit into a chocolate bar with a comically loud *crunch*. I did a double-take then laughed as she swayed to imaginary music and held up her hands to receive the accolades of her imaginary audience. "Queen of Fate! She has risen! Bow down, minions and receive your fortunes."

I bowed low as I dried my hands and waddled backwards toward our locker rooms.

"Want your wish?" Shae waved the wrapper at me.

"You know what? I'm out of here only half an hour late, and I've got a cute guy waiting for me at home. I don't need it this time. All yours." I smiled smugly as I got clothes from my locker and imagined what Seb might be doing right now. Snuggled up on the couch watching infomercials, probably. Maybe showering or cooking with Eli. All equally cute ideas, and I couldn't wait to get back to the Tower.

"Hmm. Making your own luck and all? You sure about that?" Shae called as she walked to the other side of the locker room.

I changed my shirt and rummaged through my pants pockets for my phone. "Positive."

I picked up my cell and looked at the screen. Wrong. Gut-wrenchingly, pulse-spiking *wrong*. I almost dropped my phone when I saw the seventeen missed calls and just as many texts asking me to call home immediately.

Eli: 911 911 911 911

Hunter: Do not panic, just call us
Matt: Report in.

"You okay, doc?" Shae did a double-take as I rushed past her, tucking in my shirt as I bolted out of the locker room, my shoulder bag almost smacking her as she struggled to keep up on my way to the exit.

"I shouldn't have thrown away that wish." I was a man of science. I didn't believe in hocus pocus, wishing on stars, voodoo doll taboo, but God dammit. Seb was in trouble. I could feel it.

"We all make mistakes, doc, even me. Keep your head up, babe. You saved lives today!"

It was a small condolence, but it kept me calm as I raced to my car and dialed my home number as I turned on the motor, terrified at whatever Seb might have gotten into. This was the same intense worry I suffered whenever my brothers were in strife, but I'd never felt it for someone outside of my chosen family. My feelings for Seb had blossomed since the moment we first met in the ER and they'd reached a critical point after we'd hooked up. I wasn't used to this kind of affection coming on so fast, but here it was, and I couldn't deny it.

But beyond the fear, I was deeply, painfully pissed off at myself. I should have trusted my instincts. There was serious trouble on that hard drive, and I shouldn't have left him alone with it.

Matt finally answered. "Dr. Carlisle's residence—"

"It's me."

"Seb's missing."

I sighed and pressed my forehead to the wheel as rage surged. Matt's straight-talking was a gift, and I was glad that I didn't need to drag the truth out of him, but the news was still a gut-punch. They were supposed to protect him. They were supposed to have my back.

"How long has he been gone?" I was loud and snapping, angry and desperate.

"Three hours now. No leads." Three hours? He could be anywhere.

My stomach clenched and my heart raced as I turned on the engine. "I'm coming. Do you have any more information? Any idea where he could be?"

"We checked his apartment, and Ben's. No sign. No information. Waiting for you to make a plan." To anyone else, Matt might have sounded cold and uncaring, but I could hear his concern in the way that he clipped his sentences. Not that it made me any less mad. I threw on my seatbelt.

Eli's voice boomed in the background. "Is that Derek? Can I talk to him—"

"Does he know anything you don't know?" I asked Matt.

"Unlikely."

"Tell him I'll be there soon." I hung up before he had the chance.

The effects of the pile-up crash on the city-bound traffic were still petering out, and it left me in gridlock with rage roaring in my ears and worry burning in my gut. I knew something would go wrong as soon as Ben's laptop came to us this morning. I should have listened to my instincts. Now, Seb was alone, vulnerable, with big, naive ideas about the world, but he was an adult... It was his choice to leave but knowing it didn't stop me from worrying about him. Shit. There was no telling what kind of dangers awaited him. If my brothers, each equipped with their own special skill, had no leads, then I didn't have much chance of finding him. And I couldn't help him if couldn't find him. I was beyond terrified.

The traffic crawled, Seb's phone rang out again and again, and by the time I saw the peak of Vanguard Tower, I was ready to punch someone. I practically wrenched the wheel from the column as I turned into our garage, and I was still trying to steady my breath as I stormed into the apartment.

Matt and Sean stood stoically at the entrance, Eli paced, and all three turned to look at me as soon as I entered. Hunter sprawled on the couch with Uno, gave me a quick glance over the top of his phone and a casual wave hello. I zeroed in on him, the FBI agent, his nonchalance feeding my irritation.

"We're trying to figure out—" Eli stepped toward me, but I dodged him and stayed the course toward Hunter without missing a step.

"What the hell are you doing?" If I sounded harsh, I meant to. I needed to find Seb, and as my brother who'd seen how important Seb was to me, Hunter should've known to be ready.

He looked up, eyes narrow, brow pinched. "What?"

"You're just lying there doing nothing while Sebastian is missing?" My heart was beating out my chest, and he had to know if his person was missing—somehow Seb had become my person—I would move the sun and stars to help if he needed. And I needed. Yet, still he sat with his feet on my furniture and his face in his phone.

"Whoa, all right, chill."

"*Chill*?" Was he out of his fucking mind? I couldn't chill. "Can't you *do* something to find him? Didn't you go to Quantico to learn? To help? Call someone! Fuck!" Maybe I was across the line, but Seb was small, and I'd seen his brother and the crew he hung with. Seb would fit in Pete's pocket, for fuck's sake. And my brothers weren't moving. They were standing around letting God only knew what happen to Seb while we sat on our fucking thumbs. "What are *any* of you doing here when he's out there alone?"

Eli reached to touch my shoulder, but I slapped him away, and he recoiled like I'd scolded him.

"We checked his apartment and Ben's. No sign of him there." Sean spoke with a deadpan, military monotone, but his eyes were watery and flashed with emotion that satisfied me a little.

"And for your *information*, I'm working on gaining access to the security cameras on the wharf front, so we can track which way he went." Hunter flashed the phone at me, and when he would normally give me a smug grin for being *right*, he gave an apologetic smile.

My temper faded, and it was making way for something far more uncomfortable. Fear.

Eli slid his arm around my shoulder, ignoring my efforts to shake him off. "We'll find him."

I let my bag drop to the floor and groaned into my hands. "Maybe. Maybe we won't. Maybe it'll be too late." His place had been ransacked. So had his brother's and instead of doing anything about it, I'd been here playing house and acting like some lovesick teenager.

"Yeah, *maybe*. Or maybe he'll come waltzing back in here with a pizza. It's all possible."

"I know Owen's on shift, but where are the others?"

"Brax and Richie are at work, too."

"I came home as soon as I heard." Hunter's smug smirk appeared. "It's nice to see you in dad-mode again, by the way."

I growled and Uno cocked her head as though curious about how one of her own species came to hide in a human body.

"Why did he leave? He's been here for two weeks without trying to run off. Run me through what happened today before he left."

"Sean and I were in the kitchen. I was about to make some food, came out to ask if he liked beets, and the dude was gone from his post at the computer." Eli shrugged.

"Right. The computer." I walked to the office. Matt and the boys followed.

Matt cleared his throat. "He'd had some breakthroughs, but nothing concrete. I took a toilet break, and I doubt he could have made much progress while I was gone. But he wasn't here when I got out." He shrugged, but there was a hunch in his back not usually present. He felt guilty like he was solely responsible for Seb's leaving.

"So, you don't know if he got into the hard drive?"

"No idea."

They crowded around me as I pulled out my chair. The desk was set up with Seb's laptop and the hard drive connected with cables, and it sounded like my computer was still running, too.

"Screen's blank." Eli pointed to the monitor.

I looked at the four of them, exasperated. "Have you tried turning it on?"

"We tried Seb's laptop but it's all code and weird." Eli pressed keys on the laptop and its screen showed nothing but white numbers on a black background.

"For fuck's sake." I pressed the spacebar on my keyboard and my computer screen lit up with a spreadsheet of names beside dollar amounts. The file was saved as DEBTS. I clicked away and found another file and another and a folder full of other documents. Eli gasped and Hunter leaned over my shoulder as I started opening up the other files.

"Wait, stop there." Hunter jabbed the screen at a document that looked like a check register or record of banking transactions. This was basic bookkeeping, but Hunter's eyes were wide. Matt and Sean leaned in too and made worried noises.

"What? What is it?" It took a second for him to answer. A long second that gave my stomach enough time to churn painfully. "What?"

"First of all, *that* one is an offshore account. These numbers are routing numbers. And you can tell their country of origin. This one isn't American." Hunter grabbed the mouse from me and opened a near-identical document we'd just seen earlier.

"Same dates." Sean pointed to the columns on both documents. "Different amounts."

I clucked my tongue. "Dodgy bookkeeping?"

Hunter nodded. "Probably to hide embezzlement. And this shows that there has been *big* money coming out of some companies and landing in this offshore bank account." He shook his head and straightened. "I would bet my apartment Brother Ben has been siphoning off the top of his clients' funds."

"Did Seb say anything about this to you?" Eli asked.

"No, nothing about this." I'd been at work all day, and if he knew before what was on the computer, he never let on.

"Bigger question is if he's involved." Hunter looked back at me, and I curled my fingers into a fist. I'd never hit one of them in anger before but Hunter was close. I shot him a warning look, and he held up his hands in surrender. "Okay! Just asking!"

"Wait, open that first spreadsheet again. All this money flying around, but there are debts recorded. That's weird, right?" I used keyboard shortcuts to pull up the first spreadsheet when Hunter didn't move the mouse fast enough.

Hunter hummed. "It's harder to get money from an offshore account back into the US to pay off debts like these. Not as simple as wiring it back in, that sets off all kinds of alarms. Looks like Ben was squirreling away his clients' funds into the offshore account so he could make an escape. Probably didn't intend to pay back the debts with that money." He cocked his head. "If his 'creditors' found out...they're probably doing a lot worse than trashing his place."

"And if not? What else could it be?" I didn't want to think of Seb out there on the street, in danger, with guys who broke kneecaps for a living looking for him. But here we were.

Hunter pointed to the spreadsheet. "If they're bookies, they're paying out and being repaid in cash. These are all round numbers. This is an old-school street kind of debt. Maybe not gambling, maybe it's drugs?" DC had its share of crime. Sometimes more than its share and I hated that Seb had gotten entangled in this. I had to believe he was innocent.

Matt grunted and we all turned to him. "It's gambling. These are the names of the biggest bookies in town. Heavy hitters in the DC area. Real heavy."

When it came to Matt's mysterious career change, he'd put us all on a need-to-know basis, so I didn't ask how he came to recognize the names on the spreadsheet.

There was just one thing I wanted info on. "Do you know where we can find them?"

We split into three teams. Hunter stayed at the apartment to act as a central point of contact and get more intel on the bookies from whoever he could contact at the FBI. Eli and Sean headed to the north side of the city to check a backroom poker joint a few of the bookies were associated with, while Matt and I drove west to check out the residence of the infamous 'Mr. Freo,' the first name on the list. When we pulled up to the four-story mansion, the place was pumping loud music to a pool party visible from the street.

My gut told me Seb wasn't there, but we needed information. This was as good a start as any.

I chewed my lip and tapped the wheel as a bikini-clad blonde fell drunkenly from a diving board into the waiting arms of four balding men in a pool lit by a flashing, color-changing spotlight attached to the roof.

"Should we check it out anyway?"

Matt grunted and shook his head. "They're not going to just throw open the gate and let us in, and if we force it, word's gonna get out that we're poking around."

"Right. Better to stay out of sight—" My phone cut me off and I answered it with shaky hands, anxious that Eli and Sean might have found Seb. "Eli. Any luck at the poker joint?"

"Nah, he's not here." Disappointment lowered the tone and volume of his voice. "The place is empty, no sign of anyone at all."

My heart sank, and I gazed out at the bright lights as I grumbled. "Yeah, they're probably all at this party."

"You're at a party?"

"You're not invited. Go to the next on the list, the one in Noma. We'll check out the pawn shop in Anacostia."

"Roger."

"Anacostia, huh?" Matt glanced at me when I hung up the call and put the car into drive.

"Got a feeling?"

"Yeah… Not a good one."

I turned the car around and headed east. "Then it might be the right place."

We were halfway across the city when Matt cleared his throat loudly and looked at me with a dour expression that sent a chill through me.

"What? What's wrong?"

"How are things with Sebastian?" he asked.

"Well…he's *missing*." I adjusted the AC.

"Things serious between you two?"

"No." I veered off toward the exit. "Maybe."

"You're interested in him."

"Yeah." I glanced at him. "Why? Are you?"

Another cough. "Not romantically."

"Right. Well, I am…romantically. Interested. In Seb."

"You're falling for him."

"Falling? I've never heard you sound so romantic, Matt."

He broke into a tiny grin and I took that as a win, but he wouldn't let up. "Are you? Falling for him? Strong feelings? Wait—turn left here, this will take you around the back of this place, it's a real shithole and you don't want to park out front."

I followed his directions through dark streets and pulled into a vacant lot at the back of the pawn shop we were scouting out. Two black sedans sat by the back door, and I parked close to the gate to stay out of view behind a rusted truck.

Nervous, I scanned what I could see for any sign of trouble, or any sign of Seb. In the flickering of a busted streetlight, a raccoon dug through a trash can that had spilled out onto the street. Two stray dogs cut corners down the end of the block, followed by a guy with a cart full of bags. A police helicopter swooped overhead, then dipped out of view toward downtown. No sign of Seb, but my gut told me he was here.

Matt nudged me as he dug into his unseasonal black bomber jacket to retrieve two pistols. I took one without a word, loaded it, and paused on the edge of whatever was about to happen next.

"Yes."

Matt looked at me curiously.

"Yes. I'm falling for Seb. Hard."

He nodded once. "He'll be around for a while, then?"

"I hope so."

After another of his small smiles, he nodded, more to himself this time, and threw open his door. With a hurricane of fear and a smidgen of hope in my belly, I followed his lead.

The gun was heavy and unfamiliar in my hand as we crossed over the empty lot toward the back of the pawn shop. I'd used plenty and knew how to handle them, thanks to having so many brothers in law enforcement, but I still found them distasteful. Pulling bullets out of bodies every day will do that to you. But I was willing to do anything to get Seb out of trouble. Anything.

The back door was locked, and I gave Matt a nod to go ahead and muscle our way in, but just as he stepped back, I heard a thump from inside. Footsteps. Muffled words. Matt cocked his head and I motioned for him to follow me to the window. The glass was filthy and covered in wire, bars *and* ugly lace curtains, but I managed to make out a flash of light blond hair and a sickening slick of blood.

My breath caught and I froze. Seb was tied to a chair and I could see in profile that his face was busted up. His entire jaw and throat was coated in blood that kept drizzling from his nose. Two figures moved through the room, and one of them came into view. Pete.

"Fuck."

Matt grabbed my shoulder, hard, and yanked me down just as the 'boyfriend' turned toward the window. My heart raced, but I wasn't scared anymore. When Matt cock his gun and motioned for me to follow his lead, I quickly slipped behind him. I was ready. I was going to save Sebastian.

Chapter 20 - Sebastian

Of all the shitty pawn shops in Washington, DC, I had to end up in the one with the guys who wanted me dead. The chair was fairly comfortable, and if I didn't move my face, I could ignore the pain. I started to worry the blood loss was making me woozy, but I had way bigger things to be concerned with.

I'd hit up this place first because it was the one with the biggest debt owing. The spreadsheet had said Ben owed a huge chunk to a guy named Roland, and I figured I could ask the guy if he knew where my brother was. If Ben owed this guy *that* much cash, then surely he'd be keeping tabs on him. And since they didn't want me, they wanted Ben, there was no reason for them not to give me the information. But when I'd asked at the glass counter of the pawn shop for 'Roland,' this goon came out from the back.

"What do you want with Roland?" This guy was a mountain. Shrek but not as green. "Look kid, I'm Pete. You need to see Roland, you go through Pete."

"I'm looking for Roland." It wasn't a hard concept. I didn't want to see Pete. I needed the guy in charge.

He nodded. Stared me up and down until I squirmed. "You seem familiar." He clucked his tongue and looked me over again. There was something wrong here. "You know Ben?"

"Yeah. I know Ben. How do you know Ben?" I glanced over my shoulder toward the front door. This was a bad idea.

His eyes went wide and he smiled. "You're Ben's little brother." All it took to get me the red carpet treatment. "Come on, kid. I'll take you to Roland. He'll be real happy to see you."

In retrospect, it was pretty stupid of me to follow him into the backroom. And so here I was, getting the shit beaten out of me every time Roland—a bigger, uglier version of Pete—asked me a question I couldn't answer.

"Where the *fuck* is my money, you skinny prick?"

"I don't know what you're talking about." I stuttered through the thick line of blood trickling into my mouth.

BAM! My face exploded as his fist made contact. This time, my nose broke, and terror set in. I couldn't keep calm by counting my breaths, because I could barely breathe. I wanted to cry but I couldn't take a deep enough breath to push out a sob and tensing my face muscles made me yelp in pain.

Roland rubbed his knuckles and scowled at Pete, like it was somehow Pete's fault I wasn't giving them what they wanted. But I didn't know where Ben or the money was.

I tried once more to reason with them and spoke in a steady, clear tone. "I don't have your money."

"You don't know." Pete kicked the chair I sat on, and I jumped. "Yeah, yeah, I'm sure you don't know nothin' about what you owe us."

"I don't owe you—"

BAM!

"FUCK!"

My vision went black this time, then sparked red and white as everything came back into focus.

"Fuck, little man's got a hard skull." Roland hissed and shook his hand while blood trickled down my throat.

Pete crouched to my eye level and looked me over like he was concerned about my well-being. It was a pretty good Dr. Dish impersonation, if it wasn't for the goon's fucked-up face and evil eyes.

"Why are you doing this to yourself? Is 50k really worth it?"

"Fifty what?" He couldn't mean…

"Fifty thousand dollars, you dumb *fuck*." But he did mean dollars which was substantially more than Ben had listed in his spreadsheet file. Roland kicked my shin, and I yelped like a dog. "Your piece of shit brother put you down as the guarantor on a marker, and God knows I've been patient getting it back. A little warning here, a little shove into traffic there…"

What the fuck? My wrist throbbed like it was remembering the day I'd fallen off the curb into traffic. And the bruises Derek had pointed out, the ones from the guy who'd grabbed me and demanded the money…

They hadn't been accidents after all. Roland had pushed me, warning me to pay Ben's debts. Ben, who never even told me about any of this…just put me down as guarantor and…vanished.

A rising tide of hurt almost drowned me, and if not for the pain keeping me angry, I might have burst out crying from the betrayal. He was my fucking *brother*. My brother!

I gritted my teeth and stared down Pete, who was still at my knee. "Where the fuck is Ben?"

"Who fucking knows, little dude?" Pete laughed without joy. "We were hoping you knew."

"We're looking for him. But while he's AWOL, your name's on the debt, and as long as a debt has a name, I'm going to collect it. If you can't pay cash, then I'll happily take a few pounds of flesh."

Just my fucking luck.

Two hours later, I couldn't talk, almost drowning in my sorrow. And in my blood that kept dribbling down my windpipe and making me cough a spray of red across the bare concrete floor. Roland and Pete gave me plenty of breaks to 'think about the money,' but they were still generous with the punches. I was getting close to accepting death drawing closer, and my brother was to blame. It wasn't all bad. I'd learned some lessons. Like lesson one: heroics were for chumps like Derek. And lesson two: homophobic assholes were untrustworthy, even homophobic family assholes. I hoped to take that wisdom into my next life and not be such a fucking chump.

"I've got news!" Pete came back into the room and snapped his outdated flip phone shut. "Got through to Ben. Told him we've got the little dude and we'll let him go if Ben shows up with the cash."

I let out a long, relieved sigh and allowed my head to drop forward in relief.

"Nah, man, don't look so happy. He's not coming."

"Wh-what?"

"Ha!" Roland folded up his sleeves, and my blood on his hands stained the cloth. My blood. My stomach roiled.

"He ain't coming. Don't want nothin' to do with it. Said to take *care* of you. So…" Pete shrugged and followed Roland's lead of rolling up his sleeves, cracking his neck and bouncing on his feet. "So, you got a plan to get my money, or what?"

I wished I could say it was fucking unbelievable, that Ben would give me up to save himself. But it wasn't. Brother or not. And this was way too real, and way too sad for me to even attempt to comprehend. I looked at Pete, and mentally begged him to knock me the fuck out.

But I wasn't going down sniveling like a baby. Crying like a bitch. "I've got your money, I just thought it'd be fun to hang out for a bit before I gave it to you. What the fuck do you think? Do I look like someone who has fifty thousand dollars? Or a plan to get it? How fucking stupid are you—"

BAM. His knuckles split my lip. From my good eye, I could see him winding up for another hit, and I braced myself to black out, when the door suddenly flew open and the shine of pistols made my stomach flip.

"Get on the floor!" Derek bellowed.

My heart leaped into my throat, and I let out a garbled sound because I couldn't manage much else anymore.

Roland held up his hands, then slowly started reaching into his back pocket. "Hey, we don't have a fight with you. Just the kid."

Derek looked at the blood on Roland's hands, glanced at my busted-up face, then pistol-whipped the bookie and knocked him to the floor. Damn, he looked fucking hot…and really pissed off. Despite pain burning through my whole body, butterflies burst through me, and this was the *real* trouble. And it was the kind of trouble I liked.

Chapter 21 - Derek

I'd never been so fucking angry in my life. Sebastian sat on the sofa with a defiant look under the ice pack he held to his face, and four of my brothers crowded around him.

"Should we get you to the ER?" Sean asked.

"I'm fine." Seb stared at the wall. He was alive. I clenched my hands and my jaw and kept reminding myself that even if he was bloody and bruised, he was alive and that's what mattered.

"For real? You look banged up, man." Eli peered closer, while Uno sniffed at my knee.

"Really, it's okay." He pulled the ice pack away, and a new wave of anger hit me when I saw the swelling above his cheekbone again. "Just a broken nose, maybe."

"Well, you've got a hot doctor to check that out." Hunter smirked and I almost screamed.

"Get out!"

So much shock. From brothers who knew I'd be enraged. I pointed at the front door until they glanced at each other and slowly started to make their way out.

"Not you." I practically growled at Sebastian. He sat his ass back down.

"Hey, it's not his fault—" Eli started to defend Seb, but Matt pulled him away, and closed the door behind them.

Seb looked at me with a blank expression until I knelt in front of him and checked out his busted nose, split lip, and the bulging bruises on his cheekbones. I cleaned him up in silence. Doctor mode, activated. All personal emotions pushed aside. All feelings of rage and remorse suppressed. No thoughts about how scared I'd been when I saw him in that room, or how angry I was now that he was looking so stubborn and defiant, like he was blameless and immortal. Like he didn't know what it would mean to me if I'd lost him.

With his face cleaned up, lip bandaged with a butterfly strip, and nose intact, I threw a sodden bandage at the floor and stared at him. "Well?" I wanted him to tell me what thought in his head said it was a good idea to go there on his own, to not stay put until we had a plan, to risk his life. I understood familial bonds better than most people, but even I would've waited, gathered some intel, then waited for the right moment to make my move.

He shrugged.

Shrugged. Like I wasn't a train wreck with thoughts of every horrible thing that could've happened to him running through my head. "What the fuck were you thinking? Why would you do something so stupid?"

"Stupid? Ha! I'm *not* stupid but thanks for that."

"For what?" He was defiant and angry—eyes flashing, arms crossed, bruises glaring.

"For showing me who you are. For showing me that anything I do, you'll think is stupid." He shook his head, swiped his tongue against the corner of his mouth then looked away.

A voice of reason told me that I had plenty of experience with pissed off and scared twenty-somethings. His vulnerability and insecurity snapping back at me. Seeing fresh bruises on his perfect face made me want to kill someone. "Maybe stupid was a bad word."

"You think?" And he was feisty.

And probably ready to bolt. I pulled in a deep breath, softened my voice, and blew it out slowly. "Seb. I'm a doctor. I'm supposed to heal people, not break them. But all I want to do right now is go out there and end those fuckers we left in the pawn shop, because they hurt you. That's *all* I want to do." First, do no harm meant nothing right now. "What the fuck am I supposed to do with that? With all these fucking"—I shook out my hands like I was flicking the rage from my fingertips—"*feelings*. What am I supposed to do?"

There was a long silence, a pause, and my anger simmered just below my skin. Until he looked up. "I can think of one thing."

The flicker in his eye took me by surprise, but my body reacted before my brain. I took a sudden, deep breath and filled the silence by lunging, smashing his mouth against mine.

I moaned as the taste of his blood and spit hit my tongue, he pulled me closer, and I almost crushed him into the back of the couch. He moaned desperately and wrapped his fingers around my hips, slid one around to paw my crotch, and shoved his tongue deeper into my mouth. My head spun. Rage dissipated, arousal flared, and my dick throbbed, aching to fuck my feelings into his willing body.

Seb grabbed my hair and yanked me back so he could bite my neck and my collarbones. I hissed, and he moaned, bit harder, and yanked the skin with his teeth.

I needed him, and I wanted him more than anything I'd ever desired before. I unbuttoned his pants with clumsy fingers, and he ripped open my shirt, yanked his overhead, and then panted as he looked up at me. Naked. Beautiful. Perfect, sweet, brave, and bashful Seb. I wanted him to be mine, mine, *mine*.

I hauled us both up with him in my arms, and he squeezed his thighs around my waist until I slammed him up against the wall and pinned him there. We kissed like it was the last time we'd ever be in each other's mouths, and I pulled a condom from my pants before I freed my cock. I wanted nothing more than to push into him raw, to make him feel every inch of my dick, but had enough presence of mind to clumsily wrap myself up first. We spat in my hand, and it was enough to lube his sweet little hole before I drove more than half my cock in there.

"Oh! *Fuck*!" Seb's head bounced back against the wall, and he moaned so loudly there was no question the rest of the brothers could hear us fucking it out.

"Take that dick for me."

"Yes! Yes. Fuck, yes, give it to me."

"You bossy little slut." I pumped faster, and he cried out in staccato with every thrust of my cock. He locked his ankles behind my back and moved up and down on my dick, working it as if his life depended on it.

I gripped his ass cheeks and shoved him harder against the wall so he couldn't move. I wanted him to take it. I wanted him to feel how much he meant to me with every inch I gave him. Finally, he stopped struggling to gain control and fell a little heavier in my hands, opened his legs wider, and his jaw dropped open, a guttural groan slipped out. His hard cock rubbed and stabbed my belly as I fucked him with all of the feelings he'd lit inside me, and his slit dribbled clear fluid between us.

"That's it. Good… You feel that? You feel what you mean to me now?" I grunted as I thrust deep inside him.

"Oh, fuck. Oh, fuck!" I loved hearing his excitement.

Seb gasped. He held onto my neck and shoulders, clawed, pinched the skin with his fingertips. I had him pinned and held in place. Finally, he let go and dropped his hands to my chest, his palms flush against my pecs, and my heart hammered beneath his touch.

I drove into him again and again, bottoming out at the base as my balls slapped at his thighs and my orgasm mounted. I watched his face as his eyes rolled back and a high, desperate moan broke from his throat. He grabbed my chest and arched his back as best he could against the wall, pinned in the tight space, and gasped desperately.

My heart snapped when I looked at his perfect, euphoric, bruised face. I would do *anything* to keep him safe. Without warning, I shot off a first, furious pump of cum deep inside him and cried out, shocked. It felt good.

He bucked and writhed as his own orgasm blew a stream onto our bellies. I roared as pleasure pushed hard against my agony, and I emptied myself as far into him as I could, and slammed out the last of my orgasm, riding his ass hard and fast until he cried out. I wanted his body to remember me forever. I want his ass to be mine.

Finally, my legs trembled as all the rage drained out of me, my arms grew weak, and I stumbled back to find an armchair to collapse in with Seb still in my lap, his ankles tight around my back. He slumped forward but brought himself upright to look at me as we caught our breath. It was like he could see inside my heart, and he held me pinned there just as I'd had him pinned to the wall. There was nothing that mattered that he didn't know about me; nothing he couldn't see clearly with those bright green eyes that had snatched my heart the moment I'd met him.

I only realized I was crying when he put his hand to my cheek and pulled away his fingers, glistening with my tears. I grimaced, but he turned me to face him again with a gentle touch to my jaw.

"It's okay. I'm okay. You made sure of it." His voice was soft, his head tilted, and his hands gentle as my tears continued to flow, and he continued to catch them to brush away.

I let out a humiliating sob, but he just grinned at me kindly.

"This is more than what I thought it was." I sounded croaky and pathetic.

"Us?" His gazed skirted across my face, searching.

I swallowed and nodded. "My feelings for you are…more than casual. More than I'm used to." I watched him with as much intensity as he watched me, searching for any reaction. My heart stammered when his mouth curled into a smile.

He laughed, and the vibration made me hiss, but I loved the sound. "Uh…me too. Way more than I'm used to. Way more than casual."

Relief. An ocean of it poured through me, followed by waves of happiness. I smiled and pushed his hair back from his forehead, careful not to press hard against the bruise there. "You're beautiful."

"You like my pawn shop facelift?"

I laughed and brought him into a tight hug, wanting every inch his body against mine.

"I'm so tired," he whispered.

I looked at him again, taking inventory of his injuries, and wished once more I could undo what had been done. "Mm. Shower and bed?"

"My bed…?"

I frowned and tilted my head, unsure what it was he was asking, until I realized…we'd only slept in the spare room together, never in my bed. In fact, sharing my bed was an intimacy I didn't extend to many, but one I had assumed Seb would expect. Surely, he knew what he meant to me now. I pulled back and caught his gaze. "What about mine?"

The sweet smile and bright eyes made my heart flip, and it kept flipping as we bathed each other. Flipped again when he put on my Georgetown hoodie, swimming in it like it was a dress. And again, when he beamed as I folded down the covers and motioned for him to climb into bed with me. It felt special, curling up around him in my bed, and I kissed the back of his head and held him close while I heard his breath soften and his limbs went heavy with sleep. Sleepovers had never been my idea of a good time, and I usually asked my casual hook-ups to leave soon after we were done. I wondered if I'd been missing out on this warm, tingling, happy feeling the whole time, but probably it wasn't that simple. *This* was special. Sebastian was special. And what we had was what I'd been looking for a long time, without even knowing it.

Chapter 22 - Sebastian

My fingers ached from the strength of my grip as Derek and I walked hand in hand along the docks, but he seemed okay with it. I'd gotten pretty good at reading his body language over the last two days. I'd had to. The last forty-eight hours had been a blur of sex, snacks, and intense feelings, but with a distinct lack of words. There was only so much we could communicate between grunts, thrusts, and groans, so I really had no idea what the future held for us. All I knew was I *wanted* there to be a future for us beyond what we were about to face together on the docks. It was just a shame I had no idea what *Derek* wanted.

He'd asked me three times if I wanted to go back to my apartment now that the brothers had cleaned it up, then quickly backpedaled and said I was welcome to stay with him. It was like he was waiting for the other shoe to drop, keeping a side-eye on me, counting down the minutes until I skedaddled out of there and proved myself unreliable. Well, too bad—that wasn't going to happen.

He'd admitted his feelings the night of the big rescue, but since then, nothing. I wasn't hoping for a grand declaration of love and devotion, but as the days went on, I found myself wishing for a little more than I was getting.

He was here now, holding my hand through what was probably the hardest moment of my life, but I still felt like I was on the outside. And I wanted in.

"Will you tell me how you met your brothers?"

He tensed, like he always did when I asked for details about his past. Through his stilted answers, I'd picked up enough pieces to put together parts of a story of the Vanguard Tower, but hardly enough to feel like I was part of his world. He clearly held his family as his most prized and loved possession and opening up about *them* would be the ultimate show of trust and acceptance. A show I needed him to make. But he was silent and looking straight ahead with his sunglasses on as we walked down the docks.

"You haven't really said much beyond surface stuff. Which is fine, but…you know every little detail about my family, so…" I squinted toward the bright, blue sky, and silently told myself it was okay to ask again for details about his life. It wasn't embarrassing to put myself out there. It was okay to be vulnerable. Maybe it'd pay off. Maybe he'd open up.

He let out a long breath and squeezed my hand. My stomach clenched with excitement, and he opened his mouth—this was it, he was going to let me in, treat me as an equal, trust me back, value me as a partner, and—

"Raincheck." He lifted my hand and pointed straight ahead.

My heart and my stomach plummeted, and I followed his gaze and stopped short. The hulking frame of Big Ben. I'd recognize it anywhere. And he was surrounded by the silhouettes of Derek's seven brothers at the quiet end of a dock. He didn't look so big compared to them. I should have been surprised to see him. I knew that they'd tracked him down, largely with the help of Matt and Hunter's contacts, and were giving him the chance to see me. But I hadn't expected him to accept the offer. I half-expected we'd spend an hour on the docks waiting for him to show, then call it a day and get some pizza.

"Ready?"

"Hell no." I wiped my free hand on my shorts and clenched his hand even harder. "But let's do it anyway."

I let go of Derek and approached Ben with my bruised and cut chin held high.

"Hey, Seb." He nodded.

"Hey?" My voice shook with anger as I stepped closer. "Where have you been?"

"Um. How are you, uh…doing?" He looked nervously at the brothers. His jaw ticked, his gaze darted from them to me and back, and his hands shook like their convincing him to come hadn't gone so smoothly for him. Good.

I clenched my fists and swallowed my anger, but it bubbled right back into my throat. "How do I look?" I was bruised and swollen, and the red-faced anger probably accentuated my injuries. And I wanted him to feel bad about it. Wanted his remorse and his shame. He deserved it and I'd earned it.

Ben winced and scratched the back of his neck. "You look like shit, if I'm being honest."

"Oh, now you're honest." It took all of my strength not to scream at him about everything he'd done to me. "What the fuck did you get us into?"

"Ah, man…I don't know." He ran a hand through his hair and looked around, probably scheming a way out, but the wall of testosterone I'd first encountered in Derek's apartment was here and not giving him an exit. Eight men had my back, and they weren't going to let him go without giving me an explanation. "Things got away from me, little bro."

My breath caught. We were blood. We'd shared a childhood. My dead parents were his dead parents too. I softened a smidgen and stepped closer to him. "What happened? Why do you owe every bookie in the metropolitan area?"

"I have a gambling problem." He sounded hoarse and embarrassed. "I played a little right after the accident." The one that had taken our parents. Somehow, I knew he'd bring it up, use it to his favor. He always did. Leaned on it as his excuse when he apologized for treating me like a dog. For saying shit about my sexual preference. He used our parents the same way he used me. "Then, one night turned into two, the bets got bigger, the losses too much. I didn't know what to do."

I swallowed a wad of sadness, and nodded, urging him to go on. Finally, he let me in on what he'd been going through.

"I started to lose more money than I could cover, so I took a little off my clients." His voice grew stronger, and he stiffened, stood up proudly. "You know they wouldn't miss it. Whatever, it's a white-collar crime, no big deal."

I waited for an apology. I'd been threatened, beaten, thrown into a street. He owed me an apology, but Ben shrugged and smoothed down the front of his shirt. Anger rushed through me, but so did a gut-crunching sadness.

My voice shook more than I liked. "Okay, but why did Roland tie me to a chair, if you'd stolen all that money from your clients?"

He scoffed and rolled his eyes like he used to when we were kids and I was asking questions he deemed as 'stupid.' "I *borrowed* it. I'm going to put it back, but it takes *time*, Sebastian. That's what I was saying the day you fixed my laptop, but you wouldn't fucking listen. It takes *time* to get the money, wash it, get it back on US soil. And as much as I stole, it wasn't enough. That's why Rollie came after you."

Derek stiffened, and I struggled to hold back tears as my throat closed. This was bullshit. This was Ben trying to excuse himself for all the wrongs he'd done.

"So, you gave them my name?" He knew what they would do to me. But better me than him. Typical Ben.

"Yeah." He shrugged like it was no big deal, then caught the look on my face which, if the outside matched the inside, must have been somewhere between heartbroken and horrified. "They were going to kill me!"

"No, Ben. They were going to kill me! They couldn't find you." My voice screeched and as much as I hated how I sounded, I hated more what he'd done. I hated how he shifted the blame. He made the bets. He took the money. He used my name to guarantee a marker.

"I just said you had some cash." He knew I did not. "I didn't know they were going to go after you." Of course he did. That was why he gave them my name. "I just needed to buy some time to make it all work out. I *swear, I* was about to close a major deal that would let me pay it all off, right when my laptop froze."

I groaned into my hands and my face ached and stung from the cuts and bruises I was touching. I was angry, but more than that, I was hurt. "Why didn't you come to me, Ben?"

"I did! You thawed it!"

"Not about the fucking laptop. Why didn't you come to be about the debts?" I threw my hands up, desperate for him to understand how badly he'd hurt me. "We could have run away, gotten out of here together!"

He met my anger with another roll of his eyes. And to add another layer of insult, he spoke slower like he was dealing with a child. "Seb, this is what I'm talking about. You don't get it. These guys are national. Fucking international. There's nowhere to run."

I inhaled, clenched my fists, and forced my words out through clenched teeth. "You seemed to do okay at running. But you could have warned me."

"Why would I do that?" He looked genuinely puzzled.

"Because we're brothers!" I gestured at Derek and his family, the family he'd chosen who had shown me what real brotherhood was supposed to look like.

But Ben wasn't looking, he was laughing. "Are you serious? We're not the kind of brothers who share secrets, or beers, or even talk most days. I can't tell you about the women in my life because you don't like women. I can't tell you about my business because you're a bartender. You wouldn't get it." Theft wasn't really a complicated issue, but I let him go on. "You're a baby who doesn't know about real life because you're too busy with your head in the clouds and your dick in places"—he scoffed—"it shouldn't be."

He picked Matt and Sean to shoot his smug, amused grin at, as if they were going to yuck it up with him and share some mutual heterosexism, but the twins stared back, deadpan, and quiet. No yucking it up to be seen. Then he tried Richie, Eli, and Braxton. No bites there either.

"You really *are* a dick." I sighed as the weight of years of denial lifted off my shoulders. A lifetime of trying to talk myself into liking him, accepting him, taking his insults and injuries…gone.

"Well, I guess that's good with you then, right? You like dick." Another smug grin. Another missed opportunity to be a good person.

Hunter caught my eye and cocked his head, asking if it was time to move the plan along. But I needed one more answer. I was shaking with anger, but I needed the truth. All of it.

"What happened that night?" I was clear and loud now, desperate. I needed closure so I could move on with the rest of my life. Or forming a real relationship.

"What night?" He was playing dumb, and he wouldn't meet my eye.

"After I got your computer working, you were mad as fuck. I blacked out, then I woke up in the hospital. Did you…attack me?" I took a steadying breath and mimicked the tone he used when he was being condescending, talking slow and clear.

"Yeah, I kind of freaked out." He rubbed the back of his neck like there might be some human emotion hiding back there but came away with nothing. He was going to play this off as no big deal. "I hit you over the head."

I denied my desire to rush to his defense, to make an excuse for him, to fill in the blanks of what happened next. I needed to hear it from him. I needed to hear the truth, in his own words and Ben was just shameless enough to tell the story.

"I thought you were dead, and all I could think was what the fuck am I going to do with a dead body. I'm an accountant. Dead bodies…don't fit on a balance statement." Oh. He was trying to be cute. I wasn't laughing. "I couldn't take the chance of someone finding you and connecting you to me. Last thing I needed was a bunch of cops poking around. That old lady that lives downstairs saw me go in. So…I had to get you out of there. Make it look like a mugging. But I didn't want you to die. You have to know that." Didn't want me to die. He'd actually said those words. "But I thought you *were* dead. And I was so happy when I found out you were alive. I went to the hospital." He made it sound like an abundance of concern brought him to the ER that day, but we both knew. He'd come to find me, keep me quiet, finish what he'd started.

I needed to never see my brother ever again. He was a liar and a thief and a criminal who'd tried to kill me. Then dumped me into the river to conceal what he'd done.

Before I'd finished thinking how horrible this was, how I was connected to someone so damaged and defective it had to be genetic which meant I was as bad, Metro police pushed through, grabbed Ben, and cuffed him. Through the white noise screeching in my head, I heard him shout my name, swear at me, and make promises of violence hard to keep from prison. As they pulled him away, he spat at me, but it landed short. He'd proven all my suspicions true. All of them. I was trash and everyone here knew it. The brothers had heard everything, but worst of all, so had Derek.

Chapter 23 - Derek

I turned to Seb who was shaking by my side. The dichotomy of his relationship with his brother to my relationship with mine was startling, and I wanted to comfort him the way my brothers had comforted me in my times of need. And we all seemed to have the same idea. As Ben was dragged off howling profanities, we formed a protective circle around Seb, shoulder to shoulder, with him standing in front of me, his head bowed against my chest and my arms around him. His body quivered and shook.

"Thank you all." He flashed an unconvincing, fake smile at my brothers then turned to me. "Thanks, Derek."

There was no spark in his eye, no life in his voice. He was pulling back, closing off, and I had to stand there and watch him do it.

"Come home, we'll talk it out. Or watch some infomercials about it."

He shook his head. "I need to be alone."

His words gut-punched me, took the air from my lungs, made my insides ache. My hands slid from his shoulders, and he stepped back. He needed time to process losing the last of his family. He must have felt alone and lonely. Probably lost, too. While I wanted to be there to help him, I couldn't force myself on him.

I wanted to insist that the Tower was his home, that we could make a home *together*...but I couldn't promise that. We hadn't talked about the future. We hadn't discussed anything beyond how much we liked having sex with each other. And the way Seb was pulling back made it clear he didn't *want* to talk it out, either.

"Okay." I nodded at Seb and ignored the looks Braxton and Eli were giving me.

"I'll come and get my stuff, then I'll get out of your hair." He mumbled and stared into middle space with a glaze over eyes.

"You're not in my hair—" He caught my gaze, and I lost my words. A burning pain roared just below my breastbone. I wanted him to come back with me, stay with me, let me take care of him. But a feeling of hopelessness paralyzed me. I couldn't argue or even beg. "Okay. If that's what you want."

He shoved his hands in his pockets and nodded. "Cool."

I followed a step behind him as he headed up the dock toward the Vanguard Tower, and my brothers trailed close behind. Richie tried to catch up with his long legs, but I grabbed his shirt and yanked him back before he could get to Seb's side to try to counsel him. The guy clearly wanted to be left alone.

But of course, they all filed into my apartment behind us, and each of them shot me a look when Seb didn't speak but went straight toward the bedrooms. It was easy for them to shoot me their imploring or angry or determined looks. They weren't losing the only man who'd meant something real to them. Their souls weren't dying.

I put on my no-nonsense, older brother tone. "Thanks for finding Ben and bringing him out. And for being here for Seb."

Richie raised his eyebrows. "Yeah. Whatever. You better get in there and talk some sense into him before we turn our brotherhood on your ass."

"Good threat." Sean nodded and Matt grunted in agreement.

I balked and flailed my arms at the sassy scowl Braxton was giving me. "I can't—"

"Won't." Richie held up a finger and corrected me, while Owen sniffed arrogantly and crossed his arms. Hunter's mouth was downturned in disappointment, and Eli widened his eyes and tried to shoo me after Seb. But I couldn't ask Seb to stay. He didn't want to be there, and I couldn't stand any more rejection.

My voice was shaky, but I was determined. "He won't—"

"Won't what?" Seb stood at the edge of the hallway with his backpack over a shoulder, and his eyes still vacant and withdrawn. I opened my mouth, but the moment he met my gaze, I lost all hope. His mind was made up. And the promise of a picture-perfect future for us was just words unless it was what he wanted, and right now, he didn't.

He shrugged and patted the backpack. "I think I've got everything. Um, can someone give me a lift to my apartment?"

I wanted to offer to drive him, but my mouth was dry, and I couldn't find the words. I didn't want him to leave. It was too soon. Matt cleared his throat, but Sean shot him a look, and the rest of the brothers were silent. Seb nodded in acceptance, and I braced for him to leave. My breath snagged when he walked over to me, pressed his hand against my chest, his palm flat over my heart…

He still seemed to be withdrawn, but his voice sounded sincere. "Thank you. For everything. I 'll never be able to repay you for saving me the way you did. In the ER, and out of it." He pulled me down for a sweet, lingering kiss way too much like goodbye for me to enjoy. "This was always going to happen. It's always been touch and go with us. And now it's go." His smirk was all sadness.

Richie inhaled sharply, and Eli audibly swallowed. When I glanced up, all eyes were on me. They were waiting for me to stop him, to say something to make him stay. But my throat was pinned closed, and my jaw was set.

Matt finally broke the silence. "I'll take you home, Seb."

"Thanks." But Seb's gaze was still on mine. He wet his lips like he wanted to say something, then bit gently at the split I'd patched. I took a breath to say something, *anything*. One more minute. But I was too slow. He shouldered his bag, put his head down, and followed Matt out of the apartment.

And still the words wouldn't come. Seb made it clear he wasn't going to stay, and I wasn't going to force him to do something he didn't want to do. He'd told me again and again that he wasn't a kid; he was an independent adult, he did what he wanted, and he wanted to leave. Of course, he did. The only ones who ever stayed were my brothers.

I stalked to my bedroom, slammed the door and stood there. Alone.

Chapter 24 - Sebastian

First came the slapping sound…and then the wet ear…and then the stink of dog breath. I was face-down on my couch, one of the few pieces of furniture still left in the cleared-out apartment, where I'd blacked out from too many vodka cranberries, and now there was a dog licking my face.

My sofa jolted, shook, and the room swam behind my closed eyes. "Get up."

"Go away." The harsh light of day hit me as I rolled onto my back, and a headache bloomed behind my eyes as I peered at Eli's silhouette. "How'd you get in here?"

"Door was unlocked, you idiot. You know how dangerous that is?" He didn't add the especially in this neighborhood. It was implied.

I pushed my fingers into Uno's scruff and gave her a rub while she panted happily in my face. "Yeah, some mean rescue guy and his big scary dog might walk in and make themselves at home. Again."

"Good one. Dude, you need a shower." He moved my laptop from my milk crate 'coffee table' then sat down, a huge Tupperware container on his knee.

"I was tired. I worked last night." Then I sat at the bar for a few too many rounds of welcome back drinks. Not that it was his business.

"Huh? I thought you lost your job." Eli was right. I had. Too many missed shifts while I'd been caught up in my feelings about Ben, and the bar downtown had stopped offering me hours. More proof that I wasn't worth shit.

I flapped my hand to skip over the long explanation. "New job. Old job."

He and Uno both cocked their heads, stared, confused.

I gave my face one more good rub then pulled myself into an upright position. "I lost my job at the bar downtown for being away for so long, but my friend Julie got me my old job back. At Zucino's."

"Oh, shit, for real? That place is great. It's kind of my local."

"Mm-hmm...yep." Of course, it was. And it was close to the Vanguard Tower. I stared at him, daring him to say something about Derek. In the two weeks we'd been apart, in all the visits from his brothers, no one ever mentioned him. And he sure as hell hadn't called. It made his brothers' visits all the more bittersweet. Having company helped, and the new-old job cleared my head, but my heart was still a hollow shell. Part of me thought he would have reached out, but the rest of me was quick to remember I wasn't the type of guy anyone worth a damn would go out of their way to *reach* for.

"Well, I brought you this lasagna and a salad because I thought you were an unemployed bum, but now I hear you're gainfully employed. Still a bum, though…" Eli had a smile that could have melted the anger off a blind man.

"Hey. Rude." But I smiled back.

"Rude but true. Look at you. That hair is scary."

I hauled myself up and shuffled to the bathroom. "You're not kidding." My reflection was a joke. Hair at all angles and in need of a trim, heavy bags under my eyes, and the sunken cheeks of a traumatized and heartbroken kid who hadn't eaten properly for two weeks. My face was mostly healed though, and my wrist was good too.

"Have you seen any of the others?" Eli leaned one of his broad shoulders against the frame of the door and patted Uno as she sat at his feet and watched me wash my face.

"Yeah, everyone but Matt so far." Maybe I'd done something to offend him. Or maybe he just didn't like me. Couldn't blame him.

"Cool. They helping you out with anything?" Anything like my broken heart, he meant. No. Short of one of them kidnapping me again, the chances of me ever seeing Derek again were slim.

"Yeah, they bring food. Nothing homemade though." On my way past him, I took the bowl of food from his hands and peeled open a corner to take a deep sniff of the lasagna. "Mm. Thanks for this."

"You been eating?"

"Some." When they forced me to choke down a few bites, but I didn't have much of an appetite these days. I shrugged and put the container in the fridge beside the six-pack of beer that Richie brought over and cupcakes Braxton decorated with some artsy-looking designs to matched the pajamas he always wore. At least the fridge was well-stocked. And from that, if Eli wanted to assume I was well adjusted and eating, then I wasn't going to correct him. I didn't want it to get back to Derek that I couldn't take care of myself.

I closed it and moved around Eli and Uno to make a cup of tea.

"So, what's the plan?" He looked me over, and I tried to ignore the judgment in his eyes.

"The *plan*... Keep moving. I've got a job interview tomorrow, a computer gig."

"No shit?" He looked impressed, and I hated that I liked having that effect on him. It reminded me of how Derek looked at me, proud.

"Yeah, sounds like it might be a top-level kind of thing. They want to meet me in person to give me the details. It's cool. I'm fine." Fine enough as far as he was concerned. He didn't have to know I cried myself to sleep on the nights I wasn't too drunk to know to cry it out. I couldn't even look at another man. And I would probably succumb to injury before I ever walked or was rolled into another ER. No one needed to know those things. "You don't have to worry about me."

"No one's worried." He caught my raised eyebrow. "Okay, we're all a little worried."

"*All*?" It was wrong to hope. A blight against my heart. But I wanted to know if *all* meant *all*.

"Yeah. *All*." He smiled, and I held back my sigh of relief. It wasn't wrong to be grateful Derek thought about me. It was smug. Arrogant. Wonderful. Amazing. And it made my heart lighter.

I turned so he couldn't see my tears and put a teabag in my new mug, the only one to survive the ransacking due to its previous ranking as my most hated mug, hidden at the back of the cupboard. It was bright pink with an ugly pug on one side and a handle shaped like a bone. It took all of my attention for one, blissful moment, until I remembered that Eli was staring at me with something as awful as sympathy.

"Is he...okay?" I cleared my throat. "You guys never talk about Derek when you visit."

"You want us to?" Eli picked at a piece of the cheap plastic that was coming away at the edges of the counter.

"I don't know." I stared into the mug long after I'd finished pouring in the water. "No, I guess I don't."

Eli squeezed my shoulder and slapped my back as he squeezed out of the kitchen, and mumbled something about having to get going, he'll be back soon, don't get into any trouble. I stayed in the kitchen and listened to Uno's claws clicking on the floorboards, Eli flicking the lock and closing the door, and then silence… So much silence.

The rest of the day dragged, like every other day since I'd ripped myself away from Derek and his home. I'd thought that returning to my apartment would make it easier to deal with everything that happened, to survive the trauma, come to terms with all the feelings. But the apartment was nearly empty, and I felt like I was in some kind of stasis chamber where nothing ever changed. An empty cell full of ghosts. Sometimes I saw Ben out of the corner of my eye, coming at me, and I had to sit on the floor in the area where my desk used to be and count out my breaths for what felt like hours. Maybe it *was* hours.

At least I had some lasagna. I even ate most of it. I put it down to Eli's cooking for being so good, because I sure as hell wasn't feeling any better than I had the last two weeks.

The next day, my hangover clung to the edges of my brain, was still pinching my nerves as I got ready for my shift at Zucino's, and the job interview scheduled for afterwards. I was scheduled to man the bar at the restaurant for just a few hours in the afternoon, but I was a little terrified of fucking it up.

But getting dressed was easier than it had been in weeks, since the all-black bar standard of skinny jeans and a V-neck t-shirt suited my mood, and I was almost confident when I hurried downstairs. I shoved my keys in my pocket, bounced off the bottom step, and froze when I saw a huge, looming shadow taking up most of the foyer. My pulse jolted, my mouth dried out, and I stumbled backwards on the steps, ready to run.

"Hey, it's me."

I blinked and my vision cleared enough to make out dark black hair as I landed on my ass on the stairs. "Matt?"

"Easy mistake." He knelt in front of me at the base of the stairs and smiled.

"Shit. Sean, sorry." I scrubbed my face with my hands and let out a frustrated breath. "I'm all kinds of fucked up."

"It's cool. I'm used to people being disappointed when they realize I'm not Matt…" He offered me a hand up. I took it shakily, but felt stronger on my feet with him by my side.

"Nah, I just thought…" I shook my head, trying to dislodge the sting that Matt was still the only brother who hadn't come to visit me. Well, apart from Derek... "Forget it, I'm happy to see you."

"You on your way out?" He pushed his hands into his pockets and hunched. I wondered if he was holding something back. News from Derek maybe. I scowled at myself for being so desperate for any mention of him.

"Yeah, first shift back at Zuconi's. Sorry, I'd invite you up—"

He shook his head. "Quick visit from me anyway. Came to say goodbye. And to tell you to stay safe. Eli said you're not locking your front door."

I groaned and rolled my eyes. "Whatever. Who cares?"

"I do. *We* do."

"All of you?" I mumbled.

"Yeah. All of us."

With a sigh, I fished my keys out and held them up. "I promise, it's locked. But what's this about a goodbye?"

"My leave is over, got to head back."

"Shit. I'm sorry." All that shooting. The violence of it.

He laughed and shook his head. "Don't be, I can't wait."

The world was spinning around me, moving too fast. I could barely stay upright while things kept shifting in my life.

Sean motioned to the door and we headed out. He subtly scanned the street for danger, and I told myself not to get used to feeling so safe out in the world. One of the few people looking out for me was about to leave. They always did.

"So, we're both heading back to new-old jobs, huh?" I spun my keys around my finger and pocketed them as we wandered toward the street, a casual move to try and hide how sad I felt about this goodbye. I didn't know when or even if I'd see him again, and I hated how that thought immediately jumped to wondering when I'd see Derek again. If ever.

"Yeah, Zuconi's? Near the Tower? I'd offer to give you a lift but I'm driving straight out of town now. You're my last visit before I go."

We stopped at his truck, and I wrapped my arms around my middle, as if it weren't a disgustingly humid day. "Okay. Well...thanks for coming by. And for everything."

He nodded and looked at me for a long moment. "Take care, Seb."

"You, too. I'll see you...around."

He saluted and jumped in his cab without looking back.

Two buse and a winding walk took me the long way *around* the Vanguard Tower, and I got to work just three minutes before my shift. The manager, Gary, was the same surly Italian guy who'd been running the place when I'd been there the year before, who'd given me the job right after I'd turned twenty-one. He looked up from his spot hunched over a table staring at a laptop and barely moved his head as he nodded and motioned toward the bar. That was Gary-talk for 'get to work and make me money.'

I was still nervous as hell, but the minute I stepped behind the bar, it all came rushing back to me, and in no time, I was shaking cocktails, spinning glasses, talking shit with customers, and raking in the tips from the early afternoon crowd of entrepreneurs and socially awkward middle-aged men who I liked to imagine were undercover agents.

I was five hours into my shift and dropping a skewer of blue cheese olives into a dirty martini when Julie waltzed across the courtyard in a bright yellow sundress and threw me a huge smile. I passed the martini to the nearest waiter and leaned over the bar to accept her hug.

"How you doin', Bastian?" She slipped behind the bar with me and ruffled my hair in a truly annoying fashion. She was all I had left. As close as anyone I could call family.

I flicked her hands away and smoothed my hair. "Good, good, good..."

She reached for an apron but paused and turned to look at me. "Um. No, I mean *really*, how are you? Broken heart all healed?"

I did a double-take and frowned at her. "Uh, what broken heart?"

"Oh my God! Tell me you remember the deep and meaningful conversation we had the other night when we celebrated you coming back to work here?" She pointed to two stools across from us. "We sat there. You cried in your vodka cran and told me how Dr. Dish was your be-all, end-all."

I bit my lip and shrugged apologetically. "I remember having the drinks. And I remember being psyched to work with you again?" I tugged the waist of her dress, begging forgiveness for the crime of forgetting.

"You don't remember the tequila shots?" She spun to gape at me, and a piece of pink hair flew down into her face.

My mind reeled, searching for the memory, and I vaguely remembered the taste of lemon and salt and covered my face with my hands as I groaned. "Oh, Jesus. No…"

"Or the strippers?" Her eyebrows shot up and her voice reached a high pitch.

"The what?" I peeked between my fingers and braced myself, but she just smirked and winked.

"Ha, just messing with you." She poked me in the chest where pain still lived, maybe because it was still bruised from Roland's manhandling…maybe from heartache. "Not kidding about the tequila shots though, those were real, Bas-man. But you seriously don't remember sitting in the laneway with me, bawling your eyes out about Dr. Dish?"

My cheeks burned, and I buried my face in my hands. "Kill me now, *please*."

"No way! It was adorable!" She nudged past me to grab two glasses.

"Is that all I talked about?" I peeked at her from behind my fingers, terrified I'd spilled information Hunter had warned me not to speak about to anyone, lest it corrupt the case against Ben.

"Uh, yeah, that was it." She started pouring beers from the tap. "But that was pretty hefty. Why? You got more?"

"My brother's probably going to prison." The words came out gravelly and sad, and the memory of Ben's betrayal punched another hole in my chest.

She scrunched up her freckled nose as she tied her apron. "Sorry, Bastian. That's fucking heavy."

"I really didn't say anything about it?" I caught the towel she threw to me and started cleaning the bar.

"Nope, you were completely consumed by your agony over Dr Dish. You getting back with him, or what?" She placed the beers on a tray and looked over her shoulder at me.

"Absolutely not."

"Wait." She turned to me and put her hands on her hips. Big sister lecture brewing. "Is this the guy you came in with that night? Two iced teas and the special Margherita?"

I sighed and wiped down the taps. "That's him."

Julie slapped the bar and made me jump. "Seb, you're fucking *insane* if you don't fight for him." She pushed her hair back and stared. This woman knew relationships and men. She knew me. And I wanted to believe her. I wanted hope to hang onto. But how could I fight for him? I wasn't good enough. Plain, honest truth. Sad. But most things were. "'Dishy' is an understatement. And from what I can piece together from your ranting…that relationship has potential."

I shook my head and willed my nerves to relax. "No, it doesn't. He's not into long-term." Blaming him didn't disguise what I knew as true. "I'm not the type of guy anyone settles down with."

She scrunched her nose and pulled her lips into a tight bow. She was ready to fight me for a truth I had to accept if I ever had any hope of moving on. "And why not?"

I spread my arms and turned to her. "Look at me."

"You look at you." She tucked a piece of hair behind my ear and took the towel hanging limply from my hand. "You're dreamy. And sweet, and reliable. You work hard and you make more tips than anyone else here and that's *not* just because you're cute—you're funny, smart, and always have something to say to *everyone*. Even the weird undercover agents who have nothing to talk about." She saw the best in people. Never the flaws. That was why she continued with all the positives. "You're kind, Bastian and that's no small thing."

"Don't talk about my small things." But I smiled. She was trying to help and I loved her. I just couldn't take any more pedestal lifting right then.

She lowered her voice and stepped closer, with a hand on her hip and caring eyes. "I get the feeling you've gone through some real shit lately, Bastian. Outside of the dish drama, maybe even more than the stuff with your brother. But you'll heal, boo. Don't throw out the possibility of a dishy daydream one day. Maybe even soon."

I chewed my lip and shrugged, but her words flared a tiny flame of hope I'd been carrying in my heart ever since I'd run out of the Tower. "Maybe."

She shook her shoulders like she was shaking off my bad energy and swatted me with the towel. *"You* need a self-care day, boo. And probably some therapy."

"Ha! You know a good one to talk to?" I played it off as silly, but maybe it would do me some good to see a therapist.

Julie caught the attention of a waiter and passed him the beers while she talked to me. "Me? Nah, I'm way too in denial about my own shit to start talking it through. But do you? Got someone you can talk to?"

"A few guys, I guess…" I grinned and looked down at the floor.

"Then get them on the *phone*, baby boy. Rely on those good contacts. And hook a girl up if they're cute—"

"Sebastian?"

I spun around, startled, and found the new waiter leaning over the bar. His afro was huge and his smile bigger. He pointed to the courtyard. "Someone here for you."

I glanced at the clock. Holy shit. My shift was done. Time was still wacky, spinning too slow when I needed it to race by, and disappearing when I wanted to linger. I wiped my sweaty palms on my pants, pulled my backpack from under the counter and gave Julie a nervous grimace. "Job interview. For a computer position."

She kissed my cheek and then slapped my butt on my way past. "Go get 'em."

The minute I stepped into the courtyard, I saw two things. First, there was no sign of anyone who looked like an IT recruiter—not a black polyester suit or even bad haircut in sight. In fact, the courtyard was all but empty, except for one table in the far corner where he sat… Broad shoulders, dark black hair, and startling gray eyes. Matt.

He raised his fingers from the tabletop as I came closer. "Hey."

"Hi… I, uh…don't wait the tables here." I looked back toward the bar. "But I can get someone to take your order—"

"I'm good." He nudged a basket of complimentary breadsticks. "Take a seat."

"I'm actually waiting for someone…" I glanced around the courtyard again. No one in sight.

"Yeah. Me."

I didn't have time for games. For whatever had brought him here. I raised my eyebrows. "What?"

"Please." He motioned to the place opposite him. "Sit down."

I sat before my brain caught up with me, and I hung my backpack on the back of the seat as it slowly dawned on me. "Oh. I'm meeting *you*."

Matt nodded curtly and showed no signs of being impressed by my deductive skills. I was perplexed by the need for all this cloak and dagger. "I don't get it. If you wanted to hang out, you just had to call. I would have met you whenever, wherever." The way I'd missed him felt kind of pathetic. "Or just barge into my apartment like the others. I missed you, man."

"I've been busy."

"Right." I chewed my lip and studied his face, looking for a hint of what it was he was up to.

He cleared his throat as he took a pen out of his jacket pocket and flicked open a folder on the table. "Who have you done freelance work for most recently?"

"Uh…" I rattled off a few names and threw in the big tech guys I'd been doing small jobs for before all the shit with Ben had gone down. "Why? What is this about?" Could've been anything from Ben stuff to…anything.

He chuckled shortly and kept his eyes on the notes he was jotting down. "Did you graduate with honors?"

"Um, yeah."

"What hours are you available?"

"What for?"

Matt pinned me with his sharp, clear eyes. "Working for me. This is a job interview, Seb."

"Wait, *what*?" Matt wanted to hire me. Hmm.

"If I wanted to see you nonprofessionally, I would have just called, but I really *have* been busy. So busy I need help, and I have a job to offer you."

"Shit. Okay." I sat straighter and wiped my hands on my thighs. "What kind of job?"

"I need a new cybersecurity man for my business, and from what I saw that day at the Tower… You've got what it takes, and then some."

"Thanks. I, uh, wasn't prepared for this. Do you want to see my resume?" I reached for my backpack, nervous now, even though I knew Matt and he'd helped me when I was going through Ben's hard drive. He obviously knew stuff. And I wouldn't be able to fake my way through getting hired. I was flattered beyond belief that Matt would want me on his team, but the sensation I wasn't qualified for whatever it was he wanted me to do washed over me. Speaking of which… "What exactly do you do?"

His lips twitched with a smirk, and he cocked his head to the side, as though daring me to guess. I shot out a few guesses at him, and he stayed blank-faced until I hit the right one. A security firm. And the rest was on a need-to-know basis.

I leaned *way* back and almost toppled my chair. "So, you want me to work for you. You're not kidding."

"Have you ever heard me tell a joke?"

Come to think of it… No. "This is insane, Matt." Insane not as much as surprising. "I mean, who else knows?" Had Derek put him up to this? It was the question I was too afraid to ask.

Matt brought a fist to his mouth and cleared his throat. "Hardly anyone, and I want to keep it that way. Which is why I need you on my team. I want to keep my data secure…"

I pointed at him. "And you need someone to get into *other* people's not-so-secure data." Finally, something I was good at. Something that made me feel useful.

"You got it.'"

"I mean, I'd love to, that's a legit dream job." I rubbed the back of my neck where a twinge of doubt still nagged.

"But…?"

I grimaced and shrugged apologetically. "I really don't think I'm qualified. I just graduated, and it's only a bachelor's degree. I don't have any experience working to *that* level. And I'm young. I'm not sure…I don't think I can…"

"I wouldn't hire you if you weren't qualified." He closed his folder and stared at me. "This is my business. The work I do is too important to trust just anyone. I'm choosing to trust you. So knock it off."

I coughed out a shocked laugh. "What?"

"I'm sick of you playing stupid. You graduated at the top of your class, and you're a white-hat hacker in your spare time. Yes, you're young, but that means you can pull all-nighters without falling to pieces. You're *not* immature, irresponsible, or incapable, and telling yourself that is a waste of everybody's time. Yours included." I opened my mouth, but he held up a hand. "If you want something, you have to step up and take it. Especially if someone else is being a stubborn ass about it…"

I flushed, and I'd folded the corners of a napkin to a pulpy mess. "Are we still talking about the job?" We weren't.

"What do you think?" He wasn't the kind of guy who answered a lot of questions. He was a question with a question man.

I grinned and leaned back in my chair, shaking my head. "I have to step up and take it, huh?"

"Yeah. Because it's supposed to be yours."

"Right." I nodded thoughtfully and then held my hands up in surrender. "Then I guess I better take it."

"The job?" He grinned. "Or the stubborn ass?"

"What do *you* think?"

Chapter 25 - Derek

I had become the physical manifestation of misery. Dressed in sweats and my college hoodie that still smelled like Seb if I sniffed past my two weeks of sweat. I had a super-sized bag of potato chips in my lap and an infomercial for the robot vacuum on the TV. I'd hated the stupid commercials before I met Seb, but now I watched them every spare minute of the day. I'd called in sick three times to watch them some more, and I was living on a diet of junk food and coffee.

Eli was this afternoon's visitor in what seemed like an organized roster of brothers who were assigned to nag me about Seb and lecture me on how I'd fucked up, under the guise of 'keeping me company'—or the even bigger lie, to 'cheer me up.' Uno sat at his feet, looking up at me from beneath her knitted brow, her yearning for potato chips stronger than her compassion for my plight.

"Man, that guy loved these stupid commercials." Eli sighed and slumped onto the couch beside me. I didn't have to be reminded. I knew who was missing from this scene.

"He's not *dead*, Eli. You can talk about him in the present tense." I stared at the screen and wondered when I'd started sounding so monotone. Probably around the time the first guy I'd ever really cared about walked out and took my heart with him.

Eli's tone was annoyingly carefree. "Yeah, well, maybe he hates them now. How would we know? Maybe you should call him and find out."

I grunted. I was getting good at grunting. I'd been bombarded every day since Seb left, and the onslaught was relentless. Eli's tactics were some of the more friendly——a casual conversation that just so happened to veer back to Seb again, and again.

"You miss him?"

"*Yes,* I miss him. Why do you think I'm here in my sweatpants watching this middle-aged woman struggling to peel a potato?" The video had switched. And it wasn't just that I missed him. It was worse. I was angry. I should've made things clear with him from the start. Should've talked about our feelings, our expectations, our hopes. I was the older, more mature partner. But I'd acted like a child and let things go unsaid, to the point where he didn't want to be with me anymore.

"What are you going to do about it?" He leaned forward, veering into my field of vision.

I shoved the bag of potato chips into his lap. "Go away."

He wasn't going anywhere. He shoved the bag right back into my lap and jabbed my shoulder with an elbow. "Look, I'm here for you, but you've got to do *something*."

No, I didn't. And there was nothing I could do. Seb had made his decision. I stared at Eli and crossed my arms over my chest. "How long are you guys going to keep this up?"

He shrugged and leaned back, kicking his feet onto the ottoman, and patting Uno by his side, like he was settling in for the long haul. "As long as it takes for you to go get Seb back."

I waved him off. "It's too late."

"Too *late*?" Eli exhaled toward the television. "Derek, c'mon."

"He made it clear he didn't want to be here. What do want from me? You think I should *beg*?"

"Yes." He rewarded Uno's patient, quiet whining with a chip, and I watched the woman peel her potato on the TV.

"Shut up." I motioned to the television and then crossed my arms. If he wanted to talk about anything other than the magic peeler and zucchini curler, then he'd have to find someone else.

Eli looked me over and let out a disappointed huff, before squeezing my shoulder, depositing the potato chip bag back into my lap, and standing. Uno looked from me to him and back again, then sluggishly got to her feet and followed her master out of the apartment with her tail hanging as low as her head. She looked as sad as I felt, and I worried if heartbreak was contagious to dogs.

Heartbreak… Now that was a loaded word. But what else could this be? It was beyond disappointment. My body ached and my chest pinched all day, from the moment I woke up to when I passed out on the couch sometime after sunset and before dawn. If I'd been any older, I'd have worried about having one of the doctors at work give me an ECG to make sure my heart wasn't actually shattered and little pieces weren't floating around my chest cavity in a state of suspension.

These days, I preferred solitude to having my brothers around, because being alone made it easier to lose myself in mindless TV. The infomercials were engaging enough to keep my attention, and stupid enough that I didn't have to focus too hard on them. I could become one with the couch.

I enjoyed melding into the furniture for about five minutes before Matt walked in, uninvited.

He sat down beside me with a long, low grunt. I didn't look up. He didn't say a word. He was the worst of the bothersome brothers. He gave me nothing but his cold, disapproving presence that made it impossible to shirk away from reality. He pulled me into the present, and I hated it. It was almost unbearable, and my stomach curled in while my brain begged me to break the tension. But I'd helped Sean and him practically raise the five younger brothers, so I knew a thing about being stubborn, too. I could wait him out. I'd win this battle. Then he'd leave and I'd be alone with my victory. And my sadness. The way I was supposed to be.

I just had to remain quiet.

"You don't understand what it was like!" I jumped to my feet, the potato chip bag spilling to the ground. "I had no choice! *He's* the one who left, and you're all acting like I packed his shit and pushed him out the door."

Matt raised his eyebrows and looked me over. "I didn't say anything."

Of course he didn't. He never said anything. "You didn't have to!" My pulse raced, and I couldn't stand still. So, I paced. "You think I don't *miss* him? Because I'm telling you right now, this is worse than missing him. I can't stop thinking about him. I know I only knew him for a few weeks, and we have this massive age gap and our lives are so different I don't know how we'll ever make it work, but he's all I think about. All I see when I close my eyes. All I want when I'm lying here awake, night after night. Happy now? I said it."

Matt opened his mouth, then promptly shut it as I paced in front of the television, unable to stop my verbal diarrhea.

"I've never cared about the age thing, but maybe he thought I did. I sure as hell mentioned it enough. Called him 'kid.' Treated him like he needed me to cut his food into tiny bites, so he didn't choke. But I knew he was a man. All man." Matt cleared his throat. "Shut up. You know what I mean. I mean, he was enough to make me never need anyone else. And he was beautiful, Matt. Wasn't he? He was beautiful." Matt nodded, and I didn't care. "I wanted him, and he left me, Matt. Left me standing here with my heart in my gut and my eyes full of tears. I wanted him and he left." That said it all. Except... "I loved him." And then, "I still do."

Matt nodded, his eyebrows knitted tighter.

"What am I going to do, Matt?"

His lip twitched as if he was holding back a laugh, and it made me furious. "Beats me. I'm just here to introduce you to my new computer guy."

I whipped my head around to glare at him. "What?" If he'd let me go on like that while a stranger listened to everything I said from outside the door, I'd fucking kill him.

"I got a new guy on staff. Maybe you know him?" He spoke like it was the most normal thing in the world to walk in on my emotional crisis to introduce me to one of his employees.

"How would I know him?" I didn't spend a lot of time in the security world. All I knew about it was to disable the alarm on my car, I pushed a button and to disable the one on the Vanguard Tower, I pushed a few buttons. I looked down at my crumb-covered sweats and then at Matt. "You could've told me I was going to a meet and greet. I would've put on some salsa to go with the chips."

He chuckled and stood with a smug look on his face.

"If you open that…" My threat died as he pushed the door fully open, and my heart stopped. Seb. Staring at me. "Seb…" At my door. In the Tower. Here. So close I could've touched him. Well, I'd have to take a few steps, but close. And beautiful in all black.

"Is it true?" His voice was quiet and quivered, but it still hit me like a bullet. "You love me?"

As though Matt had proudly performed his duty, he clapped Seb on the back, slipped out, and left us alone.

Chapter 26 - Sebastian

"Order yours today and get not one, not two, but *three* bonus replacement blades for The Magic Peeler and Zucchini Curler!" The television filled the silence between us, and the screen flashed blue and white light onto Derek's face. I couldn't take my eyes off him, and I couldn't unhear the words he'd spoken to Matt. And more than anything, I wanted to hear him say them to me. And I would wait all night if I had to.

I'd heard all the reasons we shouldn't be together, all of his insecurities laid out, and I heard him say he loved me anyway. That was all that mattered—he loved me. The words echoed in my mind over, and over, and over…but now he stood in front of me, mute, eyes wide and locked onto mine.

"Do you?" I stepped into the room and let the door slide shut behind me.

He gave a slight nod, and I looked down. He was barefooted, and his toes curled, grabbing onto the rug like he was bracing for a blow. "I…do." He cleared the huskiness so his voice came smooth, deep, as sexy as I remembered. "Being away from you has been hell. I…love you, Seb."

Every emotion I'd ever had flashed through me, propelling me across the room into his arms, off the floor, so I could cling to him, hang on like my life depended on it. I kissed him, hard, and his passion matched mine with just as demanding a presence. Something shifted and whatever had been holding my bandaged heart together dissolved, healing me so I was whole again.

Derek cradled the back of my head and twisted his hand into my hair as our lips met. I felt his relief too. He set me on my feet and bent to keep his lips on mine, but I put a hand on his chest and gently urged him away.

"Wait." I smiled, almost laughing with happiness, and smoothed my hair down. "We need to talk."

"I've done so much talking." He moved to kiss me again, but I dodged him with a finger on his lips.

"*We* need to talk if we're going to start this off the right way."

His eyes cleared as he straightened and nodded. "You're right. We really do."

Beside him on the couch, I wanted to touch every bulge of his muscles, the slope of his shoulder, the angle of his pecs like I was relearning the landscape of his body. But instead, I pulled myself away, gripped his knee, and took a breath.

"Sorry about the…mess." He motioned to the spilled potato chips. I'd crushed a few into dust when I'd rushed over to him. There were sweatpants strewn across a table, empty carry-out boxes on the ottoman, a couple of beer cans on the floor near the trash can like he'd aimed, shot, and missed.

"It reminds me of my place." I took his hand, and he laced his fingers with mine as I lowered my voice. "It looks like we might have taken our break-up with the same sloppiness."

He exhaled loudly and nodded. "It's small comfort to know I wasn't the only one really going through it…"

I kissed him softly. It wouldn't take away all the hurt, but it was a start.

He seemed to melt under my lips, and I moaned as he grabbed my waist. I didn't want to stop. I wanted to straddle his lap, to chase the amazing feelings that washed over me when we made love. I wanted to talk with our bodies.

But it wouldn't help us set anything straight. "Mm. Wait." I pulled back and shook my head. "This was the mistake we made the first time around. I'm not going to fuck this up again. I'm not going to lose you a second time because we left things unsaid."

He nodded and squeezed my hand tight. "You're fault for being so fucking irresistible, you know that?"

"Ha. No…but I like hearing it."

He rubbed his eyes and shook out his hands like he was pushing a reset button. "Okay, we need to talk this out, we do. So, let me lay it out first." He paused. "I never wanted you to leave. It hurt me when you walked out of here."

"I didn't want to, either. I think I was in shock, after seeing Ben...I felt worthless, and I couldn't imagine why you'd want to be with me. I really thought I was doing us a favor by ending it quick. Before you could."

His face fell, and it hurt to look at him. "Before I could?" His eyelids fluttered shut then opened to a shining batch of tears. "I would have never..."

"I know. You would've never said you deserved better than a bartender who could barely make rent and ate ramen four nights a week and skipped dinner the other three." I sighed. "And you would've never said you didn't want to be with someone who shared the same genetic make-up as a criminal." I cleared my throat. This was harder than I thought it would be. "And you would've never said you loved someone who would do something so stupid as trying to hunt down a bookie and ended up a bloody stump on the end of his boot."

"Jesus, Seb." He sighed, ran his hand through his hair disrupting the already tangled mess of all those beautiful blond locks. "I thought..."

I shifted in my seat and held his gaze. "What *did* you think?"

"I thought you changed your mind. Didn't...want me anymore."

He was all I wanted. "For being so old and experienced, you don't know shit." I smiled. "Probably because your number of real relationships is limited to just this one."

He winced like I was throwing it in his face, but I liked it. I liked being the one who was important enough in his life he gave me a chance he gave no others. "Do we have to start there?" I nodded and he rolled his eyes. "Of course, we do. Okay. Yeah...I haven't really done anything long-term. A long history of hook-ups but nothing serious, no one who ever *slept* in my bed like you did... So, I'm used to people checking out like this is a damned Hilton Hotel when they're done with me." How anyone could be *done* with Derek was beyond me. "But when you left...it almost killed me. There was nothing—is nothing temporary in how I feel about you."

I brought his hand to my mouth and kissed gently. "I left because of my own shit, not because my feelings for you changed. I didn't want to see what we shared beyond sex because it would mean I had to talk to you about all the things in my life that made me not good enough. So I left it at sex. I kind of thought that was all you wanted anyway."

He shook his head. "I wanted more. I *want* more. God, I should've told you back then, as soon as I knew."

"Me too." My heart was pounding hard, and I leaned in to kiss him. Slow. Gentle. Packed with as much love as I could convey in a single touch of our lips.

When we pulled apart, he leaned his forehead against mine. I could see every fleck of color in his eyes, every emotion in his soul. "Are you sure?"

"Yeah. I might be young, but I know what I want."

"I didn't mean… But we should talk about that."

"My toddler tantrum tendencies or your Mrs. Robinson complex?" I rolled the *r* and waggled my eyebrows, acutely aware I was making light of something that made me feel nervous as hell.

Derek gave me a small smile for my effort. "First of all, I'm not old enough to be your Mrs. Robinson."

"So I shouldn't glean anything from that 9:30 bedtime?"

He shoved me and I cackled wickedly. "That was so I could get you into bed." Oh, Lord, if he kept talking like that, we weren't going to get much more talking in. "Second of all." He took both of my hands and waited for me to meet his gaze, but I was busy imagining him naked, stroking his dick while I watched. "The age difference is a power imbalance, right?"

I hung on for a second longer then sent the image to the back of my mind for later. Balance of power. "Yeah. I suppose that's part of it." I felt small for even thinking it because he'd protected me, loved me, and taken my problems on. But he'd also made it hard for me to handle things on my own.

"What else is part of the power imbalance we have?"

I shrugged. "You seem really…put together."

"I do?" He looked down at the stained hoodie and cocked an eyebrow.

"Maybe not right this second, but for the most part, you're like a finely glued puzzle. Look at you." I motioned to him with a nod. I wished he could see himself the way I did. He was so much better than me and it must have been obvious to anyone who could see us side by side. "You're Georgetown alum. And after everything you went through as a kid, you found a way to make a home for you and your brothers, you save lives every day, you have a good income, a noble profession, you're good-looking…"

"I don't know what you're saying except I'm a catch." He grinned. He was a catch who deserved to be hooked by someone worthy, someone he could love without all these flaws I brought into a relationship.

I swallowed the knot in my throat. "Don't get me wrong, I love all of it. It's hot. But it's an imbalance. I have an apartment with four pieces of furniture, a mountain of student loan debt, no way to pay it, no friends, and my brother is…" I rolled my eyes. "He tried to kill me, tried to get me killed. I don't bring a lot to a relationship."

"Right." He searched my gaze when I stopped flicking my eyes around and focused on him, then he moved closer and held my shoulders. "I'm completely *yours.* Since I first saw you in the ER, and the more I get to know you, the more you own every piece of me. You could ask me for anything, and I'll move mountains, stop the ocean from waving, whatever to make sure you get it. And I'm terrified because there's nothing I can do to stop it." His finger stroked the side of my throat and I closed my eyes to savor the sweetness in his touch. "Does that balance the scales a little? Does it balance them *enough*?"

My pulse thumped in my ears, and I actually felt dizzy from swooning so hard. "Yeah…restores some balance."

"You're so tough." Derek pulled back and looked at me with a burning kind of passion, an intensity I couldn't fight or hide from, a need. He met my gaze again and his grin turned down as he put a hand to his chest. "I just don't know how to start something serious with someone, let alone someone I care about so much."

My heart twitched with hope, and I gazed into his eyes. Maybe… Maybe… I spoke quietly, forcing the words, almost too scared to wish. "But you want to try?"

He took my hands again, then brought each one to his lips for a gentle kiss. "I do. If you do, too?"

I couldn't hold back anymore. I threw my arms around his neck and kissed him, hard. "Yes. More than anything, ever. I want to."

His smile lit me up, and he kissed me again, deep and needy, until I pulled away and cupped his cheeks in my hands "There's something else I need to tell you."

His eyes went wide and his Adam's apple bobbed. I paused for dramatic effect then leaned in close to his ear and whispered, "I love you, too."

He barked a laugh and shoved me onto my back then covered my body with his and kissed me hard.

We didn't pull apart for long minutes of perfection, but we were stripped to our underwear by the time we got to Derek's bed. It was made. Every blanket and sheet pulled straight. "I couldn't sleep here without you." He panted the words between kisses.

His musky sweat was strong, and I breathed it in greedily. Even the sadness clinging to him was sexy. How dare he still be so hot after two weeks of depression? It was brutally unfair. I bit his bottom lip to scold him and he growled and bit back as we fell against each other.

He wrapped his leg around my hip and pulled me close, so we were pressed tight and warm as we kissed. Something inside me relaxed as soon as my skin touched his. This was exactly where I was supposed to be and the man I was supposed to be with.

Derek smoothed his thick, strong hands over my shoulders and back as we continued making out, and warm tingles raced down my body. I was hard, and my desire bloomed. I wanted more. I rutted against his hip, and he moaned like he was pleased.

His cock pressed into my leg. Long. Thick. Hard. My body reacted like I'd come home to a place I'd never wanted to leave, surging with lust, warming under his touch, and pulling me closer to him. I peeled off his underwear while my hands trembled with need. I took his hard dick gently in my fingers, caressing, adoring, sighing happily when I saw it was as beautiful as I remembered. He pulled me back for a kiss then groaned into my mouth as I cupped his balls.

He wriggled my underwear off before we lay together and laved attention on each other's cocks with greedy, demanding hands. I jerked him hard and fast until he was moaning, and I reveled at the size of his dick. With it barely contained in my hand, I eased off and massaged lovingly, and he returned it in kind as we kissed. I was obsessed with his mouth, but as he brought me closer to orgasm, I had to pull back to whisper, "I love you."

He breathed heavy and cupped my cheek as he kissed me again. "I love you."

Those three words made my arousal even more intense. "Oh, fuck, I love you."

He moaned and kissed me again. "I need you."

"Mm. That too." I was close, but I wanted more of him than just his hands. I wanted all of him to take all of me. I was desperate to feel us move as one. I eased him back and straddled his thighs, sitting up on his lap. "And I want you."

With one hand still on my cock, he reached with the other for a condom and lube from his bedside table. I smoothed a dollop of lube over my ass to get ready, but Derek just tapped the wrapped condom against his lips like he was thinking about something.

"What is it?" I tilted my head, and then poked his chest, prying for an answer.

A shy smile broke out behind the wrapper, and I couldn't have loved him more. "I...want you to top me."

I blinked and shook my head as if to clear out my ears. That was way too good to be true. My hot alpha doctor wanted me to top him. "You what?"

The certainty left his voice, and his voice wavered. "If you want to. I don't want to pressure you—"

"Um, of course I want to." I snatched the condom from his fingers and ripped it halfway open before I paused and looked him over. "But are you sure? Have you ever..."

He shook his head and smiled at me brightly. "I want to do everything with you. I want it to be equal between us."

I beamed and smashed a toothy kiss against him as I wriggled between his legs. I eased into him with two fingers while we kissed, and I worked him open until he was panting and moaning hard. His cock leaked precum against me where it pressed against my belly, and it thickened as I nudged his prostate.

"I want to feel you so badly." He held my face in his hands, and his deep blue eyes drew me in, while his plump red lips made me want to sink deeply into him, however I could.

The condom slid on nice and tight, and I was ready…and overwhelmed.

Derek ran his hands over my sides lovingly. "Have you done this before?"

"No." I gave him a nervous smile.

"Just do whatever feels good." He squeezed my wrapped cock and cupped my balls gently, until I moaned. "I want you to feel good."

He smoothed my hair and gazed up at me, love and need and want shining in his eyes. For me. And it was a lot. I couldn't hold his gaze. Instead, I focused on his broad chest and moved into position. My dick jerked when

I pressed against him, and desire ran through me so hot and strong, I moaned before I'd ever gotten inside him.

With his thumb under my chin, he tilted my face until I met his gaze. "I love you."

My first thrust was shaky. Nervous. I pushed into him and watched with reverie as his eyes fluttered shut and a broken moan escaped his throat. I did it again, and he reached up to grab at my hips to pull me in even deeper. He felt incredible—hot and tight, like nothing I'd ever felt before.

"Fuck, I love you too," I stuttered, and he let out a pleased laugh.

My cock jumped with pleasure as I pumped into him harder until he grunted with me. His eyes met mine again, and we rocked back and forth while the bed slammed against the wall.

"Yes!" He moved me by the hips, then let me go and held my shoulders as I found my own rhythm.

He was right—doing what I wanted was a good strategy. Every time I tried to do what I thought *he* would want, we lost our rhythm, but if I chased my own pleasure, he started moaning and clenched fistfuls of sheet again. He looked so good, gasping for air. I leaned forward and kissed him with all the love in my heart, and he held me so tight I had to thrust shallow, but I made up for it by fucking him faster. He moaned as he pulled back and then pressed our foreheads together.

"Oh, God. I love you so much, Derek."

He wet his lips and nodded, holding me close. "I want this forever. I want to make this work."

"I don't want to move in with you yet though."

He half-laughed and half-moaned. "Okay, we'll take it one step at a time. We'll do it right. Just say you'll be mine."

"Baby...I'm *yours*."

He groaned and arched his back. "Fuck, I love that! Call me 'baby'..."

"I love fucking you, *baby*." I kissed his neck and thrust deeper as he moaned. "I'm yours, *baby*."

He wrapped his arms around my waist and pulled me close. I rolled my hips and hit his prostate just enough to make him gasp every time.

"I'm close."

The rasp in his voice kicked my pleasure up a notch, and my cock bucked hard and deep inside him. My balls tightened and I struggled not to come right away.

"*Same*." I propped myself up on fists so I could look down and watch his eyes as we edged closer.

He held the nape of my neck and held me steady with those deep blues while he used his other hand on his cock. He let me chase my own pleasure, then gave me even more, and there was no way I'd ever been so cherished, so pleased during sex.

"Oh, fuck, I'm—"

"Now? I'm—" Derek's eyes fluttered shut, and he tightened around me.

"Yes!" I cried out and threw my head back then shuddered as I slammed my cock into him like it was the last time I'd ever be inside him. My orgasm smashed through me like a bolt of lightning. Love surged from my chest, and lust from every other part of my body, and it all poured into Derek who rode his climax, ground hard against me.

Every shot of cum felt like ecstasy, but the real pleasure was in watching the way Derek looked as he came, how he grabbed the sheets, and how his cock twitched and jerked as he blew all over himself. I rode his ass until the last tingles of pleasure faded, and then we collapsed into his arms as he pulled me down on top of him.

In each other's arms, we panted and half-chuckled as we came down. I felt at home with him, but I wasn't calm. My heart pounded, and my head spun with the *wild* idea that we were together now. I knew where we stood— and it was on the edge of something wonderful that would change my life forever.

Chapter 27 - Derek

I could feel Seb's heart thumping through his ribcage, quick and skittish. Hoping it would calm him, I pulled him tighter against me and kissed the crook of his neck, and sure enough his pulse slowed, and he let out a soft sigh.

There was nothing I wouldn't do to keep him safe and happy. I smiled into his shoulder. I was in love. Satisfied. Maybe even content.

I loved how assertive he'd become, and not just in the bedroom. His cockiness had given way to genuine confidence, and somehow he'd managed to get me to talk through our issues, and insisted we stay on topic until it was all out in the open. That confidence was hot, and I couldn't wait to see more of it. In our *relationship.*

"How long until someone bursts in here and sees my naked butt?" he mumbled.

I chuckled and shook my head. "I'm hopeful Matt spread the word to the other brothers to not disturb. We needed to make up for lost time."

"Mm." He slid off me, but quickly snuggled in close at my side. I loved how he felt pressed against me. "I need to see him again soon though, to sign that contract."

I looked at him, shocked. "You're his new recruit?"

He smiled, and the twinkle in his emerald irises lit me up. "Yeah! It's an amazing job, I'm psyched. It'll be remote, so I can work from anywhere which has always been my dream, and Matt's going to set me up with all the equipment I need. I just can't believe it...all...worked out?"

I tilted my head as I caught a little uncertainty in his voice that made me curious. "Hm, you don't sound so certain about that, though."

He sucked in his bottom lip and shrugged. "Seems too good to be true."

"We have to work on that self-esteem of yours." I pushed back his hair, and he nuzzled his cheek into my hand.

His smirk stretched against my palm. "Topping you helped."

I guffawed, and he giggled, before he rolled onto his back and sighed as he gazed up at the ceiling with a hand on his belly and the other on his chest. "Do you think he just gave me the job because of *us*?"

"Absolutely not." I moved onto my side and took his hand. "He's not one for nepotism. He wouldn't even give one of the brothers a job they didn't earn. He clearly respects you and the work you do."

A smug little grin bloomed on Seb's face, and I couldn't stop myself from kissing it.

"No nepotism, huh?"

"Mm. He's very fair." I nodded sagely.

Seb lowered his head and spoke quietly, like he was nervous to ask. "What else?"

A familiar wall rose up inside me and told me not to reveal anything about my brothers. It was a protective urge that had served me well when we were younger and I'd had to keep our profile low inside and outside the system. But that wasn't who I was anymore. Seb had been right— I'd helped us build secure housing, I had a stable career, and all of the brothers were on their feet. I didn't have to protect them anymore. And I didn't need to protect myself so sternly either.

I cleared my throat and looked at the ceiling. The words came out hoarse at first, like I needed practice speaking them, but they flowed soon enough.

"Matt is also very stubborn. Almost as bad as me. I met him in a group home when we were fourteen. Him and Sean, of course, but I didn't know that at first." The wall rose up inside me again, and I pushed my way through it. "I had no idea they were twins, I thought it was just Matt I was seeing everywhere."

Seb propped himself up on an elbow and widened his eyes. "What? That's insane."

I laughed and poked his shoulder. "Hey, I was a kid! And there were so many kids in that home, it was impossible to keep track of anyone anyway. The first few days I was there, Sean was sick and mostly in bed. But I didn't know that. I'd just see Matt in the living area, and then the next thing I knew, he'd be in the kitchen in his pajamas looking like death."

Seb snorted and rolled his eyes, but then he nudged closer, wrapped up in the story. I popped my head up on my hand and smiled at him.

"The day after Sean got better and was up and about, I still had no idea. They hardly spoke, so it's not like I was learning facts about either of them that the other would contradict. I played ball with Matt, I mean, I *think* it was Matt…then came inside, and he was already showered." It took effort to get the words out, but he listened, wanted to know. It made the story easier to tell. "I thought he had some secret passageways or shortcuts through the house, but when I asked him about it, he looked at me like I was crazy. I'm pretty sure it was Sean. He still gives me that look."

"Like the one I'm giving you right now?" His face went completely blank, his lips a straight line, and his eyes piercing but giving nothing away. It was an uncanny likeness, and I couldn't help but laugh.

"*Very* similar."

Seb's face lit up again and he ran his hand over my shoulder. I loved his gentle touch. The skin of his hands was so soft. "So how did you find out they were twins?"

I grinned as the memory came to me. One of the better ones from my foster years. "Snuck outside in the middle of the night when I couldn't sleep, and they were under the porch, smoking. Jesus, I almost had a heart attack. Thought I was in some spooky horror film."

Seb smiled up toward the ceiling. "I can see the cheesy '80s cover now."

I nudged him and growled in mock offense. "Nineties, thank you very much."

He winked and planted a kiss on my cheek before settling back into his position. "What'd they do when you caught them smoking?"

"Of course, they didn't even blink. They were just like, 'Hey, you want a smoke?' And the rest is history—"

"Uh, no, it's not." He shifted and stared at me seriously. And I was happy to accept all the help I could get. "How did you go from, 'Hey, you want a smoke?'" He put on a ridiculous low voice to impersonate the twins—"to 'Hey let's build the Vanguard Tower'?"

I smiled at him, amazed at how easily he could leap over my blocks with his sweet humor. He made me feel safe. But my voice still quivered when I recalled how serious things got after I'd first met the twins. "Okay, good question. We made the plan that night. Or started to, at least. The two of them had been through a lot in the system. Ended up in some real shitty homes because at that point they'd refused to be separated. There weren't that many places that took pairs of siblings. And that limited them to really…dangerous homes."

He nodded and put a hand on my chest.

I pushed on, determined to open up to him, to let him in. "We made a pact to move in together one day, to create a house where we could live, just the three of us. Then we got moved, separated into different homes. But we found ourselves in the same places again and again. Formed a bond, and decided we'd be real brothers. We wanted to take it deeper. We were the same ages, you know? And we had the same values, same goals. Similar experiences…" I swallowed down the emotion threatening to turn me mute.

Seb rubbed my chest and smoothed away the tension there and softened his voice. "What about the other guys? Were they in the same homes?"

"They came from all sorts of places. I mean, heaps of kids go through those homes, but we connected with a few that passed through." I looked toward the ceiling as I recalled, and counted them out, my hand on Seb's, on my chest. "I guess Richie was first…Sean and Matt got into some trouble and finally got separated when we were sixteen. They were both pulled out of the group home where we'd met. That's when Sean met Richie at the joint he got moved to. Richie was fourteen, huge for his age—"

"I'd be shocked if he wasn't." He smiled warmly and laced his fingers through mine. The comment was small, but it meant a lot. He knew these guys. He knew my family.

"Right? But he was constantly causing trouble. He'd been bullied his whole life, but with his recent growth spurt, he could fight back. To a point..." I closed my eyes and became sad as I recalled the bloody wounds and swollen bruises I'd tended to, way before med school. Sad for Richie, and sad for myself, too. "Some older neighborhood kids were kicking his ass, and Sean jumped in to defend him. When Sean got sent back to the group home, still without Matt, Richie came with him."

His voice was soft, and he gazed at me with wonder in his eyes. "The first of the little brothers you took care of."

I was flattered that he knew that was how I thought of it. I smoothed his hair back from his ear and smiled at how beautiful he was, before I resumed my story. It felt good to tell. "Hm. I guess I'd actually met Eli before then. I remember Richie picking on him the minute he walked in."

Seb raised his eyebrows, shocked. Eli did seem like the last person on the planet someone would pick on. "What about?"

"Who knows? His hair? His expression? Richie was constantly on everyone's case about the most random shit. Eli was thirteen, and looked much younger than that, so he was an easy target. But they bonded over taking care of the stray dogs out in the alley." I was surprised by how easy it all came pouring out of me. The story of my past had been locked up tight for so long, only told in segments to the brothers involved in each part of the tale, never as a whole. I counted on my fingers. "Hunter was next. Ran away from the last foster house I was at. I was eighteen, he was...sixteen? And he was adamant he'd rather be on the streets than stay in the system. That's what prompted me, Sean, and Matt to get our foster licenses. So we could help our younger brothers."

Seb sighed and lowered himself onto his belly to gaze up at me with his chin on his hand. "That couldn't have been easy."

"No. Took a *lot* of work for us to get accredited." Hard work. Back-breaking work, spirit-breaking work. Begging, pleading, degrading work.

"And the other...three?"

"Two." I smiled, touched that he wanted all of the story. "Owen was next. We were twenty-one by then, he was around fourteen? Matt brought him back with him from a house he'd ended up in when he got separated from us." I paused when a sudden swell of emotion rose and pushed tears into my eyes as I remembered the trauma of Matt and Sean being separated. From each other. From me.

I swallowed thickly, but my voice wavered as I went on. "Then Brax was the latest. It was after we were out of the system and we had our licenses for Owen and Hunter. Brax tried to pick Matt's pocket on the street."

Seb made a fart noise with his lips. "Bad target."

I laughed. His light humor had again lifted the heaviness of the moment and I smiled at him adoringly, almost in disbelief that he was real. "Or maybe he picked a good target, depending on how you look at it. It worked out well for him in the end."

He smiled at me and shook his head in amazement. "There are a lot of stories in there, huh?" His finger was warm where he pressed it against my forehead.

I nodded, took his hand, and kissed his fingertip. "They're not all my stories to tell, though. Maybe one day you can ask the brothers."

He smiled like he was holding a secret, and I tilted my head to try to urge it out of him. He just grinned and shook his head. "I know that it's probably not, like, *easy* to talk about that stuff. And I really appreciate you opening up about your side of the story. But I already know what happened."

I blinked and sat up a little. Scared. A little offended and defensive. "What do you mean? These aren't *predictable* stories, Seb. Trust me."

"Yeah, I *know*." He waved his hand but looked at me seriously.

"What exactly do you know?" My voice rose at the end with my panic.

He shrugged nonchalantly. "All of it."

"*How?*"

"Your bros have been hounding me for the last two weeks, loitering around my apartment nonstop. It was only a matter of time before we ran out of small talk and they started to yack about something substantial."

I was flabbergasted. I couldn't get past the idea my brothers had been to his apartment while I was slumped on the couch, let alone get my head around the idea that they'd opened up to him. These were my closed-off, stoic, tight-lipped brothers we were talking about, who had as a hard time as I did letting anyone in. "Wait, they actually told you their stories?"

His smug smirk was so cute I couldn't look at it without my heart feeling like it was exploding, so I covered his face with a pillow while he cackled and tried to wrestle it away from me. "What, like their *secrets*?"

"Yeah, their secrets!" I thumped his shoulder with the pillow, then looked at him seriously. "As far as I know, that's not the type of information they share with just anyone."

"Then I guess they like me."

A smile punctured my scowl. My brothers liked Seb *enough* to confide in him about their past? Or rather, our shared pasts. They didn't let people in very often, but when they did, it meant the person was all in. And their bonds were for life. It was the stamp of approval I hoped for, though I wasn't sure why I was so surprised they'd given it to Seb already—they had been nagging me to get back with him for a reason. As far as they were concerned, he was already part of our family.

"Just so you know, I'm filthy jealous." He shrugged like it was no big deal, but the hurt in his eyes was obvious. I took his hand and held it to my chest, then nodded to urge him to say more. "My brother is a piece of shit. He's going to prison. I'm going end up testifying against him. But you have this amazing…family you built."

"Hey." I kissed his knuckles. "I have some brothers to spare. Take one. Or three."

He threw his head back with force and laughed, then let out a long, heavy sigh. "I love you, baby."

God, I loved when he called me 'baby.' My entire body warmed, and I held him. "I love you, too."

He kissed me with sweetness that quickly turned into a firm bite of my lower lip, and I felt a surge of love for him rush straight to my crotch. He was on it. He knew what he'd done, and he firmly wrapped his hand around the base of my cock as he peppered my neck with tiny nips and kisses. "I don't think you heard me," he purred. "I *love* you."

"Hm? Say again?" I craned my neck and he kissed my collarbone.

"I *love* you."

I moaned as he took a nipple between his teeth. "Sorry, I'm so old, my hearing is touch and go. Didn't quite catch it…"

He mumbled a few more words and squeezed me in his fist before popping his lips off and nearly shouting, "I love you, Dr. Dish!"

I laughed, grabbed him by the hips, and rolled on top of him for a long, slow afternoon in bed with my first true love and his perfect, smug smirk.

Chapter 28 - Eli

The Cumberland State Forest was one of my favorites in Virginia, situated deep in the Piedmont plateau, and populated with pines and fertile soil that threw up mushrooms throughout the year. Uno and I were doing our rounds of the peripheral trails and documenting our fungus findings late on a fall evening. There had been enough leaf fall early in the season that our steps crunched over the orange and brown litter on the trail, and enough rain that the rapids of the Wills River roared up ahead.

Uno sniffed at the trunk of a tall pine and stuck her nose deep in the dirt, but she was no truffler. The chanterelles she was looking for were a few feet from the trees, fruiting up from the rich soil, and I spotted their orange, fan-shaped bodies. I was a search and rescue guy, but I was more than happy to help with environmental research like tracing and recording mushroom species when it was quiet—which was hardly as often as I'd like. If I didn't have such a *thing* about helping people, maybe I could have been happy as a botanist.

"Looks like foxes." I crouched by the clump of mushrooms and pointed at the small teeth marks left on the bodies where the fruit had been nearly shredded. "Or maybe a hungry dog?"

I nudged Uno with my elbow, and she gave me a bewildered look, as if shocked I'd ever suggest such roguish behavior from her. She trotted down the trail while I made note of the mushrooms in my book, pocketed it, and hurried after her.

Fall was peaceful in the woods, and I was happy to be back in my element after the drama from the city. It had been three months since Seb appeared in our lives, and while I didn't hold it against the guy, I was glad things had started to settle down in his life. His dickhead brother's hearing was just adjudicated, and Seb had done a great job testifying, and maybe now the guy—who was practically my bro-in-law—could really relax.

Speaking of relaxing, I'd never seen Derek so *content*. I was beyond happy for him. Seb wasn't the type of guy he would have seen himself with on paper, but they were made for each other. I'd known it the minute I met Seb, and damn, I liked to be right.

"He's a good egg, isn't he?"

Uno glanced back at me and wagged her tail in agreement before she took a short detour off the path to lap at the edge of the river. I followed and stood by her with my hands on my hips and gazed upstream at the disappearing light as the sun set behind the trees. The cold air blowing off the river made me shiver, and the current was so loud I could barely hear myself think. Exactly how I liked it.

Uno spun around, and I glanced over my shoulder to see what the big deal was. Nothing. Just golden light filtering through the trees.

"Squirrel?" But there were no swaying branches or falling leaves to suggest as much. The birdsong continued without interruption, but Uno still wagged her tail and lifted her chin like something was up. I was getting the heebie-jeebies before she nudged my hip with her wet snout, and I finally got the message when she barked right at my radio.

"Oh, shit." I hadn't heard the radio buzz because of the rapids, but when I lifted it to my ear, I could hear the staticky fuzz of a call-in. "Eli reporting, over."

"Miss— ike— get. Over."

I rattled the radio, blocked my other ear with a finger, and asked for clarification. "Say again? Over."

"Miss- hiker. Back to head— debrief."

"On my way, over and out." I dropped the radio to my side, gave Uno a directive whistle, and followed her as she bolted back down the trail we'd come from. She glanced back and forth for trouble, but her tail was high and wagged as we bounded down the well-worn path, sprinted through patches of brush, and then leaped out of the trailhead at the near-empty parking lot toward our truck.

In a single leap, she bounded into the back and barked for me to hurry up. I huffed and threw myself into the cab, gunned the engine, and sped the ten minutes to the headquarters at the gate of the park.

Uno barked again and jumped to the ground as I pulled up. The front door of the single-story cabin flew open and Jacob's silhouette came into view.

Our operation was a small one, but it was a tight ship, thanks to my fearless leader, Jacob. Most of the rescues I'd done at his park were of hikers who knew their shit but got unlucky, or complete novices who were totally unprepared for what nature was harboring in her depths.

I loved being stationed at Cumberland, because it was the right blend of rescues, down time, and getting to know the old eccentric veteran who was now making a weird pattern with the Thermos in his hands.

"Drunk?" I grinned playfully. "Was that you slurring on the radio?"

Jacob chuckled. "Hey, I'm as sober as the day is long. Coffee as always. With those herbs you gave me. Magic." He scratched Uno behind the ears and motioned for us to come inside. He'd been sober for over ten years, and prided himself on his sharp mind and even sharper reflexes. And I was proud of him too.

The cabin that served as our headquarters was homey, which made sense since Jacob literally lived out back. He was a veteran, nearly in his sixties by my guess, and he was an oddball with some niche interests that overlapped with mine. He was happy to accept my suggestions when it came to medicinal herbs that could help his jittery nerves, and I was happy to keep track of the health of his favorite forest fungi while I was out in the woods.

"Here's who we're looking for." He handed me a scrap of paper with a poorly printed photo stapled to it, then took a seat behind his beautifully carved wooden desk.

I quickly grabbed the picture, eager to get to the rescue, but I sat down heavily in the leather chair opposite, and tried to get my mouth to say something, anything, but no words came out. I was struck mute by how gorgeous the guy in the photo looked. His blue eyes seemed to pierce me right through the photo.

I heard Jacob set his Thermos down on the desk and clear his throat. His indication that he was in business mode. No nonsense. Ready to work. "Young guy by the name of Wyatt. Missing since yesterday."

"What?" My gaze shot up to find Jacob leaned back in his chair with his feet on the desk. "Yesterday?" That wasn't good. I should have known about it before then. If he'd already spent a night in the wilderness unprepared, his chances of survival were seriously dropping by the minute. I was anxious to get going, and Uno whined at my feet, sensing my uneasiness, but Jacob always made me stay for a full briefing before I sprinted out into the field and today was no exception. He always said that the best rescuers stayed calm in a crisis, and the best way to do that was to have all the information and to take your time. It seemed like a contradiction, to take more time to prepare for a rescue than to get to action, but in the time I'd been working with Jacob, he hadn't once been wrong. And we hadn't once failed at a rescue. I respected him more with every day, and the older man was becoming something of a mentor–both professionally, and personally.

"Signed in yesterday morning, was due to sign out that afternoon, but nada. Never did." He held up his fists and then splayed his fingers like he was doing a magic trick and making something disappear. In this case, the beautiful young guy in the photo. Wyatt.

"Why wasn't that noticed before now?" I raised my voice and held the paper up before dropping it to my side and looking at Jacob with resignation. "Oh, shit, don't tell me—"

Jacob steepled his fingers under his chin and nodded with a sigh. "Larry."

I pinched my mouth into a scowl and refrained from comment. Larry was lazy. Larry was a liability.

"He let it slip." Jacob shrugged, forgiving the park ranger for shirking his duty yet again. He pointed at the paper in my hand, as if trying to get my mind off Larry. "This guy's roommate came by looking for him."

"Nice roommate." I studied the photo and wondered which part of the park Wyatt would have gone to.

"Naive roommate. Wanted to launch a search party of amateurs." Jacob chuckled and poured himself a cup of coffee from his Thermos and pointedly didn't offer me one. "Sun's going down. You up for it?"

I raised my eyebrows and looked at him like he had to be kidding. "Hola? Have you met me?"

Jacob laughed, his loud guffaw that always made me smile, and Uno barked excitedly. "That's a lad."

I jumped up and Uno leaped from where she had been lapping at the water bowl, both of us ready for action. I shot Jacob a wink and pointed at him with the photo of Wyatt. "I'll find your man. You know I live for this."

And I truly did. After all, it was what my brothers and I did. We worked the frontlines and saved the day. Because once upon a time, we'd all experienced what it was like to need saving.

CPSIA information can be obtained
at www.ICGtesting.com
Printed in the USA
LVHW081746300622
722480LV00002B/109